W.K. Phoenix

—presents—

Peculiar Cases Of Something Devine:

Gravity Of Devotion

(Part 1)

The Prison Games

TABLE OF CONTENTS

I'm afraid I'll pass out again. At any given moment, my body will just give up. Sure, I wake up seconds after, but if it happens at the wrong time... These blinking spells are living nightmares I can't shake. The voices in my head keep telling me awful things. Some are true. Maybe some I'll do. For a moment there, I actually thought I could get better.

I keep seeing _its_

HEAD

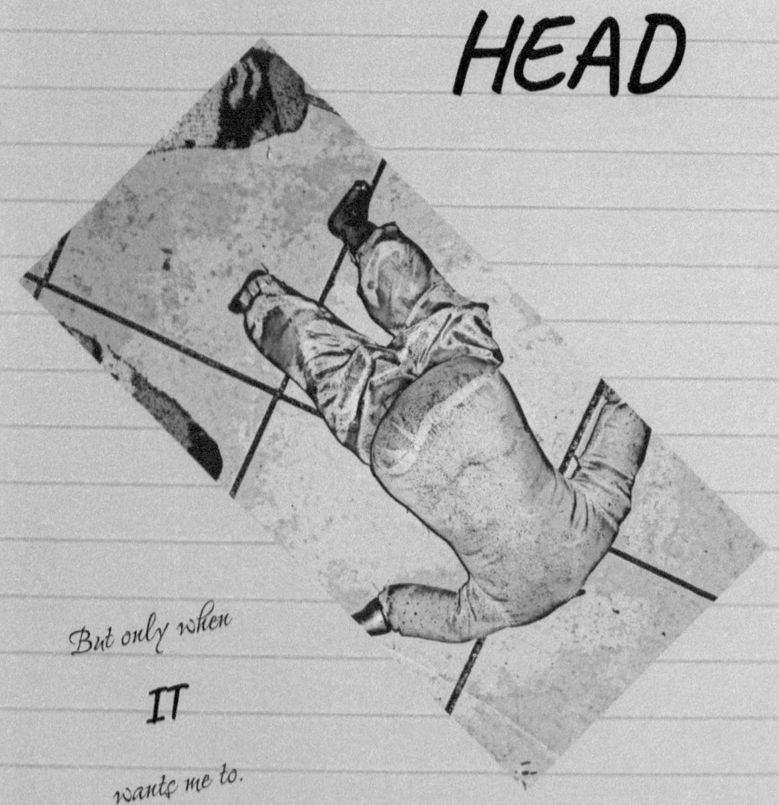

But only when

IT

wants me to.

Curses. They're only **shadows** of the people they were. Their natural <u>black light</u> must be what allows them to possess. Drawing out the worst in their hosts.

How can I use my "shadow" to draw out my aura?

Is it even possible?

I've changed so much in the past year. I don't even recognize myself...

I'm only half of what I started at birth.

—A fluster of chaotic shadows rushes across a cavernous arena clouded in gleams of white light—

—Kassandra, body without a face, watches from across a large pit— grooves in her smooth face-flesh wriggle—

—indistinguishable whispers—

—Amy's voice distorts as she screams "We can't attack her monsters anymore!" She grabs the edges of a podium. "We can find a way to win without hurting her." —

—"She made the play," a whisper in the wind said from beside her. "It was her choice." —

*—Faceless Kassandra **LAUGHS**. "Keep feeding sacrifices to my ally's ability, and I'll protect our clear path to victory" —*

—Amy fell into a pit of darkness—whispers "It's over—"

Chitter-irp-chit-irp. Chitterchitterchitterchitter-irp

—The wings of a Boeing 777 break off in mid-air—the wings spiral into the ocean—

—the aircraft seizures like a rabies-infected shark—

—a lone house on a cemetery sits on an island in the middle of the ocean—

—-the plane's turbulence increases—

—Amy stands on the roof of the house, her home watches the craft nosedive towards her—

—Amy smiles—puts her arms up as though ready to embrace a loved one returning from war—
—her watery eyes grow bright orange—a blazing inferno enlarges within her dilated pupils—

Dangle Dolly

Chitter-irp-chit-irp. Chitterchitterchitterchitter-irp

—Amy links arms with yellow jacket sleeve—
—the tip of a tongue splits and whispers behind her ear "Now or never!" —
—Amy nods. "Let's do it." —

<u>Don't let them pass!</u>

Chitter-irp

—Amy and her shadow-covered teammate speed right through a pair of linked arms—
—A giant hand picks Amy up by one of her arms—

Chitter-irp chit-i—

<u>—Don't let HER pass! —</u>

Chitterchitterchitterchitter-irp

—Amy grasshopper-kicks the giant hand, sending it into a spiralling black hole far, far away—
—Amy smiles—gasps—Plump veins swell in her face, turning grey, pulsing with an urge to bust—

ChitterchitterchitterchitterChitterchitterchitterchitterChitterchit

terchitterchitter...

<u>*—Amy* **BARKS** *mad laughter into the shadowy sky— "ITS THE*</u>
<u>*SUTBAA" —her fingers curl—mouth drips with excess saliva— her*</u>
<u>*skin peels, sizzling off her body—red streaks bombard her irises—*</u>
<u>*they turn orange—then purple—*</u>

ChitterchitterchitterchitterChitterchitterchitterchitterChitterchit

terchitterchitter
CHITTERCHITTERCHITTERCHITTER

Tormented by scum of the past.

<u>*—a silver babyhand falls on Amy's shoulder—death-grips it—*</u>

My Dreams Leak into my days.
I see Things. Sometimes they're real.
Other times, I'm sure they will be.
Living on borrowed time.
My body no longer feels like Mine.

Someone <u>Else</u> is inside.

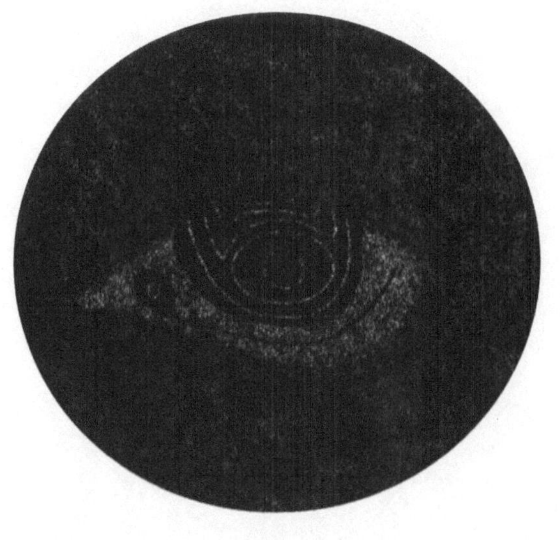

Chapter One

"Welcome to The Prison Games"

"We'll have food, right?"

Ten souls dripping wet with anticipation stood within the garage-sized elevator made of dirt *and what died in it* as it descended past the surface world. Their final pinch of light slipped away as their transport fully embraced the earth it came from. *If there's no food, we'll eat each other. I shouldn't tell her that.* "I'm sure we'll be alright, love." *Almost pitch black in here. Darkness breathes if you stand in it for too long. Is it— Is there smoke in here?*

The earth's rumble enclosed the humid space. The lower they went, the more sweat pooled around the eyes, nose, and lips.

We're going a long way down. It became dizzying the more she thought about it. Those *little pricks* that stabbed every pore She had *right before an attack* made her legs wobble. *Please. Not here. Not in front of them.* She swallowed her anxiety, but the way darkness played with shapes in her vision coughed it right back up.

Just ahead, a faint outline spun in the dark. Whispers of ghost lines swirled into each other. *It's not real, Amy.*

Remind yourself it isn't real. Don't let the schizophrenia eat at you now. We're so close to the end. Amy flinched at what looked like a face seconds ago. *Keep your bloody cool. Happy thoughts. Where do I get one of those? Who says I deserve them?* She scratched her elbow through her shirt's fabric and the ball of her right foot dug into the ground. *Maybe I should've waited till Gma got home to tell her where I was going. Would it matter? I have no intention of inheriting the family business so she can keep her death rituals to herself. Can't tell her about any of this either. For what? So she can flip her lid and preach about conserving one's secrets? She'll definitely rip my letter to shreds. I'll deal with her when I'm back. Demo's here, that's all that matters. Ol' Rezna Devine will be alright.*

Let's not forget Cloudy got to her.

Aura? You're back! Sounds like you're developing a cold. Are we okay? Aura? Are you there? I sound insane. Talking to my aura. "How long is this ride?" *Offly quiet for ten bodies in here.* "Hello?"

The silence answered back with the squirming of flesh and clatter of rocks and pebbles. Amy reached into the darkness, her hand pressing into the warm wall. "Anyone here?" She moved from one wall to the next. "Where did everyone—"

The mush and squirming of the earthly transport crescendoed to a halt. The *elevator* came to a stop. Amy froze in place, fists balled, *ready for what's coming.*

'We'll have food, right?' The thought was an infected sore deep in Amy's aching belly.

An infant laugh came up behind her. Its face, streaks of silver smoke barely there, opened its mouth over her head.

'I'm already starving.'

Light burst into life, revealing four solid dirt walls inside this *chamber.* The air was pungent with the smell of earth after rainfall. A number was etched in faded light on one wall: **10** Amy ran her fingers over it. *It's my rank,* *isn't it?* She sighed and wandered the tight space with uninspired steps. Kicked the *unimpressive* bed, one of many pieces of crude furniture sculpted from packed soil. The walls were uneven, and the roots buried deep within seemed ready to burst. The mineral-rich and bitter air coated the tongue and filled the throat with an ancient, almost fabricated texture, close to baked clay. She sat in the lump of an armchair across from the bed. *Dirt, dirt, dirt, dirt, dirt.* Her soles nestled into the crunchy floor. She stopped down and stuck a finger straight into the earth. *This soil is a bit odd. The texture is... off.*

She approached a corner of the room, bent her knees, and launched into the air. A tri-finger grip stabbed into the wall as her forefeet hit the adjacent wall before she steadied herself. After a moment of full body stiffening, her forefeet jumped to the ceiling, frigid on contact, with her shaky arms holding the pose. She maintained the position for over a minute before her feet jumped back to the wall beside her, holding the pose longer, not breaking a sweat.

Amy pushed away from the wall and dropped into a crouched stance, palm to the ground. "Gravity's intact, but the weight is absurd." She pulled her talisman out of her pocket. Rolled her eyes at the number ten on it. *Ridiculous.* She tossed the talisman to the other side of the room. *That's weird, I can still feel its weight.* She paced, keeping her eyes on the talisman. I can't shake it. *It's almost like it's tracking... me.* She stopped, her strolling eyes seeing her rank, then glaring at it, and returning her focus to her grounded talisman again. *Everywhere I turn, no matter what, I can feel where it is. How did Graves <u>do</u> this?*

"Ms. Devine?" Graves approached. Offered *my talisman!* in her hand. "It would be wise to hold on to this, though you'll find it hard to ditch." She took a seat in the dirt armchair.

"Where did you come from?"

Graves smiled.

"This whole setup is a nice little parlour trick," Amy

said. "Though I'm a bit concerned with what locking up ten students for a week will accomplish."

"I can assure you 100% nothing in here will kill or harm you."

"Nothing is 100% guaranteed." Amy sat cross-legged on the ground.

"Hm. Fair enough."

"Where's the aura source?" Amy asked. "Sorry, the <u>soul</u> source."

"You don't like the word soul? You prefer aura?"

"Soul is a little twenty-first century for me, I guess."

"Is the use of the word a part of your culture?"

They sat in silence. Graves' elegant features softened her utilitarian presence. The contrasts of her physical form stood out against the *mellow*-**buzzing** light throughout the holding chamber.

I'm not telling her too much. She's a solid Professor but I don't know yet if she's a solid human. "So. How are you doing all of this?"

"How do you think?"

"If I must guess, I'd say you're running this place off some massive bank of energy, except you can't get that much power without... I'm not even sure. It would take a considerable amount of aura."

"You are right and you are incorrect."

I don't know what that means. "So where's the source?"

"All around. Nothing's hidden. The exits are always open. The illusion of imprisonment must be kept while maintaining evidence you are always free."

A distant rumble came from under them.

"Prison games like the one you're about to embark on have been played for centuries in various forms. The earliest were played with crass tools of hand, stone, dirt, and water."

Amy lifted her feet as the rumbling grew closer.

"Upgrading to bark, wood, then steel. Since we've

gained allegiance with our spirit's energy, we've been able to link with the very World around us like never before. Crafting unique Prison Games that evolved over decades."

"You're not telling me you've actually fused your aura with the Earth to create— this place?"

Graves smirked. "Aura is growing on me. Why not? It's why and how we exist. We're meant to connect with our Earth. It's what I've always taught my students. It's only now, with society's blossoming <u>aura</u> that the notion is being criticized. Diminishing us spirit-wielding humans to a title: Peculiar. Such a dreadful term for something so beautiful, no?"

A slab in the wall pushed out in front of her. Its top half opened like a gift box. Graves pulled out a smoking mug. "Tea?"

"Think I'd prefer a strawberry smoothie, but sure."

"Ah. Give it a minute or two. Tell me, Amy, why are you here?"

To pay less attention to death. Amy locked eyes with her teacher. *I didn't want to separate from Demora so soon after her ordeal.* "Curiosity. I don't know why I'm here."

"Maybe to watch over your friend?"

"I'll always watch over her."

A slight rumble. Another wall slab shot out in front of Amy this time.

Graves waved an encouraging hand.

The slab's top half popped on a hinge, with steam rising out. Sat on a cushion at the bottom of the compartment: a glassed frozen smoothie with *delectable* pink-and-red swirls, complete with a dash of whipped cream and a strawberry on top.

"Ok." Amy picked out her treat and sucked its straw. Eyes brightened. "I'm invested."

"I'm charmed. It's my recipe. Your scores in class often disappointed, I must admit."

That's a turn. "Ouch." Amy sucked more smoothie.

"Always the bare minimum to pass. Then you realized which credits you needed to venture into a career working with the Animalia Kingdom. There you were, 12 years old, pretending you didn't have a care in the world. Pretending you'd rather be elsewhere than in your little hometown of Jadesfeld."

"I've always wanted to escape this place. But where would I go without my Gma?"

"How you spoke about your desire to pursue your dreams in Mrs. Matacin's Animalia class said otherwise."

Why is she rehashing my history?

"Four years later, we had another crucial conversation. This time, you expressed your interest in detective work. You were far behind the basic requirements needed for that space. Thought it never deterred your stubbornness to keep at it."

She's enjoying this retelling. Another Gma. "There was an easier path into detective work."

"And you found it."

"It's easy. Get enough of the right Animalia-centered credits; you can get into a position quicker working alongside the Kingdom than you could in our human realm. Felt I'd benefit more in the long run. We know less about them than they know about us. I could better my detective skills by being involved on both sides, looking in from the Animalia viewpoint."

"Harder path, not proven. Where others took the straightforward method, you created your own. Scores boasted to show your promise, too."

"Why this prison structure, Professor? *Why are we really here?* Mind is a prison and all that, yeah, sure. But why? Prison isn't the most instructional institution for students."

"I disagree."

Silence.

"What do you hope to achieve, Amy? If you had all the support and resources of the World at your disposal, what would you strive for?"

Let's be honest. "I don't know."

"Is your love for the Animalia Kingdom still there?" *—General Aba's snarling gorilla face roars into Amy's— —Archie the bat coos and hugs Amy with his wings—* "I suppose so."

"Are you still considering detective work?" *—Detective Jimmy's childish grin—*

—Bounty Hunter Praisure, air guns— "Hey there, lil lady" *— —an odd-faced detective tosses his thumb at her—* "Jimmy's pet project" *—*

"Not too sure. Where are the other students?"

"I've been meeting with each of you," said *another?* Graves' voice from afar. The Twin Graves leaned against the wall, scribbling in an old school notepad.

I'm seeing things again. The hell's wrong with my mind, fu—

"Don't let her bother you." Professor Graves waved over at her twin.

She Gma'd me. "You created an afterimage of yourself." Amy turned back to the Graves in front of her. "What's she writing?"

"What does it matter?"

"Well, I'd like to know what's being written during my unauthorized therapy session."

"There it is," Twin Graves said. "You want answers."

"Well. yes. That's not fair. I just said—"

"Tell me, Ms. Devine," *Graves OG* interrupted. "What do you fear?"

—Amy stands at the edge of her rooftop and stares down at 1000 corpses staring back at her—She turns around to the rotting face of her undead doppelganger—its face melts as

maggots crawl out—
You literally live on top of death.
Get over yourself.
Course, you'll become one of them.
—Amy blasts a mirror with her fist of white aura—
Amy massaged her temples. "I don't know if I have much time for fear these days."
—blood splatters across her face—
—Amy screams—
—Amy LAUGHS—

Graves chuckled. "This is your experience. The more you resist the power within these walls, the harder it will be for you to escape." She stood up. "Your mind, that is."

Twin Graves ceased her scribbles and placed eyes on Amy as well.

"We'll reconvene later. Remember our conversation, and next time, let's see what changes." The two Graves bowed to her and turned around. "Oh, and Ms. Devine?" The original Graves turned back. "What is your desire?"

Light left the room. Returned in an instant. *Neither*

Graves in sight.

A red square on the wall faced Amy with words above it:

TOUCH TO CONTINUE THE GAME

Amy placed her left hand in the square. It lit up.

Amy

Devine

Graves' booming voice echoed throughout the chamber.

Thank you all for participating in this Prison Games exhibition run by Ms. Genevieve Graves, Master of Games. You all have been chosen based on your hunger for undeterred knowledge, resiliency, and innate ability crafted by your curiosity.

Master of Games?

The week's objective is to escape the prison by moving through the prison floors and climbing each of the three levels. You are currently on Level 1. There will be two main challenges per level. One will be a high-stakes challenge. At the end of these types of challenges, the bottom two players on the scorecard will be sent to their cells for four hours.

"Oof." *Four hours?!*

The other challenge will be a prize fight, where players can earn bonus points and other incentives. At the end of each floor level, the two lowest-ranked players must return to the previous floor.

She's gone all out for our supposed benefit, but what's her aim?

Students will earn the names of the opponents they defeat in games. During games, you may gain insights about your opponents beneficial to your strategy and eventual escape. The numbers in your chambers are the same numbers you'll find on your talismans, 1-10. This is your identity, Numbers 1-10. At the end of each level, it will change based on your performance. Let me restate for clarity: rankings, aka, your identity, will only switch at the end of each level. This gives you time to find ways to improve your rank.

Glad we're calling it what it is. A chamber. What kind of <u>ways</u>?

The point system within games is as follows: First place is awarded 5 points, second place is awarded 3 points, and third place only receives 1 point. Whoever's in the penultimate position loses 1 point, and last place loses 3 points. Certain games may have a unique point structure and distribution, which will be given to you at the appropriate time.

Math is anal.

Amid all of this, some of you will receive roles in an ongoing game of reasonable deduction. The simple rule? Find the Most Wanted before the Most Wanted finds you.

She's clinical. Are we prisoners, test subjects, or both?

A final note. Spirit energy is everywhere throughout this prison. Including each of yours. You won't be using your spirits as normal during your stay here.

Your spirits will be using you. To train.

What the hell does that mean?
You have no spirit to use you.
Gather yourself, Devine. There are no voices in your head.

The first game starts in a few moments. Don't be alarmed, it's merely to get you accustomed to gameplay. Good luck to you all and play safely. Welcome to the Prison Games.

THOOOOOOM.

Behind Amy, cell bars made of dirt swung open. "All this magical nonsense. Professor should've been a magician." She stepped out of her *holding cell* and into the next room.

Let's review what I know.

Professor Graves
(Jadesfeld, London, England)

My old Headmaster at Highbridge Intermissionary School. A woman who knows everything without giving it off. Must stay vigilant under her eye. Mysterious mentor energy, but only gives out information when it suits her or in riddles. Calm, calculated, and commands respect without forcing it. I feel like she's testing us constantly, but none of us even realize how deep it goes. Yet. You don't gather a bunch of talented young auraists, entice them with a secret society, and drop cryptic hints about "Prison Games" without some deeper agenda. (no more detecting, Devine. Just go with the flow, observe, and keep Demo safe)

<u>Remarkables:</u>

- Coquelicot red aura

- Unknown level of aura mastery — This woman is leagues above the students. Doesn't just express herself with her aura—she controls it with pinpoint precision. And when she does she melts the rest of us just by being near. That's insane.

- Aura Manipulation Beyond the Norm - Her vast aura skills include levitation, physical altering, and possibly affecting the weather (rainstorm conveniently starting during training? Hmm...)

- Unshakable presence — No one argues with her. She'll just look at them and let them dig their own graves (pun intended).

- Has ties with a secret organization known as The Society of Great London (TSGL) which means she's not just some random teacher—she's got backing, resources, and inside knowledge.

- Ancient knowledge? That 57.65% aura sync thing? That's not random. She's working off advanced aura calculations that the rest of us didn't realize possible.

When & why did she start collecting students?

How does she know about ~~flow~~ ???

Can I <u>trust</u> her?

Demora Corbyn-McDonald
(Jadesfeld, London, England)

My best friend and top spar mate. If confidence lived and breathed on its own, Demora would be it. Can't believe I let her drag me into this. What do I expect, I'm a sucker for her. She's a natural talent when she chooses to, born for almost anything— and she knows it. Protective as hell, but just as reckless as I used to be. Demo barely acknowledges last year's events, but even she can't shake the effect of that awful curse. And her recent ordeal has me worried about her mental more than ever...

<u>Remarkables:</u>

- Fuchsia-pink aura

- Has <u>apparently</u> gained some secret abilities thanks to Graves (such as understanding the Gyaad language)

- Can probably wreck the rest of us here in a spar off of pure will

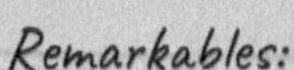

Kassandra Owens
(Jadesfeld, London, England)

Haven't heard much about her since last year. She's the only other sane person with me in that pit last year who remembers everything about the tragedy. She once told me her pronouns are sarcastic and blunt, but she forgot to add guarded in there. Skilled at aura manipulation, evidenced by her consistent use of an advanced technique like invisiauraism^{TM} (still planning to trademark that). Got a feeling she's clocked something's off with me. Observant as hell, that one. Uncomfortably too chill about some of the weirdest shit, like she's already five steps ahead of everyone else. If she ever sweats, I'll know to run.

<u>Remarkables:</u>

- Invisiauraism^{TM} - suppresses her aura's color (on purpose?)

- 1 of the tragic victims of "it" ~~(say his name, Devine)~~

- 1 of 3 "Lockheart Girls" (1 perished, 1 in asylum)

Jamari Wyst aka "The Midnight Inferno"
(London, England)

Lives for the attention. Everything he does, from his fighting style to his trash talk, is theatrical. His musical ability is multi-generational and top of our times. He may be more spectacle than skill. I don't know what's his beef with Mr. Stoicism. Partner of the Callisto's Light Org. (& believer)

<u>Remarkables:</u>

- Carnelian red aura

- Flashy moves but with staggering raw energy.

- Super showman whose ego could get him wrecked.

"Lil Sis" Wyst
(Lower NYC, New York City, USA)

She's Jamari's sister and opposite—low-key, serious, and watching everyone like she knows they're about to toe the line. Despite her brother's massive eminence, she's maintained a very private life— I searched the Internet but I couldn't find anything about her real name! Skeptical first and not afraid to say it. She's got a solid aura presence but doesn't waste time bragging about it. No wasted movement in her mannerisms, expressions, and words. I peg her as the smartest logical fighter in the group—analyze first, act second.

<u>Remarkables:</u>

- Milk chocolate aura

- So far, the only one who can keep Jamari in check, calling out his behavior

- Values trust and is hesitant to accept newcomers

- Gives off leadership qualities

Vedessia aka "Ms. Bubbly"
(Egypt?)

Comes off as super sweet, but I'm not that dense—there's something deeper there. Oddly in the know about things, and I'll have to corner and question her about them (easy there, Devine). In our prerequisites, her aura stood toe to toe with Demo's. Has an unfazed nature, by anything, a bit of a wildcard I'll have to watch out for.

<u>Remarkables:</u>

- Sand-colored aura

- May have high-level aura detection skills

- Eyes that melt your heart (what is she up to???)

- Softspoken firecracker of a woman who may have some kind of hidden emotion-manipulating abilities (I can't seem to focus straight around her.)

- Appears to be in training (for what? Sus)

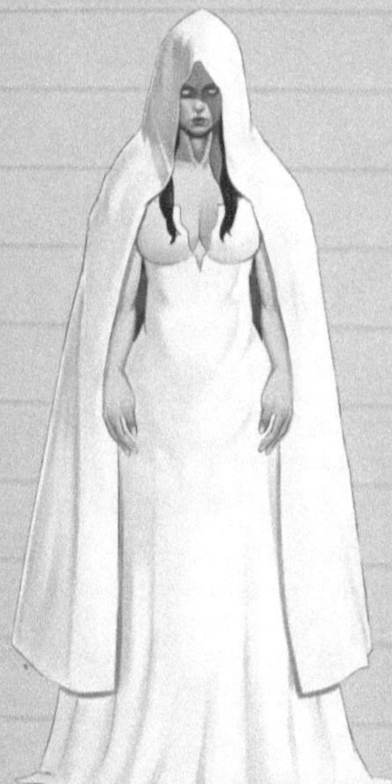

"The Gyaad Girl"

(Gyaad Sisterhood (location unknown))

I'll need to up my vocal and hearing ability to understand her, but her presence is LOUD. She's part of a rare species, and everyone respects her without hesitation (except rude-ass Jamari). Her sisterhood is in town searching for their sibling (could it be her?) Her aura work is on another level, blending multiple colors before settling into her natural one. Never seen that before. What other capabilities does her kind possess?

<u>Remarkables:</u>

- Radiates a rainbow-like aura that settles into a saffron-yellow shade

- Gyaad species, which has distinct features like blue skin, yellow eyes, & a veil-like substance around them

- Cannot communicate normally due to her species' precise voice waves

- May have other hidden abilities distinct for her bloodline

- Most likely the scariest fighter when fully unleashed.

"Ms. JellyRoll"
(Asia?)

Awesome hair. I swear she walks without her feet touching the ground. She always seems to be studying everyone like lab rats in a lab. A humane one, as she's actually quite sweet (so far). That lilac aura telescope thing? Yeah, she's not just here to fight—she's here to understand. Already taking notes on me. Iean what does she mean she can read me? I can't even read me anymore, but that's off-topic. If anyone's gonna bust our understanding of aura's potential, it may be her.

Remarkables:

- Lilac aura (with advanced demonstration including an aura ball as a telescope! Sick!)(but sus?)(too TOO nice)

- Enhanced aura visualization—she can see energy mechanics in ways others can't.

- A thinker, not a brawler—a strategic fighter.

"Mr. SmartyPants"
(Asia)

Saw his face in a Chinese gamer's magazine once. ill mad scientist vibes. What's with that weird utility belt he never parts with? Seems to be always calculating while everyone else gets lost in dramatics. Can't say the energy from his aura's been too impressive compared to the lot, but I'd be a fool to underestimate him this early in the game.

Remarkables:

- Viridian green aura

- Might be a skilled energy conserver, ready to take over in the long haul

- Scientific in approach

"Mr. Stoicism"
(London)

Tall stiff I can tell Demo's got the hots for. No idea about his skill yet but he's intensely focused most of the time. He and Jamari have an ongoing pissing contest, and it's a bit hilarious. Will keep an eye on him for sure.

<u>Remarkables:</u>

- Lapis lazuli blue aura. His aura work may be as rigid as him (brick House of power?)
- Pure strength and endurance—his aura's built like a tank.
- Probably an overachiever and a teacher's pet
- Plays Luxball. High skill athlete

Me (Amy Devine)
(Jadesfeld, London, England)

It doesn't matter who I am. People will grip their assumptions as religiously as their beating heart, anyway. Everyone keeps bringing up that damn pest, whose name I <u>won't</u> mention despite my hypocrisy in telling others not to be afraid to say its name.

<u>Remarkables:</u>

- Seashell white aura... formerly orange♥
- Annoyingly known as The Container or Newcomer
- Temporary schizophrenic
- ~~Failing in everything she does~~

Final Thoughts

STACKED group with talent here. I can't believe I'm rubbing shoulders with other auraists. They all seem confident in their capabilities and around each other. Some are probably way more powerful than they let on (looking at you, Vedessia and Gyaad Girl). Are there more groups of auraists out there? And what's Graves' investment in all of this?

Better question, who will be the first to snap?

Chapter Two

Level 1: Lab Rats

Amy entered a long narrow hall three times the size of her cell, *but still as claustrophobic on the nerves. Maybe fifty-foot end to end.* The thick smell of raw soil was inescapable. Harsh squares of white light— *aura from the earth?* — laid flat against the ceiling, beaming on her head.

No breeze. No doors, only hollow openings leading into other cells where the light doesn't reach all the way. The other prisoners stood before their cell bars, their shadows cast bigger than their silhouettes.

Amy found Demora's smiling face emerging from a cell down and across the way.

The concerned grumbling voices of the other students broke the soft hum that reverberated off the compact dirt walls.

"Have there been previous criminals here?"

"I'm not a criminal."

"I question Graves' motives more and more every day."

"I would have packed some swimming trunks had I known we'd be diving underwater." *Jamari* walked up last to meet the others in the room's center.

"Who said anything about swimming?" Lil Sis asked.

"Ridiculous." Mr. Stoicism shielded his eyes from the ceiling. "At least we'll get some false sunlight."

"There's some stairs at the end over there," Mr. SmartyPants pointed to a hole in the wall in one corner of the room. "But they're blocked off."

"I'm so excited for the games!" Vedessia smashed her fists together.

The Gyaad nodded with a smile.

Kassandra rolled her eyes.

"It's our rankings." Ms. JellyRoll pointed to a new square of white light on the wall. A *shadow-like* substance seeped from its corners and formed numbers 1-10. Next to each, pixels of light in each of the respective students' colors came together to create their faces.

Demora scoffed at the board.

"Hey." Amy nudged her. "It's all in the race, yeah?"

The test game will now commence. You're all familiar with the game Ring a Ring o' Roses. Don't fear; your ranks will be unaffected. You'll be performing two rounds. The first is a practice round, while the second game will determine who faces a mystery challenge immediately after.

"Sounds like a setup to me," Jamari said.

"Or an advantage." Mr. Smartypants rubbed his chin.

This challenge will test your form. To complete a round, your palms must fully push into the ground before your heels can touch the ground. You may find this common gymnasium routine a bit more difficult with the weight of your talismans. Good luck.

"Without our spirits?" Lil Sis scanned the prison complex for Graves' voice. "We're off balance. We could break something."

"What if we break the fifth chamber of our scaphoid cortex?" Jamari looked over his hands and adjusted his blockbuster shades at the ceiling.

"That's oddly specific, Wyst," Mr. Stoicism said.

One point deducted from Number 5.

"Hey! That's a thing?!" Mr. Stoicism threw his arms to the heavens.

"Ha-ha. Sucker," Jamari said. He checked over his hand again. "I broke it during a concert last year."

"I don't like the odds, regardless." Mr. SmartyPants cleaned his glasses and crouched, studying the ground. "This is deditrite soil."

"Who's soil?" Mr. Stoicism asked.

"It's rich soil usually found in deathwalker communities." Mr. Smartypants wiped a finger across the ground and smudged the dirt between his fingers. "Quite rare outside of them."

"It's the only soil that sparks the growth of false aura particles," Demora said. "It helps the undead keep feeding."

"Precisely." Mr. SmartyPants gave her a *sly* smile.

"Yeah, so they won't have to feed on us," Lil Sis said.

Demo scoffed. "That's an archaic mindset."

"True, though," Kassandra said. "Aura feeding originated with them."

"Blehk! Pink Blondie and Newcomer infested you with their weird word," Jamari *complained.* "You lost some cool points, yung gyal."

"Will you shut up?" Mr. Stoicism got in his face. "Your obnoxious nicknames are disrespectful! Can't wait to see you come in last."

"Oh, yeah, Mr. Luxballer? Aren't you out on injury? How's your balance holding up? Bet I take your spot before the next level."

"This is going to be a long week," Lil Sis said.

Vedessia nodded. "You're right about the off-balance. How do we complete the challenges without our spirit to guide us?" She smoothened a few of her frazzled curly hairs. "I feel like even the air down here is testing me to see if I could breathe right."

"You can never be off balance with your spirits in sight." Ms. JellyRoll glided towards them, her flowery skirt flowing across the ground in her wake. "That link never ceases."

"I see," Mr. SmartyPants said, his head lowered in deep thought. "Our spirit is never truly disconnected from us, or we'd be deceased. So this challenge must be about maintaining the link and strengthening the bond between us and our spirit."

"How are you doing?" Amy nodded over to the Gyaad, who sat cross-legged, her eyes gazing all over. "Taking it all in?"

The Gyaad's blank eyes stared at her. She gave a small nod.

Game starts in 5... 4...

The students shuffled into a circle, waiting.

... 3... 2...

Their fingertips touched one another, eyes moving from person to person.

A sensation burned up Amy's spine. *My aura's... excited?*

1...

A low-into-high-pitched **PING** echoed throughout the level.

The students skipped their feet to the side, their clockwise combined efforts creating a furious circle dance. They sang:

"Ring-a-ring o' roses,

A pocket full of posies.

A-tishoo!"

Amy sneezed—

"A-tishoo!"

Mr. Stoicism grunted something guttural—

"We all fall down!"

Amy dropped backwards and fell onto her palms. Her arms stiffened behind her as the middle of her chest gave a tiny **crack**. Her heels hit the ground last. Deep breath. **Sigh**. *Wasn't so bad.*

Well done, students. In terms of execution, only five of you would have been eliminated.

"Only?" Lil Sis said.

Did my heel touch before my palms rested? The deafening silence in Amy's mind *shatter my expectations for the round to come.*

Demora dusted herself off. Returned Amy's eye contact with a wink.

Glad she's comfy-cozy.

All right, let's reset everyone.

Amy rose and took some deep breaths. *At least I'm not the only one sweating.* Others wiped their faces from the drench of their work.

Jamari got off his knee, his talisman in hand. "This is absurd with the weight of these talismans."

The warmth in here is absurd. Must be from all our collective auras swirling around. Even so, it shouldn't be this humid, given the way dirt uses its energy to cool itself. Amy rubbed her foot into the dirt. *It mushes as though wet. This Prison... I bet none of this is real. An illusion. Graves must have some power source fueling the false image. Or...*

One more time, students. Remember, this one has a price.

Threaten us more, why don't you?

Starting in 3... 2...

I've got this.

1...

Here we go.

"Here we go." Lil Sis and Ms. JellyRoll spoke in unison. Nodded to one another.

PING!

I can do this.

"Ring-a-ring o' roses,
A pocket full of posies.
"A-tishoo! A-tishoo!
We all fall down!"

Amy blinked.

No, not this again! What happened? Amy observed her stance versus the others. *Form is top shape, thankfully, along with the others. Fucking blinking mess. It's all right. Doesn't mean I'm last place.*

Congratulations. Only four of you failed this time. Number 10, please step forth.

Fuck. Amy *followed orders.*

Everyone else, please take a position outside the square.

"Square?" Vedessia's head went one way, then the next. "What square?"

The Gyaad girl pointed.

In an almost quiet hiss, a 20x20 foot red square baked its way up from under the ground. The students backed out of it, Demora being the last, a smile on her face as she left Amy alone in the *square circle.* "You've got this." Demo nodded to Amy.

Number 10, as the last to take proper form, you will now face a mystery opponent in a wrestling match. This begins the first level of the Prison Games.

"What?! I haven't wrestled since secondary school."

"Oooooooos," from the gallery.

The match will officially begin at the sound of the ringbell. The conclusion will result from a pin, submission, disqualification, or countout.

I hate surprise match types. Amy kicked some dirt up. "Got to be kidding me."

Jamari held his belly as he laughed. "This is going to be quite the show after all!"

"For once, I agree with you," Mr. Stoicism said.

"What do you say, Mrs. Clouds?" Jamari mimed reading a book with the whites of his eyes peeking over it. "Can you <u>contain</u> this one?"

Amy cracked her neck. *I'll just have to prove his eminency over here wrong <u>again</u>.* The earth under her shook from the vibrations of Jamari's cackling. *Such a pro singer, yet unable to control his vocal waves. No wonder he can't understand the Gyaads.*

"She was once ranked number one." Demora waved him off

like a fly. "Put some respect on her name."

"Oh, our apologies, best friend of the great Cloudy Container!" Lil Sis rolled her eyes. "Please don't forsake us, barren children."

She just had to add her rendition of humorous melody, infecting my eardrums. Amy sucked air through her nose. Let it out her mouth. She repeated the sequence with closed eyes.

An angry quake ceased the noise from the students. At one end of the room, the middle of the wall split from the ground, rising with a blinding light behind it. A silhouette made its way from within the depths.

"Who the hell is that?" Jamari said.

A man in a clean, pressed suit and pinstripe pants waddled towards them. He squeezed a single yellow plume in his breast pocket twice. His *dashing* smile ate a bead of sweat. "It's... it's such an honour to be here tonight... in front of thrashing young minds." His eyes scanned the ground. "Sorry... bit nervous, it's just... doesn't matter..." He reached the center of the square. "Please to meet you, young lady. You can call me—"

No names.

"Oh, right, sorry-Professor Graves. Wow. I can't believe we're all here. Spirit wielders altogether in one space." His sweaty, tango-pink face scanned the others. "The world out there is scary. Guess you all know that. Us Peculiars bite the bullet regardless of allegiance." He grabbed his head. "Man... Okay. I should stretch. Yeah." Smiled at Amy. "Feel free to warm up, too. I won't rush you."

Amy stepped back as the man bent straight forward and hugged his legs in one clean motion. Her eyes stayed on him as She stretched one arm, then the next across her torso. *What's he on?* She took another step back as the man fell back like a domino, still hugging his legs. *We have a gymnast on deck.*

"That's a bit better." *The Dashing Man* unfolded his body, stretched his arms above his head, and down to his feet.

Fighters, take your position in the middle of the ring.

Amy and the Dashing Man met in the middle of the *squared circle*.

"Good… luck…" He bowed to her. "Yeah… Good luck to us both."

Amy returned the bow. "Good luck." *Something's off with this bloke.*

Here are some guidelines in case you need a refresher. If your opponent submits, release your hold immediately. At the third count of a pin, the one who tops must relieve their opponent from their pinned position. Disqualifications will be enforced, so keep all hits and maneuvers clean. If you find yourself outside the square, you have five seconds to return inside of it.

Amy raised an eyebrow as an absurd amount of sweat dripped off the *overly* smiling man's cheek. *He's off his rocks for sure.*

May your spirit guide you.

DING DING DING!

Chapter Three

Level 1: A Dashing Dance

Current Rankings & Points

The sharp ding rode the air in waves. Crooning sounds echoed *in the walls, angry, distant,* dying out. *Could swear something's alive within.* Amy refocused on her opponent.

"Ok. Ok, I've got this. Come on, we can do it." The Dashing Man hopped on the balls of his feet in all directions of his immediate bubble. He raised his arms to initiate a lock up.

Amy raised hers to match. Took measured steps towards the man.

His arms curled into himself *the way cats used to do when scared.* "Oh-my-oh-my, here she comes—oh! Oh-oh-oh my, ok, ok, ok..."

What is happening?

They circled each other, taking steps towards one another, only to retreat faster than they approached.

What style is this? Can't get too close.

The man pivoted away from her each time they got too close, sucking in his congested rapid breathing, followed by an utterance that became clear after the sixth false initiation of combat. "Can't believe this is happening we got this we got this we got this can't believe it okay no we can do it we can do it keep your wit keep your wit it's only a fight can't believe it we got this we got this—"

The hell is he on? Alright, if you're ripe for the picking. Amy pushed her left hand towards his while her right aimed below the waistline.

He adjusted his pivot and hopped towards her, both hands matching hers.

"Any day now, either of you!" Jamari *moaned.*

With grinding teeth and a final exhale, She stepped forward to intertwine fingers with the bumbling man. She pushed against his momentum. *Loose grip there, chum. Here goes—* Amy twisted her palms to the sky, bringing his along with **cracking** results.

"A-aachk!" Dashing Man hopped from foot to foot, trying to pull away.

Amy pulled him closer, smashed her knees into his

stomach, and dropkicked his chest.

He landed on his back outside the square.

"Attagirl!" Demora's voice echoed.

Amy crouched, smiled, and readied her arms.

The Dashing Man flustered in his recovery. He got off his butt and ran towards her, trembling head to heel.

Some challenge. Amy threw her fist through his chin—

—at least, I thought—

F a d e d... Amy, on tiptoe, shook her cobwebs as She recalled the last moments—

—Dashing Man's head jerks slightly out of range—smiles as her fist travels past his left cheek— His smile turns upside down—mouth stretches—

"aaAAAAAAAAAAAAACK!"

aMy's EaRDRUumSss— **PINCHING PIERCING PUTRID PERCUSSIONISTIC PIPING**— flooded her head. *Not enough— time— recover—*

Dashing Man's perpendicular arm flew at her— fist jammed into her lumbar, reaching into her upper abdomen— *hypochondriac region—*

"Hey-ey-**EY**-ey," his voice echoed an infinite parade that abused her eardrums. "I'm not-**NOT**-not really su-**SU**-supposed to stop-op-**OP-OP**, but I just need a second o-o-**O**-o-**O**-o-okay?"

Jitters overtook Amy's frozen body. *Can't fo-fo-o-ocus... next s-s-s-step-ep-ep... to move... where-ere—*

The Dashing Man's face fractured in three pixelated parts. His mouth moved, but the distorted words jumbled in her brain. "Here-yes-we-I know-wonderful-to me-frightened-than you are."

He's moving too fast. I can't— where is he? It's the most—so loud—

" a a a a a a **a a A A A A m m** m y y y y y y ... aaaaaAAAAmmmyyyyyy... AaaAAmyyy... Amy!"

"Ah!" Amy lifted herself off the ground with one arm. The other arm—bent behind her at an excruciating angle—held by her opponent sitting on her. *How'd I end up eating dirt?*

"He-he-hey, maybe you can tap out and we can end this more quickly, you know? P-p-please?"

"Come on, get up!" Demora yelled. "Get out of this! You can do it! Or he'll break your arm!"

Amy, barely able to turn her chin from digging into the ground, kept her left peripheral on her best friend.

"He wouldn't." Ms. JellyRoll, next to Demora, raised an eyebrow at her. "This is an exhibition. Graves wouldn't let—"

"Oh, he'll break it if necessary, I'm almost sure," Mr. SmartyPants said. "Our double jointed nature means more pain to be felt. She'd live. Heal in great time. It's our gift. We're here to be pushed to our limits. As far as we can take them, I suspect."

Demo groaned. "Don't piss me off, four-eyes, or you may need a stronger prescription once I'm done with you."

"A traditional ribbing. I respect it." Adjusted his spectacles on his nose. "Look around, class. Does this look like formal instruction? This is what we've waited for. The genuine test of our spirits. A shame the new girl had to be up first. She had no idea what she was getting herself into."

Everyone shut it for a minute. Amy closed her eyes. Her body shook with violence, pushing up against her opponent's force. *I am NOT falling here. I don't care if my arm breaks.*

"Hey, New Girl," Mr. SmartyPants' voice called. "Or, should I say, Number 10? Your opponent comes from a society of skilled fighters terrified of combat. Their obnoxious, frightened squalls are meant to disarm you. They're incredibly superior at hitting you with a ton of force in a fraction of time, coupled with the strength of their actual fear."

What the hell? That's absurd!

"I've never heard of no blokes like that," Jamari said.

"Your musical wits will only get you so far in this life."

"Watch it or I'll knock teeth from that smile and write a song about it."

"I believe it. Your uncontrolled anger is evident." Mr. SmartyPants chuckled over Jamari's growls. Anyway, thought I'd throw you a bone, Number 10. Now you can owe me one. How about it?"

"Sure." *Damn, my shoulder's out of sorts.* A sharp numbness shot down the left side of her neck to her elbow. Amy shifted that side on the ground, threw her head back into his face, and twisted out of his grip. She rolled away.

Feet away, Amy held her limp left arm. She shook it out, yet it remained a ghost. "Certainly <u>not</u> the grip of a nonfighter." *No matter. Enough of your tricks. They won't match what's coming.*

"Oh, dear!" The Dashing Man grabbed his bloody nose. "Let's end this, please!" He threw his arms in surrender. Pulled the plume from his breast pocket and dabbed it all over his face, *especially the bleeding nose.*

What the—

A spritz flew from the plume and into his face. "I just want to end this as quickly as possible. Let's let's let's let's—" His face jerked in seizure. "—let's let's let's d-do it!"

"More tricks." *Is that some type of enhancer? A toxin? No matter. All I need is one strike...*

"O-o-o-o-okay..." He shuffled towards her on tiptoes. "H-h-h-here goes."

That's right, you bastard. If you want to end this so badly, come end it. Come on! I want you to do it.

He sped forth on tiptoes. "Here we go okay okay this will be quick, miss, I promise."

Amy stood her ground. Guarded herself with her right arm, palm facing him.

His arm smacked her shielding arm away.

Gotcha. Using his momentum, Amy jumped—spun—hand on the ground as she pushed off in the opposite direction.

His fist launched an uppercut at her face.

Amy's left arm crossed the back of her right— her palm ate his attempted punch—

He swatted at her with his free arm.

Amy's other palm ate his hand. *My turn.* She tightened her grip.

"Ah-aaa-GAaaaaa!"

Amy's eyes closed at his squealing. "Shut it!" On one foot, she jumped again— flipped over his shoulder— snapped his failed punching wrist backwards— stuck a knee into his back— digging— and pushed him facefirst into the ground. Her free hand snatched his free arm. Yanked his arms behind him, <u>The Maaura Style lock in place.</u>

"Please please that hurts! My wrist!" His tears soaked the ground. "Oh please please stop it please get it off get her off please!"

"Submit!" Amy's knee dug deep into his spine, twisting into each vertebra. She squeezed his arm and clawed into his bent wrist, pulling both—*taking special attention to bend the injured wrist further back.*

"I submit! Please!"

DING DING DING!

Amy released the dashing, red-faced puddle of a man and jumped back. Landed near the edge of the square.

Your winner: Number 10! Well fought, both of you.

"That's my girl!" Demora punched the air.

Amy beamed at her from behind sweat-drenched locs. Butterflies in her gut. *Haven't felt those since I last sang. Gma raised me to be a fighter. I am a fighter. Maybe I can do this. Perhaps I belong here.* Formerly drowned out by her attention in the match, She took in the hoots and hollers that had been going nonstop since her match's climax.

The Gyaad girl jumped up and down, *more like floating.* Her mouth moved, but no words came out.

"Well-well, old girl has a little fight in her." Jamari chuckled.

"Suppose so." Mr. SmartyPants smirked. "Though that gentleman wasn't even a category B fighter. You're welcome, 10."

"I'd say her ability got her through there, glasses," Demora said.

"Wasn't too shabby." Lil Sis filed her nails.

"Appearance already suffering, princess?" Demora asked her.

Lil Sis kept filing, *unbothered* eyes sticking on her task. "I would <u>never</u> want to harm one of my classmates— oh, no!" She feigned surprise, holding out her fingertips to the crowd. "Look like they're sharper. Too bad I don't have my better filer." Her eyes crossed over to Demo. "Let's pray I don't injure someone on accident."

Jamari watched the two with a crooked smile. "It's on sight."

"Ability gets us far." Ms. JellyRoll glided over to Amy. "But our heart makes the difference. Her opponent failed with no game plan other than attempting to reverse his fears onto his opponent." She inspected Amy's body, circling thrice. "While Number 10 calculated the precise moment to initiate her maneuver, which isn't easy with the Maaura Style."

"Ack-ack, yeah, yeah." Demora shooed her away from Amy. "What's Maaura?" She pointed to the Gyaad girl behind her. "She keeps raving about it."

"Gma taught it to me. Some ancient fighting style she said I'd find useful." Amy shrugged. "Guess it was."

Demora rubbed her chin. "You'll have to fill me in. Keeping secrets?"

"You were—*watch your words, Devine, don't remind her—* unavailable."

Demo nodded *as though just remembering.* "Right, right."

"Ughhh..." The Dashing Man sulked away from the crowd, rubbing his head. He waved a hand back. "Good fight, miss. Hope we never have to again."

"Good game, mate." A laugh escaped Amy's belly. "I hope he's alright."

"He'll heal." Demo threw an arm around Amy.

All right, students. That was the commencement of the first high-stakes challenge. This will be a one-on-one wrestling match. Your performances will be scored on technique and efficiency. Remember, points are awarded to the top three performers, and points are taken away from the bottom two. The current top five ranked students will get to choose their opponent. Since Number 10 already had her challenge, she will not be available for selection. Number 1, please select your opponent.

Vedessia stepped forward, smiling as she gazed into the ceiling. "I choose... to forfeit my priority selection to Number 2."

"What?" Several voices chimed in.

"Wow."

"Is that allowed?"

"Nonsense."

"Can I <u>choose</u> to have a BYE?"

Silence answered their pleas.

Why'd she forfeit to Demo? Amy sat right outside the squared circle.

Vedessia glanced back at her and winked before turning back around.

Amy raised an eyebrow. *Did she do that for me?*

Number 2, please make your selection. Choose your opponent.

Demora strolled into the middle of the ring. "I choose Number 8."

"Ooooh!" Mr. Stoicism sneered with delight. "This should be good. Let's see Mr. Showstopper in action. What do you say, Wyst?"

No names. One point deducted from Number 5.

"Are you—dammit. Malarkey..." Mr. Stoicism sat at the edge of the ring.

"Please." Jamari flipped his token as he strolled by Number 5, his other hand waving him off. "That's a lesson in keeping my name out your mouth."

"Be careful, brother," Lil Sis said.

"Heard." He strolled right up to Demora. "You ready to give up that name of yours, Pink?"

The statuesque Demora did not stir, arms crossed, eyes closed.

Kassandra sat next to Amy. "Think she'll finish quicker than you?"

"I hope so."

"She'd place better than you."

"That's okay."

"Hm."

Seeing Demo in action again is nice, but is it too soon? Last time she fought someone other than me, they ended up dead. And she's barely said a word about her ordeal... the toll it must've taken on her...

Current Rankings & Points

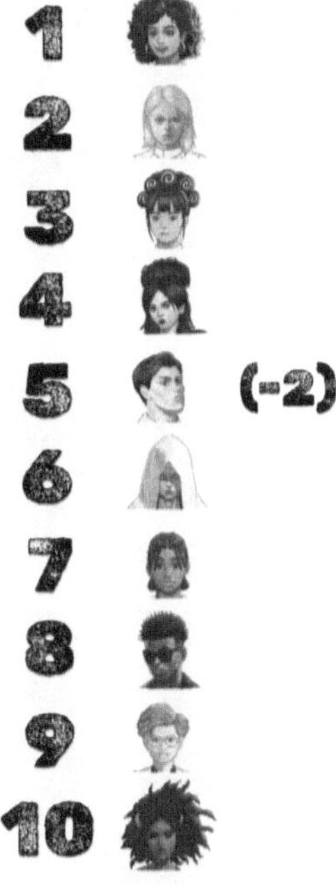

Jamari adjusted his blockbuster shades. "Let's get it."

Please remember, victory comes at a pin, submission, disqualifications or countout. May your spirit guide you.

DING DING DING!

Chapter Three

Chapter Four

Level 1: Our Demons Haunt Us

The chatter of the students mellowed to nothing as the two new wrestlers stood on opposite sides of the ring. Jamari took a few steps towards Demora. Tightened his fists at her immobility.

For the first time, Amy couldn't *feel Demora. It's a strange thing. All my life, I've always felt her there. Aside from— But right now, it's all dead air. The stench of the muddy smell is clogging my supped-up electrolarynx.* She smacked her dry lips together and apart, *loathing the earthy taste.*

Jamari bent his head and angled his body *like a staggering scarecrow.*

Demora remained unmoved.

Jamari stopped feet in front of her. "We're supposed to be wrestling. Do something or I'll have to knock you down, Pink."

Demora, unfazed.

"Whatever." He launched his arms towards her.

Demora her arms became wings, stretched to her sides, eyes still closed. Fell back.

Jamari grabbed her shoulders to stop her from falling. "Huh? What are you crazy?"

Demora's fingers clawed into his shoulders— *Did I blink?—*

and lifted him at an angle. Her head dodged his falling sunglasses as she twisted her body.

"WHAT—wait, how?!" Jamari's arms flailed, eyes wide. "Drop me!"

"Gladly."

I've never seen her move this fast! Where's—

Demora spun in midair, grabbed his falling body behind his kneecaps, and her leg straddled his neck from the front— *choked it*— landed on top of him— a **CRACK** as Jamari's back hit the ground. She pulled his legs towards her, bending as far into his torso as would go.

1... 2... 3.

DING DING DING!

"So soft." Demora released him. "Yet act so hard." She towered over his trembling body as it uncrumpled from its side position. "Those with crowns need to be taught they can be peasants, just the same." She turned her back on him. "And save your breath. I already know your name. We all do." She walked off, head held high.

Your winner is Number 2! Great match, students.

"Jamari!" Lil Sis ran over to him.

Please refrain from names. One point deducted,
Number 7.

"Man, forget—" Lil Sis cupped underneath Jamari's arm as he sat on his butt with a hand on his lower back. "Come on, let's get you up." She helped him to his feet and walked him a few paces, but he pulled away to continue solo.

Before we continue the rest of the matches, Number
10, please enter the corridor behind you.

"Huh?" Over Amy's shoulder, where there was once a solid dirt wall, an open corridor awaited her at the end of the room. She took Demora's helping hand and stood.

"Be careful." Demo patted her on the back. She leaned in close to Amy's ear. "Make physical contact as much as possible. See if you can feel their aura's strength."

"Right." Amy's eyes passed over the others before she headed for her new destination. *This is already exhausting. Now I won't get to see the other matches? Stupid.* Peering back, Demora enjoyed the praise she got from a few souls. *Bask in it, my love. Stamp your seal. I'm curious what strengths the others have. I may be out of league. Left a cheerleader. That's all I'm good for anyhow.*

She paused in front of the corridor and its unending darkness. *More of this. Here we go.* She entered. *Demo's gotten so much faster. Is it cuz of Graves' tutoring? Wonder what the others are like?*

Behind her, the opening She came through slid shut.

A faded spotlight over her head cast the only light in the corridor. It moved with her as she continued forward in the dark.

"Of course." *Graves. One twisted teacher. First, she has us fighting, now this.* "Ah fuck!" She rubbed her eye from the sting. *Something in my eye. This dusty dreadpot of a prison.* "Ah! The hell?" Amy swatted around her bobbing and weaving head. She sucked in air— hawked spit against the wall. Pressed her lips and eyes shut, intermittently peeking to see what was in front of her. Her hands slapped the air with violent abandon. *Are you fucking kidding me? Fucking cherryflies? Picking at me like I'm a child of a mazzard. For fuck's sake, Graves!*

She jogged down the corridor, hands out, *hoping to collide with something soon. This is absurd. I'm missing the matches for this? Ridic— Yes!* Her hand grabbed the edge of the wall beside her and she turned the corner. Her hand accidentally smacked her face, trying to get one of the cherryflies. *Okay, there's got to be something around here to help me get rid of these shits. Fucking hell.* She paused. *What's that sound?* Pushed her arm out *to be sure— Fuck yes*—another opening. Watched her feet walk within her cone of light.

I'm getting hungry already. There should have at least been some snacks, definitely water, after a fight. She slapped her left eye at the *invisible pest* pulling on her eyelid. Slapped her cheek, forehead, shoulder, shoulder, shook out her locs—*Where the hell does this path go?*

Turned another corner, *another corner, another corner...* She waved her hands out. *Endless corners. This is insane.* Collapsed on her knees, slapping her temples over and over. "Buzz off!" Her fists hit the ground, followed by her forehead. "Come on!"

Minutes of breathing exercises later...

This is no time for a tantrum. Amy fell back on her butt and crossed her legs, ignoring the constant insect pinches against her flesh, pounds on her skull, or attempts to insert through all her openings. She hummed low, drowning out the ceaseless buzzing of the critters and the walls combined. Stared into the bleak dark ahead. *Dalestone's dread devours me evermore. At least I got to see Demo's fight. Graves isn't fooling anyone. This place doesn't exist. Mind tricks, aura tricks. What is the answer to the trick? Gma would say to look for the source. Where's the source?*

It exists. It's the SUTBAA again.

No, this place does NOT exist. Wait, was that my— never mind. Focus, Devine. Amy closed her eyes. "Please don't go up my nostrils." She covered them and took deep, closed-mouth breaths. *Where IS the source? Perhaps I can sense it. Aura is always connected.*

The pelting against her skull aside, Amy straightened her back, nose to the heavens. *Where the <u>fuck</u> is the source? With respect. Where the fuck's the source?*

Her breaths got shallower by the second. *Where the fuck is the source? Where—*

Attagirl. You're ripe for it.

"Fuck!" *Who the fu—* Amy opened her eyes. *Who am I kidding? My aura's gone to shit.*

Hey!

Aura, is that you?

She waited for a reply. Sighed. *The cherryflies' incessant buzzing diminished to a third of their original power. If I could pull the plug on this structure...*

Amy swatted at her nose as the insect unrest grew again.

Why are they starting up again? She slapped and shook her hair out. Froze. "Ok, relax, Devine. Relax for a second." *Don't murder yourself for these annoying little bugs— language, they are mother nature's creations as well. Watch your language regarding the insects. Breathe.* She did. Her head was silent for a few moments before the buzzing of cherryflies began again.

Oh, I see. Her eyelids kissed as she took deeper breaths. *Shan... What did Vedessia say again?........ Hiska. Shan hiska. She's a little sus, but I kind of like that. Something's wrong with me.*

We all knew that.

Who— **Sigh** *Shan hiska.* She breathed in and out at <u>her</u> rhythm. Her methodical breaths matched her heart's beat and the thumps of her index fingers on her thighs. *Shan hissssskaaa...*

She grimaced and nudged her head away from the touch of the bugs. Relaxed.

Minutes passed till silence won again. *There you go. They're only as mad as the clutter in my head. That's it. Not even the cherryflies are real.* Took a deep breath. *Now stop.*

Her cheeks flinched. She stared down at her nose. "Nasty nobdickers still hanging around, huh? Welp." She got to her feet, her eyes still focused on her nose. "As long as I keep my head clear, we'll make it through. Sit tight, my little nuisances cuz I've got to get a move on. Come along, little shits."

Step by cautious step, the buzzing in her head grew and fell, over and over, *battling my head's intrusive thoughts. Invisible insects. Proves we must be in some conjured area of the Aura Realm. It can't be the Realm of Lucidity unless our bodies are unconscious back where we started. Can it? That would be a high risk, even for a master like Graves.* She licked her lips and *regretted* the salt of the wing she tasted. "So much for fake. Maybe some aspects of this prison are real." Her eyes darted ahead. "What's that?"

A spotlight of brown light many feet away in the never-ending darkness. A single figure stood in the middle of it.

"Shall we, my winged annoyances? Tuck your feet in. A tumultuous road awaits us." Amy moved towards the unknown scene in the distance, each step gaining her confidence as the cherryflies remained in limbo.

The closer she got, the warmer she felt.

Double her height stood a display case of brown light. Imprisoned inside *her <u>own</u> aura?* —Jamari's sister, on her knees. Her face cried quiet bloody murder. Her trembles controlled her, feet buckling under the pressure. She backed away from *something invisible.*

Amy circled the girl's glass-like entrapment. *How did she—* She teased a finger on it but pulled back after a teeny discharge dissuaded her. *This light's pure solid. She must be strong to produce such a clean technique.* Scratched her head as the girl trapped inside scurried from corner to corner. *What's she afraid of? There's nothing in there with her.*

Eyes shut, Lil Sis brought her hands together and bowed. She whispered something over and over, tears of makeup streaming down her face.

Tried to teach us... Can't hear the rest; her lips are moving too fast. Tried to teach us what?

The terrified girl's braids bounced, and her face shivered like a chilled wind kept slapping her around every other second. Her back angled as though icicles ran up it.

Light warmed Amy's back. Behind her, an open door of white light.

Lil Sis banged on the glass, mouthing something to Amy, *just noticing my arrival.* She jumped back. Cowered in one corner of the box like a babbling toddler.

Amy stared back and forth between the door of white light— *my exit—* and the girl. *I can't leave her like this.*

I must leave her.

Amy moved ahead of Number 7's imprisonment. *That's what Graves wants. I have to do it, right? Always have to 'do the thing.' It's not like I have an opinion of my own.* Several feet away, she spun around to face the girl's aura imprisonment again. *Because Graves said so. These childish games.* She crouched. *Won't put me in a box.*

Amy charged towards her classmate's prison. *Light... vibration... it can work.* She smashed her hands into the box, sending waves coursing through the electrifying *cage.* Her teeth clamped together as her palms sizzled against the surging wall. "Can you hear me?"

Their eyes locked again. Lil Sis nodded with urgency. "A little, yeah. I hear you," she mouthed through wet lips of sadness.

Amy's eyes examined the girl's predicament. Stayed on her shadow. *No time for a theory, Devine. But if her duress can trigger it—* "With light comes shadow! Use your shadow!"

"What?!" Lil Stumbled into one corner of the box. The sobbing girl's eyes fell on the invisible entity trapped, *seemingly looming over her.* She flinched at its threatening movements and mouthed more unheard things.

I'll admit, what I said was vague. "It's your light!" Amy pointed down. "Let your shadow overwhelm it! Use your sha-dow!" She raised her voice a hair above the surging of the electric aura walls. *Throat's starting to itch.*

Lis Sis' widened eyes searched the ground. She nodded. Closed her eyes. Held her arms out over her shadow.

An unseen force threw her hair back on end, nearly sending the girl off balance. Lil Sis flinched, inching herself deeper into her corner. She clawed at her neck, *trying to free herself of hands only she could see.*

Dammit, she's not gonna make it much longer in there. Amy banged on the cage. "You got this, come on!" Took turns shaking out each hand, returning them to push against the trap. *My hands can't take much more of this! Damn, it burns!*

Defiant lines poked out of Lil Sis' forehead and temples, and she tried to stand tall, her closed eyes squeezed together. But her body wouldn't budge against its invisible captor's presence.

Think, Devine, think. "AH, fu—" Amy backed away from the muffled shotgun sound below her, shaking the singe off her hands. Patted the waking nerves in her leg. Her sneaker and sock on that leg had their front blown off, a small smoke trail rising. "That's insane!" *Her power is immense. The electrical field it's generating nearly took my damn leg off! How?* Amy removed the sneaker and sock from her aching foot. "Okay, we can do it." She hovered her hands over the box of light, leaving inches between her and the surface. "Careful…"

Lil Sis' body rose off her feet, held around her neck by the presence.

Amy's eyes narrowed on her. *What am I doing? Fuck!*

Great Cloudy Container who?

Shut up shut up shut up shut up shut up—

The top of Lil Sis' head reached her trap's ceiling. Her eyes rolled back in her head.

Come on! This is no time to be useless, Devine! Just cut me a fucking break— "AH!" Amy didn't have time to scold herself for screaming as her vision went white. Her scarred right hand clamped around her own throat— *meaning to massage—* but forcibly squeezed the burning sensation down her esophagus. Still, it was nothing compared to the scorching, scraping pain her exposed foot on the ground experienced; the foot tensing up in its seizure of hot stabbing. She slammed her right hand back on the Lil Sis' aura prison.

Amy blinked.

The world of the prison pixelated back into her vision.

Lil Sis stooped over her, lips moving, but no sound. The black landscape of the corridor they were in scattered away *like locusts looking for their next meal.*

Amy sat up and despite Lil Sis's shaking of her shoulder, time was still slow and delayed, yet fragments of what happened came back to her. *Jamari's sister… trapped… in her own aura… my shoe blew off…*

Sound came back as the *ringing of ball bearers at an undead scrap for survival. Lutherson vs Mathymer, what a match.*

"Girl, are you alright?" Lil Sis asked.

"Yeah." Amy coughed at the settling smoke show she now noticed all around them. Behind Lil Sis, the aura trap she was in was gone. "What happened?"

Lil Sis wiped her face aggressively with her yellow jacket sleeves— *wiping away her tears*— and fanned away the remaining smoke.

An orange-brown electric spark struck between their accidentally touching fingers. Both girls immediately withdrew their hands. Lil Sis' eyes quivered in full sight of Amy.

"What?" Amy asked.

"That's—" Lil Sis looked down, *trying to find her words.* "Callisto once said a spirit's light can't grow dark…" She stood up, her face screwed up in her thoughts. "It's a hypothetical."

"What is?"

"I'm not sure what I saw. But your spirit energy grew dark. And it looked— mean."

Mean? "I don't understand. What did you see?"

"Almost looked like it had a face."

Amy's eyes widened.

"But it didn't! No, it was the— the detail in your energy. I've never seen anything like it before."

"What— what did it do?"

"It ate my spirit's prison."

"Ate?"

Lil Sis nodded to herself, pacing in spot as *her mind worked overtime.* "Theories of dark photons being tangible have been debunked for ages. I'm not sure what I saw, but… you manifested something that shouldn't be. Even Callisto was skeptical about dark matter's potential and she was a raging optimist."

"I— It was an accident." Amy stared at the girl, stumped. *My spirit grew dark? Dark photons?* "I did?" She looked down at her busted sneakers. "Those were my favorites."

"You sure you're alright?" Lil Sis helped Amy to her feet. "Does this whole blackout thing you've got going on happen often?"

"Lately. I get more confused each new time."

"I'm assuming you're getting that checked out?"

"It's a work in progress." *Like shadow work. Did I really create... black light? Shadow light?*

"Thanks, by the way. I owe you one."

"Please." Amy threw up a bored hand.

Lil Sis stared into the door of white light waiting behind them. "Graves knew the one thing that haunts my nightmare's nightmares. I wasn't ready for it." Her eyes scrolled Amy from top to bottom. Her eyebrows tightened *making a decision.* "My name's E'oné." Her voice echoed. "Shit." After a few moments of silence, "Guess it's fine, no one else is here. Now we're even cuz I don't like owing favors. Keep this quiet."

"Say no more."

"Us sisters gotta stick together." E'oné took out lipstick and reapplied the shade of green on her lips. "This place sucks."

"I got got with cherryflies. What was the thing haunting you?"

"Something that should have stayed dead a long time ago." E'oné shivered head to toe and put her lipstick away. "Okay, let's move, come on, girl."

Lil Sis/*E'oné* walked in stride, leaving her previous shattered disposition behind. Amy followed with hesitant steps.

"Do you really watch undead scraps?"

"Just the once when they were legal and streaming. I was 8. I thought they were all staged for entertainment. Once I learned about the nature of the fights, I tuned out. Can't support forced cannibalism, even if the parties are already dead."

"That's real."

Amy took a deep breath and returned E'oné's nod as *her unlikely ally for the moment* guided them into the dazzling light.

Chapter Four

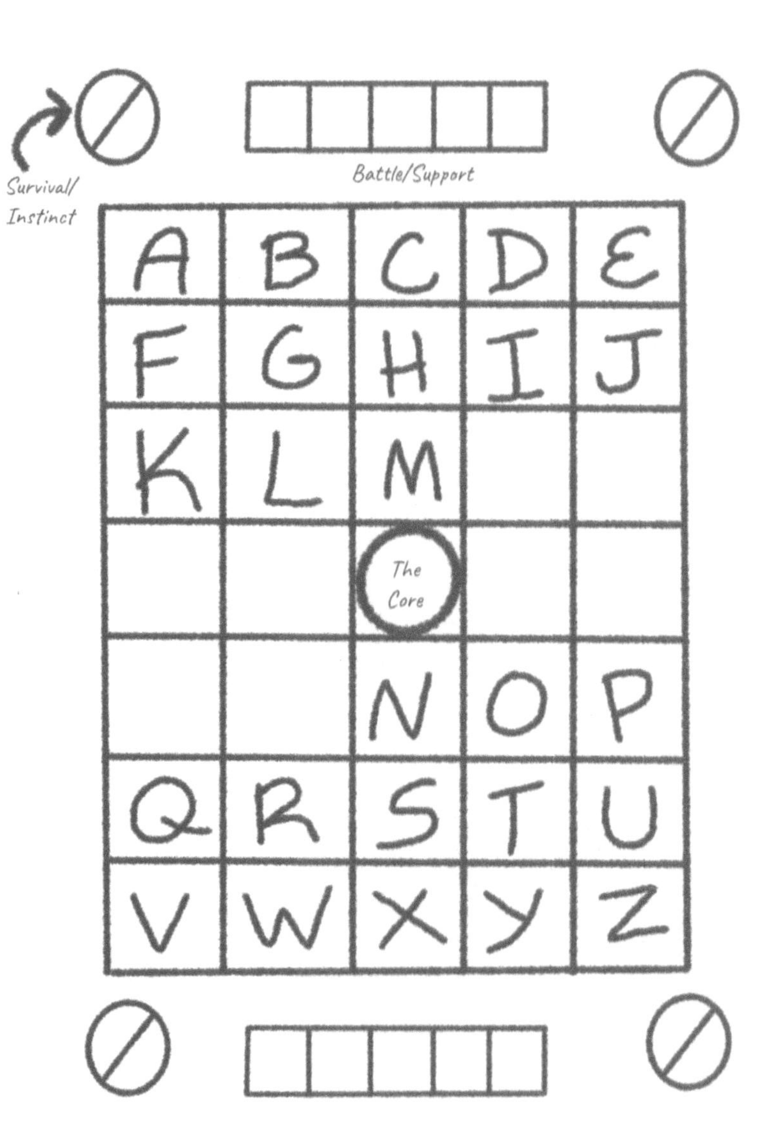

Survival/
Instinct
Battle/Support
A B C D E
F G H I J
K L M
The
Core
N O P
Q R S T U
V W X Y Z

Chapter Five

Level 1: Soul Game

The tight space of mudded dirt contained their two souls, stooped, light casting their shadows bigger than their frames. "Those matches sure going slow, huh?" Amy chewed through her words.

"I got sent away during the match after mine." E'oné picked a taco while smiling at the other on her ceramic plate. "I could get used to this service." She waved her taco like a wand.

"Cheers." Amy met her waiting taco. They dapped their tacos together.

E'oné stood to study the menu items carved into the muddy dirt wall before her. "Number 1 versus Number 6 was taking forever."

"She must be getting this stuff delivered. No way she's got cooks on location for this fake prison." Amy looked up. "Huh? Wait, how many matches have gone on?" *How long have I been here?*

"Fake prison? My match was after my brother's, then 1 and 6 were up next. Damn, they could go." E'oné stared past the menu for a moment and then returned to it. "When I was sent off, their match was at the twenty-five-minute mark."

"Twenty-five?!"

"It was amazing. I haven't seen the others brawl, but I must admit, those two are top fighters in our group. I have work to do if I want to catch up with those two in the ring."

Amy slurped her strawberry smoothie and sank back against the wall. "Was my friend sent off anywhere?"

E'oné's nose flared up, her eyebrow raised. "No. She was still there." She eyed the ceiling. "Ok, I'd like to order the curry chicken and sweet plantains with the mellowbread." She folded her arms and turned to Amy. "So, black light, huh? How'd you do it?"

Amy shrugged and threw her head against the wall. "I've been working at that for months. <u>Apparently</u>, I finally succeed. But I'm too busy being unconscious to realize." Amy peeked at her through her locs. "It's weird having someone new to talk to this about." She frowned into space. "Shit. I haven't talked to Demo about this yet."

E'oné smirked. "Since I witnessed it, mind keeping me in the loop?"

Amy's face considered her options. "Sure. Is this pleasure or desire?"

"Desire. You could say I'm something of a scientist myself."

Scientist??? ME? HA. Not this Amy Devine; maybe someone, somewhere else. "What's your study—"

"Tell me. Did you <u>actually</u> battle with that Cloudy spirit?"

Amy shrugged. *She'll hold deets of my discovery quiet unless I tickle her fancy.* "I wouldn't call it a battle. I survived. Found a way for everyone to survive."

"What did you sacrifice?" E'oné asked.

"What do you mean?"

"Your aura color is lost, yes? Why? How?"

"I don—"

A portion of the wall rumbled open behind her.

From its depths came Mr. SmartyPants. "Ladies." He stroked his chin and approached a new menu that formed on the wall.

Behind him came Kassandra, Vedessia, the Gyaad girl, and Ms. JellyRoll.

"Have you been waiting here long?" Ms. JellyRoll asked, re-fluffing the worst of her trampled-looking jelly roll buns in the middle of her hair. "This place is brutal."

"Define long," Amy said. "I've lost track of time."

"See my brother?" E'oné asked.

Vedessia's sad eyes laid on her. "I'm afraid he got sent to his cell."

"What? Damn, I forgot he lost... How long ago? When did the final match end?"

"No idea," Kassandra answered, sitting on the ground. "The timing's off in this place."

"Our GCIDs are wonked. Do you think it's a side effect? An infection in the brain?"

"Nonsense," Mr. SmartyPants didn't even examine her.

E'oné's face *couldn't believe him.* "Can't touch base with the outside World; no symmetry in that. Let's get this game sped up. Who's the Most Wanted?"

Amy rubbed her chin. "It's odd..."

Mr. SmartyPants chortled. "Whoever they are won't tell you."

E'oné pressed him. "So you're it?"

Amy stood up. "What kind of equipment do you think Graves uses to run this place?"

"Equipment?" Ms. JellyRoll inquired forward.

"No one's broken in the equipment yet?!" Vedessia marveled over every inch of the room.

"Equipment?" Amy spun to her.

"It's all in the carvings." The bubbly girl's fingers scaled and fell down the slushy wall, this way and that. "Let's see..." She put her ear up against it. "On my way to the ladies' room, I stumbled on some gym equipment by touching the carvings."

"Carvings?" Mr. SmartyPants dropped his plate of sushi and moved over her shoulder. "What carvings?"

Vedessia tapped mud onto her sleeves as she thought with her finger. "They're not exactly hieroglyphics; there's some deviance. I saw some similar ones when I was on holiday last summer. Hmm." Her fingers pinched against the wall. Symbols, the color and texture of butter, flushed to life all over before dimming out. "This room doesn't have equipment. I think it might be some sort of cellar, but it won't open." She bent and pointed to a lower point on the wall. "There's a symbol here that signifies a lower region."

"This structure is remarkable," Mr. Smartypants said. "There must be decades of secrets hidden within."

"How do you figure?" E'oné asked.

"I thought I saw markings when we arrived but shook them off as imperfections. On second thought, it reminded me of a sea creature's mark. I wish I could remember which..."

"It's all a ruse," Amy said. "Did you all have mini-challenges, too?" *Fucking cherryflies.*

The Gyaad girl sat against the wall, hugging her legs and nodding between them.

"If by mini you mean being dangled above a tank of sharkittens," Mr. SmartyPants said.

"Challenge is a polite term." E'oné downed a bottle of champagne cola.

The wall opened up again. "I'd have to agree." Demora strutted in, hands behind her back. "Too easy." Her demeanor dropped into softness as she smiled at Amy.

The two friends met in the middle of the room, holding each other with a squeeze.

"What mini-challenge did you have?" Amy asked.

"Challenge?" Demora pulled back. "What do you mean?"

"Apparently, we all had to go through something dreadful after the wrestling matches."

"I just walked the halls a bit." Demora leaned into her ear. "I was trying to solve that little riddle we were discussing."

"Glad someone had time to relax," E'oné spat.

Demora smirked. "Yes, you and your brother should try it sometime."

E'oné approached her. "Show me."

Vedessia's smiling face darted in between them. "Come on, girls, let's try to get along. We can work out this prison stuff together."

"Ugh." Demora marched off. "Your constant need for acceptance is beneath you."

"Hey! I'm just saying. It's important we cultivate a positive prison culture so we can leave this place with substantial lessons intact."

Amy held her beaming smile behind her exposed, scarred right hand.

Demora looked like she swallowed a stinkbug. "Are you joking? Positive prison culture? You're joking."

"She has a great point," Ms. JellyRoll said. "It may be beneficial to foster alliances here despite our differences. I suspect Graves wouldn't have us all together unless for a purpose."

"We work together when we can," Mr. SmartyPants said. His attention fell on something else. "Your hand."

Amy's eyes went wide.

—white swirls clash like derailed trains—Amy watches her own body from a distance—she blinks and falls to her side—blinks and falls to her side—blinks and falls—blinks and falls—blinks and falls—

She stared at the split in her glove, perfectly exposing the scar on her right hand. She hid it with her left hand.

Students, your next challenge awaits. A Prize Fight that will test your communication skills. Your choices carry guaranteed consequences. Make them matter.

Vedessia bit her nails. "What kinds of consequences?"

Today, you'll be playing a game that has remained hidden throughout our civilization for decades. It is known to some as the Soul Game, though tonight you won't be bargaining any souls.

"The Soul Game..." Mr. SmartyPants's frown grew into a smile. "Is it? I can't believe she's found it. What a rare treat!"

"Soul Game?" Amy raised a brow.

"Doesn't sound too friendly." Vedessia cornered herself next to the Gyaad, the two sharing anxious glances.

"It's banned in several vicinities. Known in less!" Mr. SmartyPants cackled. "They say this game was created using technological advantages of the alien kind. And finally, I get to play it..."

"<u>His</u> excitement doesn't make me feel any better," E'oné said.

This game will be played with a cooperative effort. The top five leaders will act as captains going forward, except Number 5, who forfeits his leadership position to Number 6. Here is your updated leaderboard with points added:

Current Rankings & Points

"Ouch," Kassandra said. "Shake ups already."

Since they were at the bottom of the last challenge and are currently in their cells, Number 5 and Number 8 will get to pick their teammates first. Number 10 will get the last pick since she has not faced another student.

Amy rolled her eyes.

"This _is_ brutal," Vedessia said, sharing a look with Ms. JellyRoll.

"Brother…" E'oné muttered. Her face hardened. "Let's do this."

Number 8 has made his selection. He will team with

Number 3.

"What?!" E'oné pitched forth.

Ms. JellyRoll stepped forward. "It would be my honor."

E'oné watched her. "Doesn't make sense..."

Number 5 has made his selection. He will team with Number 6. Selections will continue from the bottom positions, going up. Number 9, please choose your captain.

Mr. SmartyPants closed his eyes and smiled. "I choose number 2."

Annoying. Amy placed a loving hand on Demora's shoulder. "Good luck out there."

"And to you," her best friend smiled back.

Number 7, please choose your captain.

"I choose Number 1." E'oné's scowl fed itself into Demora's vision.

Demora checked under her fingernails.

That leaves Number 10 to team up with Number 4.

"Maybe we'll team up on the next one?" Vedessia smiled at Amy and bowed to both her and Demora. "I wish you both the best of luck."

"Seriously?" Demora folded her arms as the girl skipped off. "I hope we meet in the ring soon."

"That would be so much fun!" Vedessia shouted back.

"Unreal."

Amy chuckled.

Demora gave *me the look.*

Amy cleared her throat. Straightened her spine.

Let's set things up.

Light **snuffed** out of the room. A royal rumble awoke as angry as a hurricane passing over a bunker.

"What?"

"Hey!"

"Are we going up?"

Had just about enough of this.

Light sprinkled back into the room *like raindrops.*

Amy balanced herself on the rumbling ground, almost losing the battle until the rumble grew quieter.

The decayed yet spectacular theatre surrounding her seemed to go on for ages. A black mass of cotton-like material circled and topped the theatre, each rotation giving glimpses of the dirt wall behind it. An almost silent *mouth blowing through a fan* paired with the sensation. *Just like my wrestling match against the Dashing Man—it's all distractions. The darkness, loud rumbles, and lack of clarity in what's real and what's not. What are you hiding in your shadows, Graves?*

In the middle of the theatre, a field full of several species of greying flowers swished around. Each end of the field had two transparent pods with a console behind them. In front of each set of pods were five looping circles of light protruding from the playing field.

"Is this like chess?" Mr. Stoicism's voice asked. He and Jamari walked up behind the smaller group beside the field.

E'oné hugged her brother. "Thought you wouldn't get out till later. How was the cell?"

"Time works differently in those cells," he told her.

Mr. Stoicism nodded.

Jamari took off his blockbuster shades; his eyes focused on his sister. "Listen, sis. We have to rise out of this structure in one piece. I gave us both a fighting chance, so let's make the most of it."

More rumbling shook the room's core.

Your Captains.

Five log-shaped mounds of dripping dirt dropped from the ceiling. From left to right, on each in throne-like seats: the Gyaad, Ms. JellyRoll, Demora, Kassandra, and Vedessia—*The bubbly pop of color she was, did the cutest little dance,* riding the waves of the rumble that moved them all.

Mr. Stoicism stared at his feet. "I should be up there. I'll earn it back."

The first match will start with Numbers 2 and 9.

Demora's pillar moved down towards the field, made a sharp angle over the lower-ranked students, and hovered over the right end of the massive field. Her seat's wondrous branches clawed above her head, settling into the furthest pod from the low-rank group. A bright orange light-filled Z pressed out from the wall behind her team's station.

"Dwaaak!" Mr. SmartyPants' voice called, but he was nowhere to be found, though the hole in the ground suggested his whereabouts.

What?!

"Whoa. Mate's gone."

"What in devilish might?"

"This is not it."

Mr. SmartyPants's head reappeared as he rose into place at the pod to Demora's left.

This will be Team Z.

"This is c-chaotic." Sweat ran down Mr. Stoicism's face. He stared at the token in his hand.

Three white screens of light/*aura?* blinked into existence and flew around the arena. One angled below the high-ranked students, one faced Team Z, and the last screen faced Team A's positioning.

I'm not seeing the usual off-yellow glow and spark of ziccolights before the screen is formed. If she's using aura for all the white light, whose aura is she using? Far as I know, I'm the only one here with a white aura. At least I should be.

Numbers 2 and 9, Team Z, you have one minute to select your opposing team.

DING

Demora grabbed Mr. SmartyPants by the collar. Whispered something in his ear.

He nodded, chuckled, and relayed a response before they stood apart.

Amy's eyes narrowed. *What was that?*

"Interesting..." Mr. SmartyPants rubbed his chin. "Guess we'll have to choose Numbers 5 and 6 then."

"Huh?" Mr. Stoicism looked down. "Oh, noo**ooo**..." He dropped into a hole twice as big. The hole closed itself up.

Above them, the Gyaad's pillar moved into place within the pod on the left of the field. A blue letter A lit up on the wall behind her.

Besides her, a floundered Mr. Stoicism popped up into the pod on her right.

"This is madness!" He inspected the console in front of him. "How do you play this game anyway?" he asked his partner's blank stare.

Each team will see half of the alphabet on their side of the field. This is how you'll make your moves.

Light particles came from above and rested in front of each of the four players. The particles combined into unique colors representing their auras—Demora's pink, her partner's green, Mr. Stoicism's blue, and Number 6's yellow. The auras formed into five rows of ten auracards for each player.

Your decks contain fifty cards. Each card within a deck is unique. The cards were chosen by your spirits.

"What type of sorcery is this?" Jamari said. "How do we play without knowing what's in our decks?"

We all come from the same deck. We have our unique qualities and we share miraculous abilities. These are reflected in your cards. This game has been played with souls tethered to yours through generations. This game is in your hearts. You may not know it, but you will feel it.

Mr. Stoicism's fist quivered on top of his pod. "Playing a game we don't know sounds a little absurd, no Professor?"

Earth's aura is ours. Trust your souls. No cell time will be served for the lowest ranking players in this game, as with all Prize Fights.

Jamari sighed. "The mercy of Callisto exists, after all."

Please. Amy folded her arms. *Forgot _he's_ a believer.*

For ranking, the number of moves it takes to defeat your opponents is the measuring stick. The fewer moves made overall by your team, the higher you rank. Teams will be awarded a set number of points based on rank, and each team must decide how to split the pot of points amongst themselves.

"Time to rack up, sis." Jamari made a fist. "Let's show them!"

"Yeah..." Voice trailing away, she just watches him.

"We will catch up on points." Mr. Stoicism nodded to his partner. "Ready, partner?"

The Gyaad girl nodded.

Amy stared at her best friend's concentrated face on Team A. *Something's off. What are you after, Demo?*

Your cards will now be shuffled.

Each deck maneuvered into a single auracard, then spread into sets of five single auracards that floated in front of each player's face.

Five cards are drawn to start. Your next draw is on your second turn. Any player who runs out of cards when it's time to draw forfeits the match for their team. No attacks are allowed on the first turn of any player. Each player has three minutes to make their move or forfeit their turn.

The left side of the field blinked with shimmering light. It blinked out but reignited on the field's right side, then zipped back and forth between the two sides.

The first match will be Team A, Number 5 and Number 6, versus Team Z, Number 2 and Number 9. The field will randomly select who starts.

The blinding light **POPPED** and steadied on the side of team Z. The light blinked in and alternated underneath Demora and her partner.

After the first player's turn, the player across from them goes next, and so on. You'll find the gameplay quite intuitive, so trust in your decks. Good luck to

all.

The field light stopped on Demora with another **POP**.
DING DING DING

Chapter Five

Chapter Six

Level 1: Game Time for Everyone

"Right into it then." Demora's eyes zeroed in on her starting hand. "All right, so what here? We just play one of these cards?"

"Careful," Mr. SmartyPants said. "Careful consideration is needed during every single move, from beginning to end."

"I'm sure. Think I'll play this…" Demora selected an auracard in front of her. "There's a number one in the top left corner of this fellow. Reaper's Defense. I assume this ally is level one, and I also assume I can move one space ahead onto Z."

Over the field, pink speckles of light. A creature burst to life within them. The Reaper's Defense. Its shadowy over-cloak danced over its head down to its knees. The ripples from the mysterious cloth created small pockets that small eyes peeked from, sucking in air around them. It floated its way onto the square marked Z.

"Brilliant start. Our path to victory forms already." Mr. SmartyPants smacked his palm behind his floating auracards, inches from touching. *The wind of his smack violated the link between him and his cards.* Each of his fingers pinched forward and gestured down, bringing the auracards along. He lifted his palm and his auracards hovered over it.

"This isn't fair!" Mr. Stoicism pointed across the field. "He knows more about this game than any of us do!"

"Ah, you lack knowledge, both inner and exterior. Don't be angry with me for your lack of knowledge." Mr. SmartyPants pressed his glasses against his nose and studied his floating auracards. "Look within."

"Calm down, boys," Demora said.

"Huh?" Amy peeped a breath of mist over her shoulder. A jolting shiver left her spine as quickly as it came. *Don't lose your mind in here, Devine.* She turned back to the matchup.

"Although it's still my partner's turn—" Mr. SmartyPants picked one of his auracards and flipped it around. "I have an Instinct card— Helping Hands!"

A pair of enormous yellow hands welcomed Team A into its embrace, floating towards them. It disappeared.

"This allows me to automatically place a support or battle card onto an ally that my teammate played this turn. So I'll play this one, facedown." He flicked the card onto the field.

The green card enlarged in the circle behind the Reaper's Defense.

Demora shrugged. "Guess I'll end my turn."

"That's malarkey!" Mr. Stoicism's head was on a swivel. "Can he do that?"

The Gyaad girl watched her teammate with large eyes and a half-opened mouth.

"Need to get a hold of yourself, Number 5." Demora crossed her arms and turned away from him. "To think I even found you the slightest bit attractive. Mistake rectified."

Knew it!

Mr. Stoicism's reddening face swallowed hard. He shrunk behind his console.

Ah. I did not expect to see one of two rare card types tonight. Congrats, Number 9. Students, this game consists of survival and instinct cards, which are extraordinarily rare and have special abilities that help tip the scales for their owner. These one-of-a-kind cards can only be used by the owner, regardless of any other effects or circumstances. Number 6, it's your go.

"This is going to be a slaughter, isn't it?" E'oné's body cringed.

"I wouldn't bet against the young Gyaad just yet." Amy shrugged. "Though I am still rooting for my friend."

"Right. Wish we could hear from the others up top."

"Me too." Amy stared up at Vedessia.

Vedessia caught her stare *and kept eye contact.*

Bold one she is. What's her deal...

The Gyaad mimicked the hand sequence Mr. SmartyPants had shown off before with her auracards. They moved with her hands as she studied each one. She placed a card face down. Her mouth opened, no sound escaping.

Number 9, your move.

Mr. Stoicism's shocked expression faced his partner. "Why would you tell them you're not playing an ally, although you have one?"

The Gyaad opened her mouth to him. *"Hhhhhhhhhhaaaaaaaaa aaaaaaaa HHHHHHHHHAAAA AAAAAAAAA"* Closed it and faced the field.

"Really?" Mr. Stoicism shook his head. "How—"

"Did you hear that?" Amy searched the others' faces for a similar shock but found none.

"What?" E'oné said.

"That sound. Coming from her mouth?"

"I ain't hear a thing," Jamari said. "Prison's got you wired."

"Excellent." Mr. SmartyPants pinched his chin as he glossed over his three remaining auracards. "Here, I'll play Avrid's Ankle with Acrid Apple." He flicked two more cards.

Avrid's Ankle blinked atop the letter V as a dislocated human foot stood at an elderly magician's side. The crusty red robes of the magician draped underneath him as he scratched his crooked, long nose. Behind him, an apple with a devilish wide smile bounced in place. The magician pointed a wagging finger at it.

"Is he mad at the apple?" Jamari asked.

"I'll end my turn with that."

"Finally." Mr. Stoicism jabbed at his aura cards. Electric sparks resulted, causing him to withdraw his hand. "What in Dalestone's name?! Ouch!" He shook his hands out.

Mr. SmartyPants cackled. "You'll make this thing too easy if you don't ask questions, friend. The connection between you and your cards is sacred. The cards are an extension of your aura; therefore, you must show them the proper respect. If you don't respect the cards, you don't respect yourself. Which we can already tell you don't. Is that clear enough for you, or must we pause the game to babysit further?"

"You overcompensating piss beetle. Huh? What?"

The Gyaad's mouth was open. She mimicked her earlier hand movements over her auracards. She pinched and retracted her hand, showing her partner the maneuver.

"Oh." Mr. Stoicism followed along, pinched his hand, and retracted. "I see..."

"It's a shame they don't give points for gaining new insight," Mr. SmartyPants said.

"We're going to show you something." Mr. Stoicism took two cards and flicked them out towards the field. "HA! Try these on! Parasitic Boots! Move onto G! Anvil of Desire, onto H!"

A pair of snail skin boots blinked onto square G, accompanied by the golden Anvil of Desire. The anvil floated above H, its shadow in the square.

"I'm allowed to play my Anvil with another creature, thanks to its magnificent effect."

"<u>Ally</u>. The only creature is you. I suggest you play something to protect your partner, 5." Mr. SmartyPants sneered. "As a precaution, you know."

"What are you getting on about? I'll play this card face

down and end my turn."

"Wow." SmartyPants threw his hands up to the heavens. "Today must be my lucky day."

"Will you quit it?" Demora grilled her partner. "Is this the game? It's just a bunch of fake monsters on a board."

"Just…" Mr. SmartyPants grasped his console, shaking. "Fake… on a <u>board</u>?" His fist struck the heavens, a chaotic look in his eye. "I will teach you all exactly what these <u>monsters</u> on a <u>board</u> can accomplish!"

"Touchy, touchy. You're a little too into the cards, 9." Mr. Stoicism shook his head. "She's right."

"You're pathetic, 5." Demora grimaced with closed eyes.

"Huh? Why me?"

"Don't kiss up to your opponent. What's wrong with you?" Demora rolled her eyes.

Number 5 retreated below his console.

"Your incompetence reeks." Mr. SmartyPants turned to Demora. "I've got something for them. Don't attack yet."

"You better be right." Another pink aura card appeared with the others. "Oh, what's this? Interesting. I'll play a card facedown and end my turn."

A new yellow aura card blinked in front of the Gyaad. She flicked it onto the field.

We found her.

Amy looked over her shoulder.

"That card…" *Mr. SmartyPants' voice came from further away.* "I've seen one like it before. Its category has multiple types. Tread careful, partner."

Number 6, open mouth, pointed towards Demora.

The card's effect has been revealed as Number 6 has activated it on Number 2's Reaper's Defense. This also ends her turn.

"What?" Demora said. "She can do that? What does it do?"

The silver marble was no longer on square E. It blinked

onto square Z, right beside the Reaper's Defense.

This card is P-Bomb 3. It can link with an enemy ally. Each turn, it moves with its linked enemy ally and can also move the one space permitted by its level. After three ally turns, it evolves into its next form, letting Number 6 pull the card needed from her deck. Her deck is then shuffled.

"Atta girl, 6! Let's show them this won't be an easy game."

"What's going on, 9?" Demora said. "Your little plan still good?"

"No worries. I've already adjusted to the situation." A new auracard blinked in front of him. "Excellent draw. Avrid's Ankle, move forward to square R, and I'll end my turn."

"All right, let me get this started." Mr. Stoicism peered at his fresh auracard. "Let's go!" Threw it onto the field. "I play Mr. Manchy! Take square J."

A pair of furry pink, monstrously muscular arms pounded onto square J while its tiny white torso and legs dangled in between. There was a pocket from which steam rose where its head should have been.

"A bunch of level twos, huh?" Mr. SmartyPants snickered. "Overshooting yourself early."

"Quiet. I'll move up my Parasitic Boots to K."

The hard-to-look-at boots slimed their way onto the square.

"And now I activate my face-down card— Winds Revealing!"

A gust of wind hit the field with treacherous force. All players grabbed onto their consoles.

"This allows me to reveal one of your face-down cards at random, Team Z! If a support card is revealed, I get to use it immediately."

Demora grimaced while Mr. SmartyPants grilled the other side.

The green auracard behind Reaper's Defense flipped over

and disappeared. It reappeared on Team A's side.

"Uptown Journey?" Mr. Stoicism studied the foreign green auracard in front of him. "Interesting. I guess I'll use it on my Parasitic Boots. It says it can protect my ally from all danger."

A cage dropped onto the Parasitic Boots on square K. It lowered itself and the squealing boots into the field. Sunk until it disappeared.

"Where's my creature?" Mr. Stoicism shouted.

"Your <u>ally</u> will return," Mr. SmartyPants smirked. "Patience."

"I don't like it, but as long as it's protected. Your move 2."

"This is boring," Demora said. "Time to liven things. I play Fear Monger on square S."

A line of purple smoke rose from square S. At the top, a grey head formed wider than its lengthy, slim, grey body, with each eye almost half the size of the head. Its smile was modest as it peered towards Team A.

"What the hell is that <u>thing</u>?" Mr. Stoicism said.

"Fear Monger," Demora continued, "reveal his anvil's effect!"

Although it occupies a square, the Anvil of Desire allows any other ally or enemy to join its square. Enemies lose the ability to attack, while allies gain the ability to strike twice. Only level 3 and up can pass the square without this effect activating.

"Dammit." Mr. Stoicism pounded his console. "There goes my plan. Still, you can't cross it!"

"All right, Fear Monger, take over his anvil."

The Fear Monger wormed into the ground. Slid back out seconds later towering behind the anvil. Fear Monger opened its previously minuscule mouth, showing off a whirlpool of sharp teeth. It CHOMPED the anvil whole. Slithered back into the ground.

"No way…" Mr. Stoicism's eyes bore over the spot where his

ally got swallowed.

"Your Anvil can move two squares, right?" Demora asked. "Fear Monger, bring our Anvil Of Desire to the middle space on the field. The Core."

We found her, too.

Amy peered over her shoulder again at the solid wall with narrowed eyes. *Something's not right here...*

Pay attention.

Aura? Who else is there with you?

The Core illuminated the same orange as the Team Z logo on the wall. Purple smoke sauntered up from the circle as the Fear Monger's long body and colossal head returned to complete form. Its eyes grew vibrant red.

The Core has been crossed. Team Z may now move their allies into enemy territory.

"Dammit." Mr. Stoicism studied his cards. "There must be something here..."

"This is not looking good," E'oné said.

"Wanna place bets?" Jamari asked. "Yo. Yo!" He waved his hands in Amy's peripherals.

Amy watched Demora. *What aren't you telling me?*

Many.

"Alright, Fear Monger, let's lose the dead weight!" Demora pointed with authority. "Unlink from the Anvil!"

The Anvil of Desire reappeared on square N.

"She's not even announcing her squares anymore!" E'oné kept her eyes on the match but turned to Amy. "Have you all played this before?"

Amy tried to reply, but her mouth wouldn't open. Her arms were glued to her sides, no matter how much she budged. She stood silent, her intense eyes on the gameplay. *I can't move.*

Chapter Seven

Level 1: Hearing Voices Again

Amy's eyeballs did a swirl, from the ground and up to her classmates, whose muffled voices clashed around her. Voices on the field **boomed** against her eardrums.

"Why would she drop my Anvil on their side? Does that mean?" Mr. Stoicism shook his head. **"That gives us an open play on their field, right?"**

The Gyaad nodded.

"True, but I'm not done yet." Demora flicked two more cards into the field. **"I play Matter of Decadence. This field card increases the attack power for every move made so far for all allies on the field. However, defense drops double the amount."**

The field decayed; flowers wilted; flies buzzed; the squares turned a murky grey.

Amy's face strained against the invisible weight, which kept her looking forward.

"Finally, I'll play Stubie's Quarrel! This battle card forces allies and enemies who are aligned to move again and initiate combat, if possible."

A bald man in overalls appeared, stomping his feet as he paced the field, complaining about something.

Mr. Manchy joyfully strutted onto square M.

"And I'll move my Reaper's Defense up as well." Her ally moved into the space designated. A hum came as all companions on the field glowed before returning to normal.

Mr. Stoicism nodded. **"This means my Manchy can attack your Fear Monger."**

"It must." Demora *waited.*

"So be it. Mr Manchy, let's make a pie out of them. Show them who's toughest!"

Mr. Manchy clapped his hands together with increasing zealous vigor each second. Electricity escaped from the contact between its palms, and the happy beast extended its arms. A huge blueberry pie formed from nothing in the middle of his grasp. His slimy head, with mad eyes full of rainbow-flickering streaks, crept out from the socket between his shoulders. He leaned back, a devious smile worn, and slammed the blueberry pie on top of the Fear Monger, the echo *BANGING* in decreasing increments.

"Ooooh, that's a wrap!" Jamari cheesed. **"Cold, mate, cold! Huh? Ay, new girl, you good?"**

Mr. Manchy picked up the pie and faced Team Z. An imprint of the Fear Monger was the pie's central design. Mr. Manchy snickered as he turned the pie back around and disappeared behind it, with only the sounds of him hungrily devouring the dessert heard while blueberry bits flew from either side.

Mr. Stoicism, hands on his hips, beamed. **"That's how you clear the field!"**

"Charming." Demora waved a bored hand. **"Your move, 6."**

Amy gasped for air as her body broke free of its invisible prison. Turned to E'oné. "Did you say something?" E'oné stepped back. "Uh, yeah, like a million things. Like, have you and your friend played this game before? She's caught on quick."

"Oh, no." Amy watched Demora. *I don't* think *she has.*

"Are you good?" Jamari asked, pushing his shades down.

"Yeah, I just... What a match, right?"

"Listen to it." Mr. SmartyPants cupped his ear. "Seems like your journey is about to reach its destination."

A rumble came from underneath the field. An explosion of dirt and rock blasted through the surface of K's square. The Uptown Journey cage shot up. The cage broke apart and faded. The much more putrid-looking Parasitic Boots stood five feet taller than its previous state. Drooling yellow goop, sores all around it, pulsing and dripping a red substance.

Mr. Stoicism's shocked face turned to greedy ambition. "It looks worse than before, but a lot more powerful, at least by three times! Solid!"

"Don't forget you must discard two cards since your ally returned." Mr. SmartyPants winked.

"What?!"

"It's terribly important to understand all the effects your card has. How can you win otherwise? Blind luck will get you so far. Letting your partner down like this. **Tsk tsk**."

Amy dug fingers into each of her ears from the ringing that came.

Mr. Stoicism's nose was in his cards. "Piece of shit," he muttered. "Dammit. No matter." He chucked two of his auracards to the side. "Mr. Manchy, move to square N with my Anvil. Gain more strength!"

Mr. Manchy #1 moved forward, glowing until it rested in a spot. It licked its lips at the target on square T.

"Parasitic Boots, move to the middle, and finally, Mr. Manchy, move to square O. That's right! Now, my allies, destroy her Reaper's Defense!"

Another pie attack commenced with Mr. Manchy taking away the reaper.

"Do you feel in charge now?" Demora said, leaning back against her console, checking under her fingernails. "This game's boring. Can't bear to watch your sorry plays any longer."

"You..." Mr. Stoicism quivered as he stared at Demora's back. "I will. After this—" He shot his hand out towards his partner.

The Gyaad opened her mouth. *Her long-forgotten* face-down card flipped up.

"My partner activates Storm's Coming! This allows all of my allies to make another move."

"And I activate my face-down card," Demora said, eyes back to the match. "Scramble! All field positions will be randomized."

The allies on the field became blurs of light zipping from square to square.

They stopped.

Field changes are:

Parasitic Boots on Q

Mr. Manchy on I

Anvil Of Desire on E

Mr. Manchy on P

Winds Of Destiny on D

P-Bomb 5 on K

Boy Who Could on N

What's the plan here, Demo?

You're losing—

"Huh?" Amy searched around for the familiar voice. "Come ba—"

"What?" E'oné asked.

"Nothing." *What's happening to me?*

"—doesn't matter," Mr. Stoicism said. "We can still move. Now—"

"Hold on," Demora interrupted. "I activate Show Your Grace!" She flicked an auracard.

Mr. Stoicism threw his hands up. "You can't do that! Is this allowed?"

Number 5, Show Your Grace! is a unique battle card you can activate from your hand, given the right conditions. It ends the current turn immediately if any allies or enemies have moved more than once during this turn.

Mr. Stoicism's head lay in his palms. "Of course it is, of course, it does." He pointed at Demora. "Who's stalling now?!"

"Stop your crying, 5," Demora said.

"Someone sure does not do well under pressure," E'oné said.

"Nope." Jamari shook his head. "What I will say is our time in our cells was… different. Poor bloke rambled now."

"What happened in your cell?" Amy asked.

Jamari wagged a finger at her. "Wouldn't you like to know? Y'all gonna find out on your own."

"If I were you, I'd worry about that P-Bomb over there," Mr. SmartyPants said. "Has your partner even told you its effects? I've already figured it out."

"Why don't you stop with your backhanded advice and worry about how you're going to stop us from winning in the next round?"

The Gyaad opened her mouth, glaring into 9. **"oooooaaaaAAAAh."**

Amy held her belly. *Something's **inside me**.* She gasped at the foreign voice in her head.

"My partner wants to know why you're being so helpful," Mr. Stoicism said.

"It's simple," Mr. SmartyPants said. "The more knowledge you have, the more knowledge I can eventually gain from you."

"What is wrong with him?" E'oné asked.

Beats me.

"Cocky know-it-all, what else is there to figure?" Jamari said.

"So, who do you all think is the Most Wanted?"

"My bet's on glasses. She good?"

It could be him.

"Hey, Number 10, are you all right?" E'oné tapped Amy's right shoulder.

Or her.

"Yup, just need to move around." Amy held her flushed cheeks and backed away. "Legs get jammed if I'm still for too long." She paced behind the others, eyes scanning the field.

There's space in here.

Comfy, isn't it?

We can nest in here...

Forever!

Who's up there?! Amy held her head. Off the stare of the others, She feigned a back of the hair scratch while pacing, studying her surroundings. *Am I possessed?* Gave an uneasy smile towards the siblings next to her. *Keep it cool, Ames.*

The Gyaad opened her mouth. **"Aaaaaaaahhhhhh ooooooooaaa."**

Am I hearing things? Amy frowned. *Well, I am, but...*

"Wait, WHAT?" Mr. Stoicism, besides himself.

"That's right." Mr. SmartyPants sneered. "After three more ally turns of your own, the next evolution of P-Bomb will destroy all your collective allies on the field."

"6, why would you play such a thing??"

6 opened her mouth, face scrunched.

"Your people?? 'Fearless action in light's obscurity' can include your partner's input, I'd think!"

6, mouth opened, closed. She nodded.

"Trust you??!" Mr. Stoicism lowered onto his console, staring helplessly at his sole auracard in hand.

Demora groaned. "I've got a minute left, so I'm just gonna play this."

Demora... such clarity. She's not even worried about the match's outcome. How can she be so confident, given the past few weeks? Amy smiled. *I remember when you charged into Bryzen Hemley's house, broke his nose, and slapped his sister with her ziccoscope. Then came back to me with a cut above your eye and presented my unicorn backpack that the little shitter had stolen in math. If only unicorns existed, you'd be one, Demo.*

If the rich brat has a telescope that can see the Mumauds on Mars, she can _pay_ more attention to her little brother's nonsense.

Got that right. Amy froze mid-pace. *I am possessed. Or who the hell was that?*

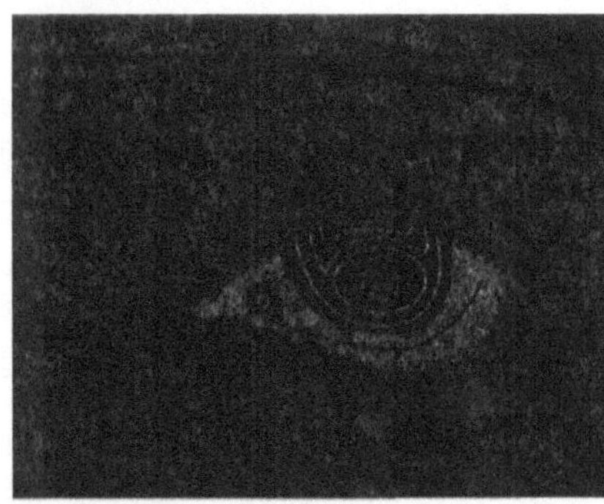

Don't fear. The voices you worry about are not your enemy.

I'd like to be the judge of that, bloke. Now, <u>who</u> <u>are</u> <u>you</u>?

I am called many names by various entities.

I want to know... Amy nodded reassurance to Demora's curious face. *What do your enemies call you?*

You've created...

Created what?

A swarm of mountain ticks the size of bears crawled towards her. "Oh, shit!" Amy backed up, soon finding herself against the wall. The ticks were gone. *They were never there.*

You've lost the plot once more.

Aura?! Where have you been, I've been calling you! What the hell is going on? Who are you inviting inside me?!

We're not going to win with you in a state like this.

Wha— Never mind that! How many of you are in me?

Damn near catatonic.

For my aura, you're a bit of an annoying little—

"Number 10! <u>Girl</u>—you're sinking!"

"What?" Already up to her knees, Amy's feet sank into quicksand. It crawled to life around her knees like hungry piling ants. *NO—fuck!* She shut her mouth as her chin got gobbled by the coarse texture rubbing against her flesh. Her eyes widened as the earth ate the scene above her.

She blinked.

—Panic—Amy's arms flail, swimming through dirt—

Wait. Stop. Stop! Stop stop stop! PLEASE!

"**STOP!**" Her voice echoed.

Chapter Eight

Level 1: Distant Remembrance

Amy grabbed her throat, in the fetal position, her head between her knees. *I'm still breathing.* She uncurled herself. She was a pebble in another arena, this one more like a cavern. Mildew and sweat rode the air. Sculptures of pumice origin dripped from the ceiling, with tips leaking black goo. A thin, uneven glow—thin, fractured, *hesitant*— seeps from sources of light behind craters in the ceiling and along the walls. The jagged recesses of unfresh-darkened-blood red hold the light at bay, only allowing it to cut through darkness in ghostly ribbons.

Amy got to her feet, her back foot sliding *down?* She caught her balance before stepping back to her death. She faced and peered over the edge of a pit that had no end in sight. "Super."

What would you do without me?

You again. Amy sighed. *I don't know. Technically, I'd be dead. Otherwise, I wouldn't have so many panic attacks.*

Thrive! Survive! That's the attitude you need to always have!

Always sounds tiring.

It's more tiring to waste away our potential. Then you wonder why we're lost.

Who else was in our head?

How am I supposed to know? You're the captain.

Fireworks of light exploded all around, lighting the rest of the arena.

"Graves. Sending me off alone again. What now?"

"You never exhaust hopelessness, do you?" Across the bottomless pit, Kassandra sat on her throne-like seat like a queen of the UnderCity. Her cheek rested on her fist. "Welcome." Nets made of dark brown vines dressed the walls and dangled behind her. Inside the nets stood stone carvings of various beasts from the Animalia Kingdom, squaring off with one another.

Dolphin v. Shark. Wolf v. Coyote. Elephant and rhino. Cobra, mongoose. Famous rivalries in Animalia history. What's this about? "How come she gave you such a stellar set-up?" Amy pointed to Kassandra's side and then to the uninspired stone poles on her end.

"She didn't. I got comfortable."

Welcome Number 10 and 4! Your match will be two on two despite the lack of a physical body beside you.

Lightning aura strikes, white and purple, struck right beside their owners.

The white light sparkled together and formed Aura Amy. She raised an eyebrow. *"We are doomed."*

"What's with the negativity?" Amy asked. Her gaze fell to the ground. *Wait a minute.*

Swirling purple aura mixed with shadows took human form beside Kassandra's *throne.* Aura Kassandra unveiled from the shadows, arms crossed, glaring at her opponents. "Let's get this over with."

A rumble **roared** as a rustic board on the wall pushed out into place. The letters A through M on one side and

N through Z on the opposite, with The Core's circle in the middle.

Behind the Amys, a pink-lit letter A brandished into the wall.

The letter Z in purple and black burned in place behind the Kassandras.

This feels familiar.

You both watched some of the match going on upstairs. Your game will be even more refined as you'll be playing war style.

I wonder... Amy's quivering index teased the air. "May I make a suggestion before we start?"

Yes, Number 10?

"I think the education would be more beneficial if I worked with her aura and she worked with mine." *If this plays out...*

Kassandra raised an eyebrow.

Aura Kassandra scoffed. "I don't want to work with her!"

"If Number 4 agrees, of course," Amy added with a smile to her opponents.

"Whatever." Kassandra slumped back in her seat. "I don't plan on losing either way."

What are you up to? Aura Amy glared at her owner.

I think we need a little distance. If we're gonna be as good as Demora, then I need to do this without you.

So you want to work against yourself?

"It'd be more challenging to overcome our auras despite our joint journey." Amy shrugged. "I think."

I see. Very well. I see some gains from this exercise. This is your prison. Your rules.

"Since when?" Amy's head snapped at the ceiling.

YOUR REQUEST HAS BEEN GRANTED.

A flash of white light obscured the entire room, then faded.

Purple swirls of aura beside Amy formed into a grilling Aura Kassandra. She leaned in close. "I don't know what you're up to, Devine, but this won't pan out."

"This should be fun." Amy nodded. *Oh dear.* She stared into the eyes of a snarling Aura Amy across the way. *Odd. Seeing her next to Kassandra... a betrayal... one I orchestrated. Hope that was the right call. Am I dreaming again?*

"You're going down for ditching me!" Aura Amy shot a finger at her *traitor.*

"Will you settle down?" Kassandra side-eyed her.

Amy and Aura Kass stepped back as an enormous glass gorilla head with a *familiar* scowl rose from the earth in front of them, facing their opponents. A bright pink A flashed onto its forehead.

These are your idols.

Across the field, a glass leopard's head with a raised eyebrow rose. A purple Z came to life on its forehead.

Your decks will be evenly divided amongst your counterparts, with twenty-five cards for each player. You'll be playing "I Declare War" style. In each round, every player's top three cards on their ever-shuffling decks are to be played facedown. Each player will draw a fourth card and put it face-up. This card is used for the round's battle. The other

three cards may support your team this round, or they will be shuffled back into the deck. After battles have been decided, cards played this round are tossed into the pit. However, surviving allies of a round can return once to guard against direct attacks. The first player to have no cards to play during their turn is out of the game, and their team loses.

The lettered spaces on the wall burned bright yellow light.

The field on the wall adds another element to gameplay. As you play allies on letters, their level dictates how many spaces they can move toward the middle square, The Core. Lettered spaces landed on have one of two effects that are unique to the player who landed on them. These special rules are individualized based on each player's spirit.

"What sense does that make?" Kassandra said. "Wouldn't our spirits have the same goal? Think the same? Same rules and all?"

Though you and your spirit may share an existence, imbalances always exist.

"Sure," Kassandra said.

When you play an ally, declare a letter on the board, and that letter's effects will be given to you to choose from. Each turn allows players to move further on the board based on where they last landed. Once The Core is passed by a team, that team may initiate a direct attack on their opponent's idol before the round ceases. Five direct attacks on a team's idol will end the game and the team whose idol still stands are the winners.

A stack of white auracards blinked in front of Amy.

Be advised if your fourth card is not an ally, you can use its effects but may be vulnerable to direct attacks. Any unresolved battles between allies equal in level may use other allies drawn from the facedown set to weaken the opposing.

WHISTLE

Amy's eyes bulged and darted across the field. *Why would you—*

Smiling and twirling her fingers, Aura Amy's palm faced the ceiling, showing off her hovering stack of—

<u>ORANGE</u>?! —auracards.

"How..." Amy's eyes stayed on the orange set. *I haven't... in over a year. How could she... when... wait, what?* "How did you do that?"

Aura Amy twirled in her spot. *Maybe you'll beat me. Maybe we'll find out.*

"Your bickering is wasting our time," Kassandra said. She touched the top of her purple auracard deck. Her eyes flashed purple. "Seems this deck really knows me, after all."

Aura Kassandra touched her purple deck. "She's right. The energy is remarkable."

Amy placed a finger on hers. *I don't feel a thing.*

Aura Amy grilled her with crossed arms.

Let the game begin.

DING DING DING!

Aura Kassandra flicked her hand over her deck. Sent three auracards across the pit.

They hovered over it. Kassandra's set met hers there.

The Kassandras locked eyes.

Aura Amy flicked her top three cards. *"Hurry, slowpoke!"*

"Wow." Amy rolled her eyes. "I'm sure the great-great-great-grandmother of Gma used that one." She flicked three cards over the pit. Placed a finger on top of her auradeck.

Her eyes met the others.

They all flicked their fourth card—

The glowing auracards hovered over the facedown ones. Turned up.

Number 4, I'd advise you not to play such a card. It requires a certain level of skill to master it, and I mean that with no offense. I'm not even entirely sure how a beginner like you has such a card in their deck. I will offer you an exchange for it and restart the round.

"No thanks, I got this." Kassandra stared at her face up auracard. "It's my Instinct card, isn't it? It's calling..." She nodded. "I activate my Instinct card: <u>Your Mother's Dread</u>."

The room darkened with the only light coming from the auracards. A ghastly green mist rose from behind her.

A puff of silver smoke zoomed out of the clouds around Team Z. Something zipped out from the depths —

Amy gasped, frantic eyes following it. "Is that a—"

"Silvabee??" Aura Amy dipped into a hug around her knees. *"Shoo it, shoo it. Partner, get it away!"*

The silvabee flew forth—a PURPLE VINE WRAPPED around its black-banded neck—SNATCHED it BACK—into a bubbling hole that shrunk like a tight anus.

A sea of log-sized purple vines slapped the air around a grotesque sequoia. Thin purple vines wrapped around its warped, burnt crimson trunk, with gaping holes, excreting green sud-like fluids.

Since Number 4 played an Instinct card, none of the field's squares are occupied. The other cards will be revealed now.

The other face-up auracards over the pit morphed.

Amy blinked. Opened her eyes to a penguin with green bushy eyebrows nose to nose with her. "You're huge."

The penguin leaned up with an open mouth. Diamond shards shot from it.

Amy shielded herself as the shards stuck to the ground, circling her. A hint of white light flashed in the center of her eyes. "Support. I can't battle for three turns? What use—oh. My ally, on the next turn, gains two levels. Ok, fine."

"Flutter of Heart! On Z!" Aura Amy waved a hand across the sky.

The light on the wall's square Z extinguished.

In front of her, a feathery pink web floated by, shooting tiny strands that stuck to passing shadows. The fluffy web spun in place as webbing shot out and grabbed an auracard from Amy's deck.

"What gives you twat?"

"Glad you asked, my humble host. My lovely ally allows me to feed an ally at random from my opponent's deck!" Aura Amy beamed with a fist in the air.

She's rather chipper.

Amy!

Amy peered over her shoulder. *Something's following me—us. Who?*

That's a good question.

Huh? "Huh?" Amy spun around to face the wall.

HA HA HA HA HA.

Amy looked across at her aura self. *You heard it, too. Yeah...*

"Will you stay focused?" Aura Kassandra said to Amy. "You've got one less card now." She turned towards the pit. "Immaculate Knight onto F!"

Square F's light on the wall's board extinguished.

Over the pit, a knight in blue-diamond armor stood using a sparkling sword as a cane.

Players, choose your effect.

In front of Aura Amy, two words formed from gathering white lights: *Zeal or Zig-Zag*

"Okay…" Aura Amy's nose twitched. *"Let's go for zeal."*

The Flutter of Hearts grew twice its size. Its webbing shot out and stole another card from Amy's deck.

"You're joking! C'mon!"

Aura Amy beamed. *"Now my ally is level two and gets to use their effect again."*

"You're standing in your own way," Aura Kass said. "How shocking."

Amy grilled the diamond shards around her. *And what are these things doing—nothing!*

Two more words formed over the pit in front of Aura Kass: *Feint or Force-field* "Feint," she *chose.*

Her Immaculate Knight shimmered.

Let the War begin.

The Immaculate Knight jumped forward; its sword swung above its head.

The sword met the webbing of the Flutter of Hearts.

"Ha! "They're the same level!" Aura Amy said.

The Immaculate Knight vanished.

Reappeared behind the Flutter of Hearts and sliced it in half. The Flutter burst into ziccolights.

"Hey! How is that fair?" Aura Amy pouted.

Since when do we pout?

I can hear you!

So can we.

The Amys froze.

"My feint attack was successful," Aura Kass said. "It's a brilliant effect of my Knight. My round. Huh?"

A card from her deck and a card from Amy's deck zoomed out. Burst into nothing.

"What the hell?" Amy looked over at the smiling Kassandra. "What's so funny?"

Kassandra shrugged. "An effect of Your Mother's Dread. Eliminates a random card from my opponents' deck every turn."

Aura Kassandra growled. "Absurd."

Her Immaculate Knight bowed to her before it burst into light particles.

Great first round, students. Good luck in the next.

The players flicked three new auracards off their decks, then a fourth.

"eDeeno, take S!" Kassandra said.

A white form materialized in front of her over the pit and grew limbs. **POP** of light.

A green baby raptor wearing a tiny half-eggshell jumped and roared at Team A.

Sink or Swim

"Swim."

eDeeno dived into an invisible pool, its tail the last to disappear.

"Oh, c'mon." Amy rolled her eyes at her own face-up card. "I play Happy Trails. This allows me to draw three new cards and send three back to my deck. Ridiculous." *Whoa.* Her eyes stared at the auracards in front of her. *It's that card... from my dream. I can feel it.* She looked across at Team Z. *But if I use it now...*

—Amy ducks as the shadows close over her. "Should've activated my facedown card"—

— "And next turn, this match is over." —

I'll save it this time. May come in handy later.

"I'll play The Golden Archer! Take square O! This is so much fun!" Aura Amy clasped her mouth, eyes zipping left and right.

"What is wrong with her?" Aura Kass asked.

Wish I knew.

Obscure or Overwhelm

"Overwhelm, please!"

The Golden Archer glowed and split into three of the same.

"Cheeky!"

"Desperada Jinxx," Aura Kass said, "on square K!"

Four pairs of stringy noodle arms slithered through the air, connected to a green ooze-dripping sack. Mud-colored puffs of gas pushed out from multiple holes in it.

Amy's eyes squirmed. "I can't unsee that."

Karma or Kinesis

"Karma."

The Golden Archers all shrank to pint size.

"Hey!"

Aura Kass smirked. "Guess your ally is now three times as useless." She pointed across the pit. "Jinxx, massacre, please."

The stringy arms of Desperada Jinxx shot out.

Purple vines intercepted with a **SMACK**. They wrapped around the arms and reeled Desperada Jinxx across the pit—and into one of the sucking holes of the tree of Your Mother's Dread.

"Excuse me?!" Aura Kass said.

Kassandra winced as purple vines wrapped around her outstretched arm. "Protects the babies, just like an ideal mother would. My round since your partner can't string together an attack. Oh, and goodbye to another card from your decks."

A pair of auracards shot out from the decks of Team A and burst into thousands of lights.

"This is the card Graves tried to ban?" Aura Amy laughed. *"Glad I'm not on the receiving end."*

So damn chipper for what? Stole _my_ _orange_. Few more rounds like this, and I'm done...

"I'm gonna punch your spirit in her teeth." Aura Kassandra said.

Ditto.

Aura Kass grilled her host. "Where's your other summoned ally?!"

"Patience." Kassandra flicked new auracards. "I play Bland on N."

A white blob of gunk jiggled over the pit.

Necrosis or Nightmare

"Nightmare. Activate Pawn Scheme."

The room's color tone dropped to a cold greyish-blue.

This is familiar, too. It won't end well. Her eDeeno returns, crosses The Core, and starts mayhem. If it happens... Let's see. Amy scratched her head as she stared at the card in front of her. "I don't know why, but it feels like I've played this game before."

"I know the feeling."

Amy shot a glance at her partner. "Really?"

"Yeah." Aura Kass stared at her auradeck. "This exact game is so familiar to me..."

"Yes, exactly!" *She gets it! First time any version of Kass agrees with me.*

"Like I've known this game my whole life. I've played it one hundred too many times..." Aura Kass *chuckled?*

"Yeah..." *I don't know about all that.*

The game has been pau—

Howling winds, followed by shadow, spread across the entire room, obscuring the field, walls, and everything else but Team A.

Amy scanned the dense atmosphere of nothing but purple clouds. "What's happening?"

Aura Kass pointed above them. "Look."

Shrouded in passing clouds, Kassandra hung in midair with dead eyes. Her neck cracked to the side.

Aura Amy floated from behind some clouds. *"Uh, partner?"* She waved at Kassandra. *"Let's get back to the game, huh?"*

The shadows devoured Kassandra.

"What did you do?" Aura Kass got in Aura Amy's face.

"Nothing! She turned to me and said, 'This game's ending soon.' I don't know why she brought us here, of all the places."

"Here? Here where?" Amy asked.

Welcome to My Realm within The Spirit World. You love spirit play, don't you, Devine? Your precious aura.

"Kass?" Amy moved deeper into the darkness. "Where are you?"

Aura Kass jumped and hovered in the air. "Professor, can you hear us?"

She's always lingering, isn't she? She won't disturb us, don't worry. She won't disturb the end.

Aura Amy gulped. *"The end?"*

Before anyone could answer, a whip-cracking gust snatched everyone off their feet in one swift scoop. Their screaming voices mangled with the gathering, tornadous air. Rock chunks ground to dust, giving the circling air some texture. Purple clouds and violent invisible winds tossed the bodies of the players in different directions.

Chapter Eight

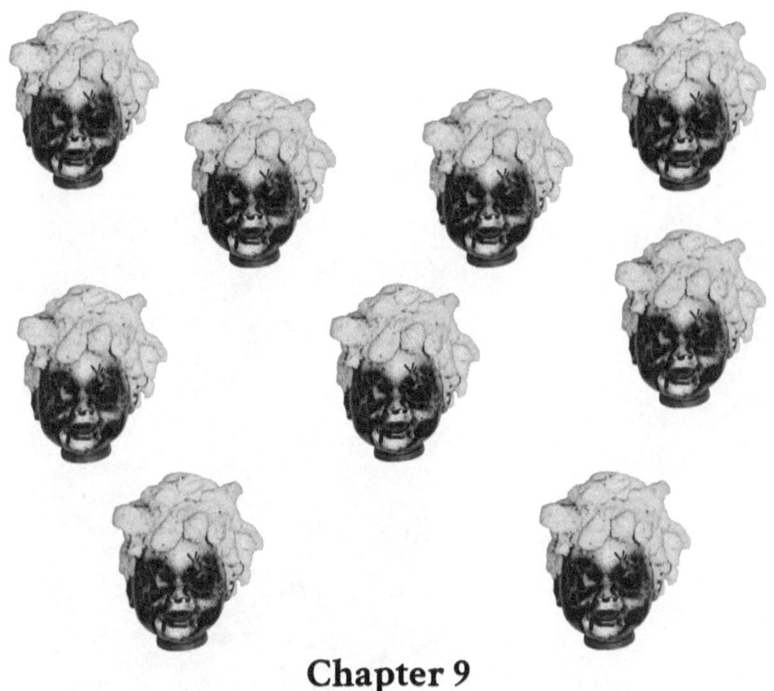

Chapter 9

An Unexpected Visitor

A dust-filled vortex settled in the dense, black, cotton-like atmosphere. A solo figure unmoved inside of it. Amy, on all fours. "What happened?" Her eyes searched, but she was alone for miles in vast nothingness. "Kass? Auras? Graves?" *This isn't good. I've seen enough possessions to know. Gotta snap Kass out of it somehow. But I couldn't even snap Demora out of hers last year.*

Your World's intriguing.
This one, however... unsettling.
Though, it is easier to talk here.

Speaking of possession... Amy stood tall, still alone. "Who's there?"

A shadow crept high behind her.

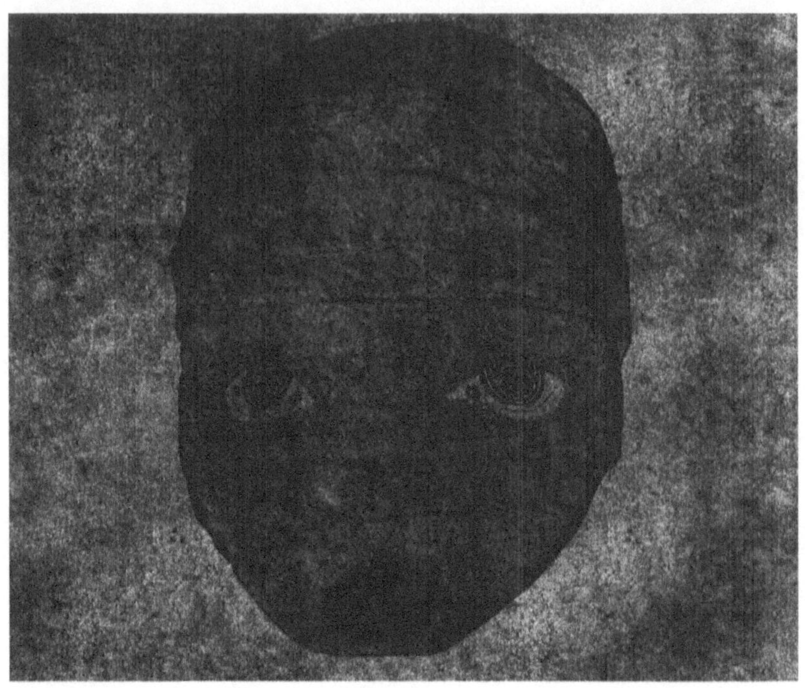

This is maddening. Have I gone—
Who can qualify insanity?
Who <u>ARE</u> you?
You've created your destiny; you must accept it.
What? ... HELLooo? ...
You seem to upset most you encounter.
<u>—Kassandra's eyes burn into view—</u>
That's not true. Who—I can't—I'm in the middle of something if you don't mind. Whoever, whatever, or maybe in my mind.

Definitely in your head, but you seek a source you haven't found.

What are you actually—I DON'T care anymore. Leave me alone.

Maybe you care too much. Or too little.

Gma? Is this a test? I don't know how you'd get in here, anyway.

Do I sound like a 150-year-old woman?

Depends on the woman. How do you know her—

Knowledge comes easily to me.

Still, remarkable resemblance.

Touche.

Listen, mister, can you stop your intrusions? I'd like to finish this <u>dreadful</u> game and be off.

I have a visitor for you.

Oh? Another unwanted visit—

A light blue aura rose from far away. It floated towards Amy. The closer it got, *the more human its form.* Its arms reached out.

Amy backed away, but her eyes stayed on the mesmerizing glow. "Wait..."

Jonathan Jones, in aura form, stood in front of her. "Why haven't you left your house?"

Amy shivered in cold sweat. Rubbed her eyes. *Jon?* "How can I see you?" She took trembling steps closer to the heat waves surrounding her floating auradeck. Pointed at it. "Are you doing this?"

"More people need you out there. You said you'd be

there. Instead, you've been shackled at home."

"How are you—" Amy watched his feet. "Why can I see you?"

"I don't know!"

"Am I dead?"

They stared into each other's eyes. His figure shrunk away from her.

"Jonathan, am I dead?" *Where is he going?* She opened her mouth but remained silent. A tear betrayed her. It led more. A rebellion of sorrow soon followed. She squeezed her fist. *AM I DEAD?!*

He watched her from far away. Looked away. "Only if you want to be." He shrugged. "No, you're not dead."

Her eyes narrowed on him. "You little—"

He zoomed up face to face with her. "Now, how did that feel? Knowing you're dead? You didn't like it, did you?" Jonathan struck a finger at the darkness behind him. "Imagine those kids out there, living, breathing. Those souls being tortured by some menace." Pointed to her. "You've got breath to spare and some spiritual prowess. Why not use that?"

"Jon, there's a lot more to being human than jumping your gun with every shot you've got. Perseverance." *Oof, I sound like Gma.*

"I never could understand you adults!" The boy of blue grabbed his temples. "Always squandering in your booze, and your currency, your game-playing, your fucking—"

"Hey, tone there, young man."

"—Self-entitlement. I'm DEAD!"

"All I'm saying is that you don't understand—"

"What, cuz I'm a <u>child</u>? Been there. HEARD that."

"I'm not gonna have a shouting match, so if that's what you're after, I suggest you—"

"All of you are the same! You forget what it means to live in your present. Fiiine, fine! Go on, then."

Amy stomped her foot. "You don't understand what it means to find meaning in a meaningless existence."

"Yet I'm horrified that a part of me started to and may still believe that Cloudy had proof to his message."

Silence except for the **WHOOSH** of clouds passing by.

The dead have a way of breathing... Amy rubbed her elbow. Firmed her stance. "I'll prove Cloudy wrong."

"You've been there, said that." Aura Jonathan faded from existence.

"Wait! Jon! Don't leave, I'm sorry!"

You won't escape. Where is she?

Amy wiped her eyes and looked off in the distance to where Kassandra's possessed voice came from. She drifted towards it. Her auradeck zoomed behind her.

—LATER—Amy sits on the ground of her cell—her finger writes in the dirt—

This whole game is pointless in hindsight. Though parts of it intrigue a deeper part of me. Tedious mechanics. What is Graves playing at? are in play, so you skip 10 pages just to get to the good stuff. That's what I'd do for this part of the story.

— Amy looks up. "What's this?" —

—a trail of insects crawl single file out through the bars of her cell—

Amy walks outside her cell—

—outside her cell bars, another trail of insects move alongside the precious one—

— several more lines of insects crawl up the walls—

—all lines of insects crawl into a hole in the corner of the Level 1 ceiling—

Something's attracting them.

Maybe.

My dreams have married my reality. Yet they aborted the child that was me. I grow more embarrassed of the past I left behind me. It wasn't a matter of time. It was a matter of my ego. An ego too shaken to deal with the promises I made and the souls whose lives were damaged by the truths I ran from.

I failed.

Now I'm haunted by my failures. A fit punishment...

Chapter Ten

Level 1: The Unsanctioned Battle Continues

"I'll play Pension Plan!" Kassandra, eyes glowing purple, laughed. "This raises my eDeeno's level by two."

eDeeno's body glowed. His figure grew several feet. His limbs stretched, and he grew two tails and three extra arms on his back. The white light diminished. eDeeno LVL 3 roared into the ceiling, striking the massive claws on its seven copper-colored arms in wild directions. Its same-sized eggshell hat spun as it expelled pins of purple aura.

Kassandra pointed below with a vine-covered arm. "Crush her!"

The happy eDeeno stomped his way forward, snapping its king-sized jaw.

Aura Kass, on a knee, reached towards her auradeck, inches from her fingertips.

eDeeno gained speed, closing on her.

"Obey me, my spirit," Kassandra said. Both arms and legs outstretched, entwined in vines. "**Accept your fate.**" She **barked** laughter into the black sky.

Beside her, Aura Amy's sad eyes watched Kassandra, then fell on Aura Kass. *"I'm sorry."*

"Desperate Champion, rush forth!" Amy tossed an auracard

that morphed into an emerald-suited soldier, his yellow coned hat covering his eyes. He raised two staffs in either hand that sparks raged off of.

eDeeno's jaws clamped down onto one staff.

Desperate Champion stuck the other one in the dinosaur's ear. Electricity PULSED as eDeeno burst into falling lights.

Aura Amy's eyes brightened. *"There she is."* Smiled.

"My ally steals a level from your attacking ally and self-destructs after his duty." As Desperate Champion burst, Amy stepped past the lights and stood beside Aura Kass with a glowing white hand. "Why is she in vines?"

Aura Kass took her glowing hand and got up. "Your Mother's Dread. She's used it to block every attack. But it overtakes one of her limbs each time it does. I'm not sure how to stop it."

"She can't help you!" Kassandra glared down. "She can't even help herself."

Amy grilled the airborne, possessed girl. "The rules of your realm aren't superior to the whole, Kass. Or should I say the thing possessing Kass? What are you after?"

Kassandra laughed. "There are no rules in this world. I was under the impression..."

...allows her to play the same ally as Kass. There she goes, on and on. That's not Kass. Who or what's inside her? Same as my dream, and then my overly cheerful spirit says—

"Great minds think alike! We're floating on the—"

—Stars and beyond! WAIT. It really is—

—my dream! Aura Amy's eyes go wide.

Thing is... Amy's eyes widened. *This part never goes well.*

"They're already on their last leg." Kassandra turned to her partner. "Keep feeding sacrifices to my Instinct's ability. I'll protect us and clear our path to victory."

Aura Amy nodded *with a nervous smile. "If you say so..."*

Kassandra pointed at Amy. "First, I sacrifice my eDeeno..."

"What?!" Amy's eyes searched the field. "How? I smashed it!"

"You smashed his reflection. Don't you remember? He went for a swim before I even brought us to this realm. Now, I sacrifice him and my partner's ally to bring out the level four—Consequential Disrupter!"

An electrified sword fell from the sky. A figure dropped down beside it.

A warrior clad in sparkling grey witherstones picked up the sword.

A wicked smile grew on Kassandra. "If my opponent has two allies on the field, my ally can move and attack twice."

Amy raised an eyebrow. "We don't have any allies out."

"I do," Aura Kass's stern eyes bore *past my shoulders*. "We do. They're hidden in the shadows."

Behind them, several dozen silhouettes of white and purple aura, all shapes and sizes, dimmed to their actual forms—the undead allies of Team A. They swayed in the distance. **Moaning grumbles** echoed from them.

Amy turned to her thin auradeck. Only a few cards left. "Our decks!"

"She killed them all," Aura Kass said, "then forced them back from the grave as tokens. Our idol's been attacked three times. I only got to attack theirs once."

On opposite ends, the cracked gorilla head idol lay on its side across from the leopard idol with a single chip in its forehead.

"There's no other choice." Aura Kass shook her head. "We've got to let her Instinct card swallow her. Keep attacking."

Amy stood in front of her partner. "This isn't Graves' game anymore! And you heard the warning she gave <u>you</u> about Your Mother's Dread. What does attacking her mean for Kassandra? We'll find another way."

"ENOUGH!" Kassandra spread her arms. "Consequential Disrupter, ELIMINATE my allies!"

The sparkling Disrupter grabbed its sword and charged the field.

Now's my chance! "I activate my Seal of Deception!"

A raging burst of spinning white lights formed into a golden circle with a heptagram in the middle.

"Oop—" Amy levitated. Her seal **swooshed** past her body. "Huh?" Her arms, legs, head, and torso snapped back and stiffened against the seal.

The Consequential Disrupter changed course and leapt into the air. Towards Amy.

Oh dear.

SLICE.

SLICE.

Amy winced from the blows.

Consequential Disrupter dropped to a knee. Broke apart into a dust cloud full of tiny grey sparkles that vanished in seconds.

"Devine!" Aura Kass ran below her partner's levitated body. "Are you alright?"

"Peachy." Amy caught her breath, eyes on Kassandra. *I've gotta play this smart. Only seven cards left. It's fascinating. Not all the details are correct, but the movements... the language... all the same. The feeling, however, is worse.*

Aura Kassandra raised her <u>glowing white aura-covered fist</u> to Amy. "What is this?"

"It's a Palm Share, an aura technique. Looks like it's finally ready. You'll be able to use my auradeck for a limited time while I'm strapped up here."

"Aw, how sweet." Kassandra stroked her cheek. "Next round's up, and you're almost out of cards, Devine."

"Hey, do you think I could get a turn, pretty please, partner?" Aura Amy's eyelids fluttered.

"QUIET!" Kassandra raised a finger at her. "Another word, and I'll feed you to Your Mother's Dread."

Aura Amy tightened up and raised a finger with her mouth ajar. She closed it and stared into space. Nodded.

Kassandra lifted an orange auracard from Aura Amy's deck. "Aaah. Now, this is a card. A level four that doesn't require any sacrifices. I play Phoenix Fire!" She flicked it down.

It formed into a fiery golden sphere that hovered above the floor of shadows. Golden ripples flushed under Aura Kass's feet, disrupting her balance.

How is she using MY cards?

Good question. Aura Kass raised a brow at Amy.

You can hear me?

Aura Kass waved her glowing white hand. ***Thanks to your technique.***

I've got an idea.

Let's hear it. So do I.

Kassandra crossed her arms. "<u>Your</u> Phoenix Fire brings back an ally I lost in three turns, making them four times as strong. Too bad your team won't last two more rounds. But I've guaranteed victory just in case. The vines on her arm turned to ash. "Huh? NO!"

Aura Kass crossed her arms and shook her head. "You have so much left to learn. Playing Phoenix Fire card burns away everything that you have."

"How did I not see that?"

Aura Amy scoffed. *"You thought you could just use my auracards without my permission?"*

Kassandra stared daggers into her. "Did you—did you hide that effect from me?"

Aura Amy's upturned nose turned away. *"Serves you right."*

Amy smiled.

Aura Kass tossed her auracards out.

"We can't attack her anymore!" Amy said. "We have to find a way to win without hurting her."

Aura Kass shrugged. "She made the play. It was her choice."

"Do you not feel her pain?"

"She needs to feel the pain first!"

Kassandra's frown crept into a smirk. "That's my spirit, for sure."

Three ravens with mighty jaws swooped down in front of Aura Kass.

Aura Kass glanced back at Amy. "She's almost worse than you. Crying about Maddy and Tilly all the time. On and on about last year…"

Kassandra's smirk died.

"Whatever," Aura Kass said. "Poe's Ravens hit the skies! Bring me cards from her deck!"

The giant ravens followed her command and soared through Kassandra's body.

Six purple cards burst into lights.

Think she bought it?

We'll figure soon.

"Amy, she's bringing it back!" Aura Amy got swallowed by purple clouds.

"Huh?"

Kassandra floated backwards into the darkness. "This is no longer a <u>fair</u> game."

Purple clouds filled the space between both teams. Team Z—nowhere in sight.

"Find them!" Aura Kass shouted.

The ravens soared in and out of the purple obscurity.

Sudden death rules.

Thick and thin purple vines whipped out of the darkness as the towering Your Mother's Dread tree shed shadows around it.

"Absolutely not." Aura Amy's hand lifted an orange auracard through the shrouds.

The tree backed into the darkness with a **SCREECH**.

YOU PIECE OF SHIT! YOU DEACTIVATED MY—

Limbs shot in and out of the evaporating purple clouds.

Kassandra's mad purple glowing eyes dug into Aura Amy as their limbs connected with lightning speed and accuracy. Neither landed a solid blow, but their persistence grew as their fight's violence escalated.

"Should we stop this?" *Wait.* A smile crept on Amy's face. She removed it.

The white aura around Aura Kass' hand shot straight up.

BURSTING into the Seal of Deception.

Amy rubbed her freed wrists and cracked her neck. The top auracard of her deck flew in front of her. *Now I <u>really</u> feel it. I can feel my aura's power through these cards.* Her eyes found her aura form's blows clashing *with brilliance* above. *My spirit's fighting again.* Amy's eyebrows furrowed. *I'm fighting again.* She flicked her auracard. "Now I play my Survival card—Shadows of Oracle!"

The air behind Team A circulated into a purple-grey sphere. Lightning struck its core as currents bounced off the sphere and into the darkness surrounding it.

"Whoa." Aura Kass took steps back to avoid the growing sphere.

"Shadows of Oracle, bring me Your Mother's Dread!"

"What?" Kassandra paused—right as a fist from Aura Amy smashed her nose.

"Why'd you bring that back?!" Aura Kass said. "You can't use its power without her."

Amy raised a palm. "I can't <u>use</u> its power, but I can <u>activate</u> it. My Shadows Of Oracle allows me to not only steal a card my opponent has played but also lets me use the same number of card types you've used for the last three turns. If I don't have the right types in hand, I can search my deck for them. Or my partner's."

"I see." Aura Kass gave a small smile. "Brilliant." Her auradeck zoomed up—

In front of Amy, the cards spread out into even rows. Her eyes lingered on one of them. *The weird machine from my dream.* "This'll do. I play Eaglot's Nest—for my partner."

A purple auracard torpedoed in front of Team A. From within its dazzling lights, a mechanical nest made of wires and barley stalks crawled out and around Team A on chrome legs.

"And finally, to end my turn, I play both Kassandra's Instinct card, Your Mother's Dread, and her Survival card, Ruins of Vengeance!"

"You CAN'T play those!" One of Kassandra's eyes went normal.

"I know. Which means they're discarded at the end of my turn."

Aura Kass smirked. "Eaglot, you know what to do."

Two of the ten arms of Eaglot's Nest extended and snatched the purple auracards falling from Amy's hand.

"I'll take over from here." Aura Kass flicked two auracards. "Your Mother's Dread—Ruins of Vengeance—Come home to me!"

The wicked purple vines snapped and whipped as the monstrous sequoia tree returned from the shadows behind Aura Kass' defiant pose.

The entire realm flashed. The blinding white light dimmed to the shade of purple Kassandra knew best. Amy, Kassandra, and their aura versions took on a negative color against the purple backdrop surrounding them.

"Our Ruins," Aura Kass's distorted voice said, "helps me bring back three fallen allies with half their strength."

Three grey forms rose from below: eDeeno, Consequential Disrupter, and the Immaculate Knight.

"It also allows me to bring back a Battle card. Same one you used to get us here. Pawn Scheme!"

"No, you won't." Purple aura exploded around Kassandra's body, She dove down at her opponents in a furious auraball.

That's an incredible technique. Amy flew up—charged at her. *Come on! It's my time to throw down.*

Kassandra stopped mid-flight. Dozens of purple-turning-into-red aura strands mimicking fingers yanked her face back. "Get. Off. Graves."

Amy slowed to a stop in midair. "Professor, can you hear us?!"

Kassandra shook her head, mouth getting stretched by the

aurafingers. "Get off me. Spirit— stop this— parasite!" More aurafingers gripped the rest of her limbs.

Aura Kass frowned. "You'll be back to normal soon, my host. I have to complete the game now. Pawn Scheme! Send two tokens to her partner!"

Two beams of light shot from the auracard in her hand and landed. Twin spurts bounced into form and raced to the other side. Their pruned faces snarled and screeched as their vine-like arms slapped around them.

Aura Amy squirmed.

"What the fuck?"

The spurts held hands and did a circle dance, their leafy limbs blowing in the wind. Puss dripped from the boils all over their bodies.

"Now, Consequential Disrupter can attack twice since you have two tokens. Along with eDeeno and my Immaculate Knight." Aura Kass threw a finger toward her host. "Go forth and end this!"

Kassandra's eyes went wide. Her purple eye flickered back and forth between its normal color.

Aura Kass grilled her. "Game over."

.

.

.

White light flashed throughout the room.

.

.

.

Hm. Seems the idol for Team Z has been cracked.

Team Z's CRACKED leopard idol shattered over the arena floor.

Team A wins.

Kassandra's arms pounded on top of her throne's armrest. She _laughed_.

Scary. Amy turned to her partner. "Nice job, partner."

Aura Kass' blank expression stared into space. "How did she still win?" she muttered. She dispersed into small lights that flickered away.

"I don't know how." Amy watched the empty space beside her. "I trusted myself. And my aura..."

Aura Amy gave her a smirk and a wave from across the field. She dispersed.

Kassandra's nose jerked to the side with a rottweiler grill. "You know my name. And fuck you."

A flash of light obscured the room. Dimmed to normal.

Kassandra—nowhere in sight.

What happened here? Amy grilled the ceiling. _Were we really transported into the Aura Realm?_

A rumble.

"I'd appreciate not going through the dirt again."

Off to her right, a rusty door opened.

"Where did that come from? You mean to tell me you have actual doors here?" Amy shook her head. "Unreal."

Blinding white light waited on the other side.

The words **LEVEL 2** pushed out from the dirt above the door.

Amy rolled her eyes. "Dramatic enough..." The nails of her fingers scratched meat off her palms.

CHAPTER TEN

Chapter Eleven

Level 1: Strangling the Opposition

nother long, dark passageway. Becoming too predictable, Professor. What the fuck happened back there? And Jonathan... I'm sorry I failed you. Maybe I don't deserve to live.

<u>*—Amy's burning flesh sits frozen on her bed as the inferno takes over her bedroom—the room's ceiling is missing, revealing the night sky—Amy's corpse melts under the moon's light—*</u>

Voices from the other side of the wall in front of her filled the corridor.

"I don't see the value in these childish games." Mr. Stoicism's *voice cried.* "We should receive some compensation for that complicated prize fight."

"Did you pass your mini-quest?" Mr. SmartyPants' voice asked.

"Mini-quest? What mini-quest?"

"Sis, you should be lower on this board. What gives?"

"Don't be a hater. Keep your eyes open, and maybe you'll catch on. This place is riddled with puzzles. I can't be the only one who found two more."

"Two more?" Mr. Stoicism said. **"Where?"**

The wall slid open.

Amy wandered into the cramped hall space. Met the already

approaching wide smile and embrace of Demora.

"We've got this."

Amy peeped the leaderboard on the dirt wall.

Current Rankings & Points

1   = 7

2   = 5

3   = 4

4   = 2

5   = 2

6   = 2

7   = 2

8   = 2

9   (-3)

10   (-3)

"I'm seventh. Who's we?"

"C'mon." Demora playfully pushed her. "We both know you're gonna fight your way up to the top with me. It's child's play."

"Children shouldn't play dangerous games." Amy walked off.

"What's with you?"

Amy ignored the stares of the others. She stopped next to Kassandra's nonchalant carcass, chilling in one corner of the room, *arms always crossed.* "What happened in there? Are you alright?"

"Nothing." Kassandra turned away. "Course I am. Are your eyes blind?"

"What's going on?" Demora stepped beside Amy. "What do you mean if she's alright?"

"She knows what I'm talking about." Amy's eyes stayed on Kassandra's grill. "Our match was a lot more intense than yours." She stirred in her spot despite the attention She was gaining. "This <u>education</u> we've been blessed with seems to come at high costs. You could have been seriously hurt."

"Will you quit it, Devine? I'm fine."

One point deducted from Number 4.

Number 4's death eyes locked onto Amy. "I'm going to kill you."

"Don't worry," Vedessia chimed in. "It's only a point!" She nodded, hands on her hips. "You'll have plenty of opportunities to make it up, I'm sure!"

Kassandra's growl reverberated as she moved to a distant corner of the room.

"Graves' intentions are unknown, but she's been honest with us from the start." Ms. JellyRoll sat crossed-legged on the ground. She stretched her neck from one end to the next, grunting at the cracks that came off it.

"She can be barking mad." Jamari flipped his token in the air.

E'oné pushed him. "She can definitely hear us, so take care."

"But you're right. Solid teach." Jamari crossed his arms. "Just wait till you all have to experience what happens when you're sent to your cells…"

"Never again." Mr. Stoicism shook his head at the wall. "This whole process is exhausting."

"Not to mention we have no perception of time," E'oné said. "Our GCIDs can't get a signal, and we're still drawing more blanks than conclusions about who the Most Wanted is."

"I forgot we were even playing," Amy said.

"Whining about what can't be changed is exhausting." Demora's eyebrows jumped in E'oné's direction. "Taking action and getting better is the key to your boredom."

"Intriguing." Number 8 stooped down to study something the Gyaad girl drew into the dirt with her finger. "What is this marking?"

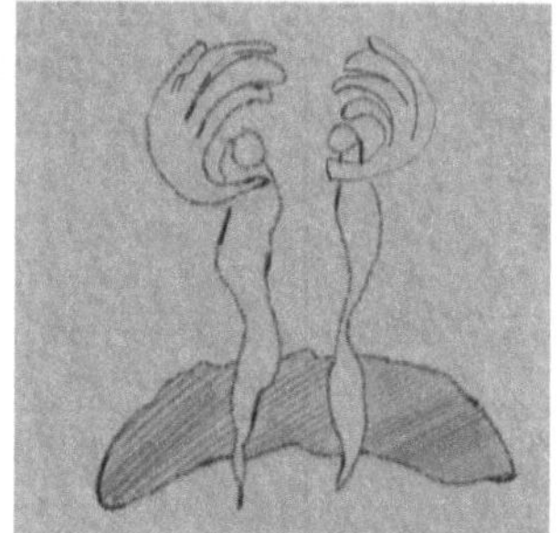

The Gyaad opened her mouth. ***"Eeehhhhhhhaaaaaaaaaaeeeee."***

Not this again.

"She says she saw it in one of her puzzles." Mr. Stoicism stooped down next to her. "Did you solve that one?"

The Gyaad opened her mouth.

Amy winced at the high-pitched squeal in her ear.

"So we've got these puzzles." Mr. Stoicism trailed around the room. "We're fighting for each other's names and respect, but also to escape the prison."

"Maybe escaping the prison isn't the real objective." Ms. JellyRoll retrieved a ceramic teapot and cup from an opened portion in the wall and placed it on the ground before her.

"Yeah, we're supposed to knock each other down in the process." E'oné sat on the ground.

"And catch the Most Wanted." Vedessia looked at all faces. "It's one of us here. Right now."

Everyone kept an eye on their neighbor. Casually shuffled further apart.

"All's fair, and I appreciate the team aspect," Demora said. "However, there can only be one clear victor. An undenied leader of the board."

"Let's guess, in your fairytale, it's you," E'oné *mocked.*

The two held eye contact as others broke into small chatter.

"Even the fiercest warrior can fall to the might of the many." Ms. JellyRoll mixed her tea with a finger. "I grew up in the middle of three provinces, led by who many say is the greatest

Zhigzi ever to rule. That is until he went against the royal order and started a project for which he did not understand the cost. He was a spirit-wheeler and sacrificed his ruling status to give life to human-made beasts he could never control." Her face scrunched tight as she stared at the ground.

Mr. SmartyPants patted her shoulder and passed her a tissue.

"Thank you. It was the pinnacle of scientific and biological achievement at the time. Until they fought. The Dragon and the Phoenix."

"You don't mean an actual..." Jamari put a hand out as though wanting to pause the story.

"Both. The Phoenix's tech was revolutionary. A near-perfect mesh of metal and organic matter. Like the Phoenix, the Dragon was also built to survive most forms of death." Ms. JellyRoll rolled her eyes. "Naturally, the two were set up to fight. Put up for show. The Phoenix kept rising against The Dragon's traumatizing fury. I will never forget the scattered muscle and fat excess that was a regular part of the <u>entertainment</u>."

The Gyaad girl opened her mouth.

"Yeah, me too," Mr. Stoicism said. "I remember the rumors, but I assumed they were only that."

"My uncles went to a show." Vedessia's doe eyes shrunk. Her face scrunched up. "Although one said he wouldn't return, the other kept returning. He was a little twisted in the brain. Then, one day, there were no more shows."

"The last show was exclusive for the Emperor-at-the-time's son." Ms. JellyRoll finished a cup of tea. "The Phoenix was still marred from the last battle, an eye hanging from its socket. The scientists hadn't yet developed a stable way for the Phoenix body to reconstruct itself. The Dragon's structure was nearly indestructible. Both beasts were too stubborn to quit this time. It was a nightmare in the Tokyo sky. They fought for weeks."

Mr. SmartyPants handed her another cup of tea.

"One day, their battle finally stopped. I guess their aging did it to them, but the Dragon and Phoenix started communicating, wondering why they were fighting for human amusement. They figured out that this was what they were created for, to fight each other forever. So, instead, they leveled an entire city. And many more after that. So many families left in shambles…" She failed to sip her tea, moving the cup away from her lips.

"How come we never heard of something like this?" Amy asked. "Even local news should've covered something of that magnitude."

"Prestige needed maintaining. Contain the catastrophe. When the fifth province was attacked, spirit-wheelers came out of hiding to help quell them. I've never seen my people more united. It's what drove me to seek the answers to my soul."

I hear that.

"Both Dragon and Phoenix are still out there, snatching humans bit by bit, and they are more patient as the years go on. They learned torture. Began skinning their victims and left strips of flesh across rooftops as a reminder. Reparations for their pain."

Sizzling flesh under an angry Sun.

"Why not offer them something worth their anger?" Demora leaned against the wall. "Like the man who created them?"

"My great-granduncle has been long dead."

Silence.

"He took his life before they could sentence him for the creation of those beasts. You tell me what you can offer screaming infants who don't understand why they're in pain."

Demora nodded. "My condolences for your losses."

Ms. JellyRoll sipped her tea. "I think what the professor is trying to teach us is that there are more squirrels to strangle than there are—"

"Hey!"

Wow.

"Whoooa."

"Took a turn."

"Seriously?"

"Why are we strangling squirrels???"

"Oh." Ms. JellyRoll placed her fingers on her lips, stifling a quaint chuckle. "I apologize. I sometimes forget when I am outside my province. Where I am from, we have been overrun with the species known as Chim-mook squirrels. This species is ravenous in its intention and in no way friendly. Keep your eyes on theirs because if you're not careful..." She finished her cup of tea. "They leap down onto your face as they enjoy sucking both eyeballs out while choking you with their oversized bushtails. All while scratching you endlessly with their four-inch long nails."

Jaws dropped.

Kassandra, bored but interested.

Mr. SmartyPants— *impressed.*

Amy shut her jaw.

"That's mad," Jamari said.

"Have you tried rehabilitating the squirrels?" Amy asked.

"My uncle once tried to rehabilitate within his megalab funded by the World Committee. It backfired as the Chim-mook began studying him." She poured herself some more tea. "My uncle nearly choked to death on several occasions, but on the last one, his eyes were taken. What's worse about all of this..." She sipped for moments.

The students watched her in silence.

"This species retains the scent of its victims for quite some time. For the few victims who live, these squirrels can even adopt and spread the scent. It is like an addiction for them, seeking it out whenever they can. They'll stockpile food within the shelter of nearby trees to their hosts or burrow in the ground and wait for you. Wait for that scent to return. My uncle keeps windows and doors locked at all times, as it is a must. Little peepholes in every room so he can monitor the squirrel's favorite spots to hide. Usually, it is in the cherry tree right outside his house. Definitely more than one nest on my uncle's plot now. When I was younger, I found a burrow the squirrel must have made. Luckily, it was empty at the time, but I still have nightmares thinking about what could have happened if the squirrel was home..."

She finished her cup, staring at the ground. "If the squirrel cannot find the original victim, it will seek similar scents. Family or anyone who spends enough time with the host of the scent. No one visits my uncle anymore."

"He can't... he can't move?" Jamari cleared his shaky throat.

"Several times, he's tried. Last in his thirties, I believe. That persistent squirrel acted as a beacon for others. The last time I checked in with him, that cherry tree had at least thirty-three nests."

"What?!" Several voices roared.

"Different Chim-mook live in it now, but they are all protected by the Animalia Act. The cooperative skills of this species of squirrel are lesser than most."

"They must be an infant species developed within the last quarter century or so," Amy said.

"Precisely. Too young a species to understand how to coexist with humans."

"I've seen similar behavior before." Amy hugged her arms. "Racooroaches. Devilish crits." The stench of roasted brussel sprouts invaded her nostrils. A wave of nausea rose in her throat.

Chitterchitterchitterchitter-chit-irp Chitter-irp-chit-irp-chit-irp

Ms. JellyRoll leaned forward. "Racooroaches? I've never heard of them."

"My Gma told me about an aunt of mine who had them. They are despicable, little treacherous, leeching creatures. Jadesfeld had an infestation once." Amy's head shivered, and the rest of her body followed. "They aren't something you want crawling through any of your crevices at night, especially when you're trying to shower. The little crits jump out your bathdrain. Their furry bodies poof up to the size of your average cathound." Amy itched at her arm with fervor.

Ms. JellyRoll passed Amy a cup of tea. "It's a special brand. Surprised the professor had it in stock. It'll help your nerves."

Amy whiffed it, "Hm," and took a sip. Raised a brow. Delightful. "Thanks."

"Your town, Jadesfeld," Mr. Stoicism piped up. "You've got, well, that's where the bulk of those missing folk come from, yeah?"

"Yeah. What of it?"

"Nothing. Just sad, that's all. Unfortunate when people have to suffer."

Amy nodded. "Anyway, the intention of raccooroaches is insane. My Gma saved me before they did their thing."

*—Rezna runs into Amy's bedroom—waves a hand—her green aura washes over a kneeled Amy covered in the fuzzy critters, with the sound of **shallow slurps** rising in **symphony**—*

Amy's dead eyes bore into the wall. "They'll latch on to any open holes in your body, doesn't matter, and pump you with some of their special pheromones. It paralyses you in this sort of catatonic state. Seconds go to hours, hours to days. Whole time, they're licking you until they're full. Three days max, at least for the adult raccooroaches. They're more efficient in their goal. The babies are the worst. They're always accompanied by an adult who can pull them off before they burst. Otherwise, they'll lick you like an IcyJel! Nonstop. Longest case recorded by a baby attack was three weeks."

Silence.

Jamari's nervous laugh broke it. "I could use an IcyJel! Right now! Cookies Strawbaganza would be wicked." A compartment pushed its way out of the wall in front of him. He reached in and, with a smile, pulled out a wrapped dessert. He ripped off the wrapping, marveled at the attractive cinnamon color, and then chewed a bit off the top, leaving its reddish core exposed. "Ahhh, oh yeah. Best flavor in the world. Mmm."

"We could use a shift." Mr. Stoicism held his stomach. "IcyJel! it is."

Voices filled the spot as students ordered various flavors of the frozen treat.

Halfway through their treats, Ms. JellyRoll moved closer to Amy. "So what happened to that aunt of yours?"

Jamari threw his hands up and walked away from them,

mouthing something.

"She stayed in a mental facility till the end of her life." Amy shrugged. "After that experience and the Old War, I guess her brain and soul just had enough."

"I hear you. I am sorry to hear your home is dealing with such chaos right now. Please accept my prayers and hope your people will recover soon."

My people. Hm. Never considered them that way before. I guess neighbors can grow into family under dire circumstances.

"I'll have to research those raccooroaches. Thank you for your input, Number 7."

"No worries." *Happy to pass on the nightmares.* Amy shivered. "And thanks for your prayers."

Congratulations on reaching the second level, students. The bonus pot from the last Prize Fight contains thirty points, as your efforts will always be worth at least three times the weight.

Amy rolled her eyes.

First place for the Prize Fight goes to the team of Number 1 and Number 8. They are awarded fifteen points.

"Excellent," Mr. SmartyPants said.

Second place will go to the team of Number 2 and Number 6. They are awarded ten points.

E'oné and Vedessia high-fived.

"Let's get it, girl," E'oné said.

And in third place, we have the team of Number 7 and Number 4. Due to the unique circumstances of their match, Number 7 is awarded three points, and

Number 4 is awarded two points.

Kassandra's subtle growl came from somewhere behind.

Teams can divide points amongst themselves as they see fit. Due to glitches in the system, Numbers 9 and 10 have been spared from remaining on Level 1.

Current Rankings & Points + (Points not added)

1	= 7 (?/15)
2	= 5 (?/10)
3	= 4
4	= 3
5	= 2
6	= 2 (?/10)
7	= 5
8	= 2 (?/15)
9	= (-3)
10	= (-3)

"Score!" Jamari punched his fist into his palm.

Vedessia had a finger on her chin. "What kind of glitches are those?"

What kind of glitches cause possession, you mean...

The dirt characters and faces on the leaderboard shifted.

"We should take our lead right now," E'oné said to Vedessia. "We have no idea what the next challenge will be, but we'd be on <u>her</u> tail." Her eyes burned into Demora's glare.

"I concur," Vedessia said, averting Demora's gaze. "Evenly is best?"

"Let's do it."

"Professor!" Vedessia yelled into the ceiling. "We'd like to add our points now. Evenly, five each, please!"

Demora rolled her eyes.

Your request has been granted. Five points are awarded to Number 2, and five points are awarded to Number 6.

Current Rankings & Points + (Points not added)

1 = 7 (?/15)

2 = 10

3 = 4

4 = 3

5 = 2

6 = 7

7 = 5

8 = 2 (?/15)

9 = (-3)

10 = (-3)

Your cells will remain open for you throughout the rest of your experience. Rest well, students.

A portion of the wall reeled up, exposing a large room on the other side.

Demora made her way into the next room.

"We'll hold on to our points a bit longer," Mr. SmartyPants said. He followed *his partner.*

As the others made for the exit, Amy turned to the approaching Kassandra.

"Hey, we can split the points else—"

"We don't have to coordinate," Kassandra said, moving without pause. "Don't get in my way again." She exited without making eye contact once.

"Right." Amy let out a huge chunk of air. "Will do."

Chapter Twelve

Level 2: Hypse A New Strategy!

The Level 2 floor was a replica of Level One, but with all the cell bars wide open, and each cell in order from five through one, on one side, and ten through six on the other. The students wandered the floor, some taking refuge in their cells, others loitering about.

Jamari leaned against the wall near his cell, a bright red ten above it. E'oné approached him *and inspired something in him* as his arms went frantic.

Shit. Can't talk to E'oné right now about my black light experience. I need to know what she saw. Amy touched the bars of Cell 1, *hardened and melded gravel, same as some of Gma's tombs, crafted for those with a drop more in their wallet.* A bright pink one above. She peered inside at her best friend's pushup routine. "You're off to the races."

"You're not?" Demora said, still going. "How's your cell looking? Our layouts are different all around."

"Haven't checked it yet." *Not too keen on revisiting, either.*

"Well, then." Demora popped up on her feet. "Let's go explore, shall we?" She winked and passed Amy, who followed after. "What's up with you and that Egyptian princess of delusion?"

"How do you know she's Egyptian?"

"Have you gotten her contact?" Demora devilishly slid back close to Amy as they made their way across the room. "Don't pretend I haven't noticed."

"She's a little friendly, that's all. You and Mr. Stoicism make up yet?"

"**Hark**. He's a lost cause. And yes, she's <u>too</u> friendly. Like a cancerous growth. Careful with that one. Don't get too attached. Remember why we're here."

"Why's that?"

"Ha ha."

They pulled up in front of Cell 7. A bright *white* seven above.

Amy's shoulders slunked.

"Looks about the same. Hm." Demora entered first. She pushed around the dirt chair and dirt bed. "Strange. Number 8's cell has moving furniture."

"What's up with you two?" Amy peeked out at the green lighting within the **Cell 8** marked on the opposite side of the floor.

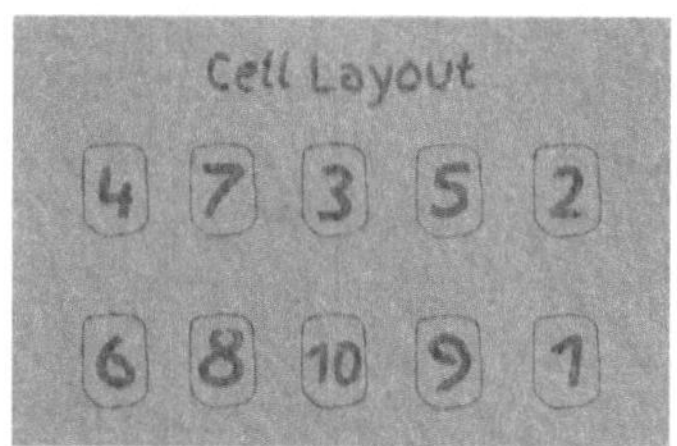

She frowned. "Did the cells rearrange? I <u>was</u> across Number 5." Turned back to her snooping friend. "Hello?"

Demora searched every inch of the walls around the cell.

"Saw you chatting before your Soul Game match." Amy sat on the edge of her bed. "My feet are killing me. Walking through this place is like walking through a swamp."

"Pretty sure it's another one of Graves' tricks." Demora stopped her search and faced Amy. "8 has a secret alliance with Number 5. He asked me not to select her team, so I obliged."

"That's it?"

"I had to make sure he kept his nose in the game. He had some sentimentals, but we made it, and now I know two more names."

"Can't we build an alliance… if not already formed?" Amy's eyebrow raised high.

"Sure, sure. I just can't give up any names, you understand. Part of the game. Although, I do hear the names may be a part of the puzzles."

"Where are you getting this?"

"Come on, Amy, look around. This place is littered with whatever Graves gets up to when she's not," quotation fingers, "teaching us." She leaned down on her knees in front of Amy. "We need to crack whatever the SOGL is all about. I think we need to find the Most Wanted. That person may be the key to the rest! This place could hold secrets to Graves' prowess. We'd be aura masters."

"Please." Amy brushed her off. "You can't be falling for it? Look around! If secrets exist, they're all coming from Graves' memories. I think there's something to unlock that we can use to learn how to control this prison ourselves."

Demora rubbed her chin. "That's quite the outlook. What are you saying? This place is some sort of…?"

"Space she crafted within the Aura Realm. *Like Kass did.* Making us think we're somewhere we're not. Gma does it all the time. I just don't get how we're able to be in here for a prolonged time without feeling totally drained. Our auras <u>should</u> be taxed by now. During my Soul Game's match… *I hope she's buying all this. She's so eager to prove herself my words may go over her head. Retelling what happened with Kassandra brings back memories of last year. But she doesn't seem possessed any more. What gives? Possession. Such a nasty bug—oop. Language.* **Sigh.** *No wonder Aba hates us…* and whatever possessed Ka—my opponent, seized control of the game when it took us into the Aura Realm." *'Glitch.' Sure, Prof.*

<u>*—Amy pounces and punches and slams and tosses her weight down onto a squelching heap of flesh, blood spitting around her—*</u>

"An old Rezna trick, huh?" Demora smirked. "Delicious. I've been curious about this Aura Realm she trains you in. If Number 4 can crack it… Maybe it's part of the game. Either way it should be easy to crack this with you on The Alliance."

—A rabid gorilla pounces and punches and slams and tosses her weight down onto a squelching heap of flesh, blood spitting around her—

"4 was possessed. I don't think she— Wait, how many people are in this 'Alliance'?"

Demo shrugged. "8 started it. Pretty sure Number 5 is the only other member apart from us." She folded her arms tight together. "Wait, what do you mean, <u>possessed</u>?"

"Oop—" Vedessia froze in the doorway with wide eyes and a rigid body. She bowed. "I'm so sorry. I didn't mean to intrude. I'll just… yeah." She dipped out of sight.

"Told you," Demora, still between Amy's legs, said. "She's bonkers for you."

Amy slapped Demora's arms and pushed her off. "Quit it. I need to go find out what she knows. She seems to know a lot about these carvings on the walls and then some."

"There it is." Demora stood with fists on her hips. "Now, get her contact."

Amy mocked her face. "Don't mess up my cell." She ventured back into the complex, turning right.

She ran a hand along the wall as She moved down the hall. *Everything looks like a carving. Simple crack in the wall. How bout that one? Nope.* "This place… She's trying to drive us insane. What's her end game?" She retracted her hand as she passed Cell 3. Stared at the bright yellow three.

Inside, the Gyaad girl hopped from spot to spot as she drew symbols into the earth.

My point exactly.

Amy passed Cell 5.

Ms. JellyRoll levitated, eyes closed, deep in concentration.

She's another marvel.

The lilac five flickered above the cell.

Amy clenched her fists. Moved forward.

Put her nose up to a *strange marking* on the wall.

Amy rolled her eyes.

She reached Cell 2. *Ignoring* the sandy yellow two.

Vedessia sat on the bed, head down, blind to the world around her. Her lips moved at an incredible pace. Lines of hieroglyphics filled a third of each of her cell walls.

Amy leaned inside. "Hey."

"Hoh—Hey!" Vedessia jumped awake, out of breath. "Hi, hey, how are you?"

"You alright? Is this a bad time?"

"Yeah, No! Just some Hypse, I'm in training."

"Hypse?"

"Did you want to come in?" Her caramel cheeks grew red. "Are you here to see me?" She looked away. "Silly, of course you are." Back at Amy. "Not that I expected you to be or anything."

"It's chill. Can we have a chat?" Cocked her head. "Hypse?"

Vedessia scooted over, patting beside her. "Or there if you'd like." She pointed over to a golden seat across from her.

"Did you make that, or it come like that?"

"Little of both." Vedessia sent one of her brown-golden curls flying back over her right ear.

Straight to business, Devine. Amy sat across from the fidgeting girl and settled into the golden seat. *Comfy.* "What did you mean when you said you 'knew it'?"

"What? When?"

Stupid cute doe eyes. "The first night we met. When my friend overstepped her knowledge."

"Ooo, I get you now. Your scar." She pointed.

Amy shifted her scarred hand into the palm of her left. "What about it?"

"The Hieros in my culture are those who possess the ability to exude their essence, their spirit. Hieros are blessed by our community to take on any matters where their abilities may be required. They have almost as much influence as our Pharaoh." Vedessia leaned in. "Depending on the matter, their word could be held higher."

Amy leaned towards her. "Egypt recognizes auraists? Officially?"

"That word you say is exquisite, I quite like it very much. Yes, they recognize <u>auraists</u>, but only unofficially. The world isn't quite ready for that, I'm sure you know."

Amy leaned back. "Must be freeing to live there…"

"Everywhere's got problems. Before I left, my cousin tried to strangle me! It was a nice rush as I thought I was having an entirely different dream at first…" She squinted into space. Shook her head. "Waking up to my cousin's frothing face wasn't on the breakfast menu."

"Is he…"

"He caught a nasty leprosy virus. Long story. Nearly a short one for me! Luckily, us spirit-wielders are immune." She chuckled with a hand over her *angelic lips.*

Pull it together, Devine! I can't tell if it's appropriate to laugh. "Back to the scar."

"Yes, so. Once you've been officiated as Hiero, you're given the Eternal Scar, burned from your <u>aura</u>." She lifted her hands and showed off an inked pattern on her left hand. "I'm still training for mine, so I have this for now, and yours reminded me of the scarring pattern Hieros share. You see, it's—" She reached for Amy's hand.

Amy pulled back.

"Sorry."

Cool it, Devine. Don't be weird. "It's fine." Amy rose and sat beside Vedessia on the bed. *It's cool.* She uncovered her right hand and gave it over. Watched curiously as the girl marveled over the marking of her past trauma.

"Incredible. Sort of looks like a Phoenix." Her bashful eyes gazed into Amy's.

Amy threw her a small smirk. *Least someone thinks so.*

Vedessia released Amy's hand. "The pattern Hieros share is the mark of a great warrior only known as So-bek-Nu. My dream is to one day find their real name and solve the mystery of their disappearance." She shook herself loose *of whatever thoughts* and pushed back her unrelenting curls *over each perfect curve of her ear.* "It's so nice to have normal conversations with people again." She looked off. "Extracting information from a corpse is rather excruciating."

"One more time with that."

"I'm also an archaeologist in training. It's the family business, after all. The training camp back home is exhilarating but maybe a bit overwhelming on the soul." Her eyes got lost in the shifting light within the hieroglyphics on the wall.

"So why do it?"

"Oh." Vedessia shrugged. "It's my culture. I need to honor it."

"You can honor it without succumbing to torture."

"Yeah. I'd be a bit sad if my Mom was disappointed, though."

"It can be growth to disappoint. Think I'm learning that. I love my Gma, but she's suffering from scars of wars long gone."

"I've got one of those, too." Vedessia's frown turned around. "A suffering grandmother. Though I don't agree with her racist—" she finger quoted, "'factuals', as she says. I always try to remind myself that her pain comes from some truth. Whoever, whatever, hurt her long ago left a permanent scar inside of her. I just remember to heal the scars and not dwell on the pain they caused. Or that caused them."

"What type of truth can a racist have?"

"For some reason, they are afraid."

"Hm. Heal the scars." Amy's eyes widened. She stood fast. "Thank you. I've gotta run, but this was enlightening." She wagged her index like a mad scientist. "Yes..." *Before we go—* "Oop!" She leaned over, adjusting her shirt's v-neck. "Hot in this prison."

"Oh!" Vedessia turned away with flushed cheeks.

Amy smirked. "I'll see you around, cutie." She made her way out.

Wish I could see her face. My black light was able to break E'oné's prison. Maybe I can do the same for Graves' prison. If I can just control the black light, I can break out using Graves' weaknesses. What her mind fears... The answer could be horrifying.

Demora's face, still by Cell 7, mouthed something in her direction.

Amy quickened her pace to hear it. A little closer, Demo's message—

"Did

You

Get

The

Contact

?"

Amy lobbed herself into Demora and swung the cell bars closed. Air slapped at her friend's continuous mouthing of her *nonsensical* phrase. "Will you stop?"

"Did you get it?"

"I got it alright."

"Delish! Marvelous!"

"The secret to cracking Graves' prison."

Raspberry "Boring." Demora plopped down on her bed.

Amy's finger twirled at the ceiling. "You think she can hear us?"

"Well, if she can, it doesn't matter now." Demora grew a devilish smile. "You've got a scheme in mind?"

"Let's link up." Amy took a seat on the ground.

"Think we can?"

"Aura's always connected. Can't hurt to try."

Demora stretched her arms out. "We've got the time." She closed her eyes and pointed her fingers out to the sides.

"Will you get level?" Amy pointed to the floor.

"Ugh." Demora scooted off the bed and sat across Amy, sticking a tongue out before closing her eyes.

Amy shook her head, closed her eyes, and took a deep breath.

Both young women stretched their arms, pointing their index fingers to their sides. They both took three deep, shallow breaths, followed by tens of seconds of silence.

Amy breathed deeply.

Demora breathed deeply.

Amy's eye peeked at her best friend. "Match with me."

Demora's opposite eye peeked back. "Match together."

"You're impossible."

Both girls shut their eyes again.

Amy breathed deeply.

Demora breathed deeply.

Deep breaths in unison.

There's her heartbeat.

Lub-dub Lub-dub Lub-dub Lub-dub

                    Lub-dub Lub-dub Lub-dub Lub-dub

Little slower, Demo.

        Lub-dub Lub-dub Lub-dub Lub-dub

        Lub-dub Lub-dub Lub-dub Lub-dub

That's on me. Almost there...

       Lub-dub Lub-dub Lub-dub Lub-dub

       Lub-dub Lub-dub Lub-dub Lub-dub

Perfect sync.

            Amy's breath. Hers.

            Hers. Amy's.

Intertwined into one soothing melody.

Immediate thoughts between the two fused into a single purpose: <u>Unity of the Two</u>.

In unison, the women snapped their arms forward, index fingers pointing at one another, beads of sweat running down their faces. In the space between their pointing fingertips, minuscule specks of white light formed a transparent bubble.

Amy's nose wrinkled. *"Can't believe it worked."*

Demora beamed. *"I never doubted us."* Frowned. *"How much control do you think Graves has over this place? She **must** have help."*

"Good point. She's only human."

"Did you get a clue about the MW from Ms. Shan Hiska?"

"Something better. I know how we can escape without playing her games."

"Oh? How?"

Amy got her up to speed on her shadow training over the past few months, and how she accessed black light. *If only I can remember how my body did it. And do so without going unconscious immediately. Is she... alright?*

Demora's face *was not* the one she anticipated. She resembled a protective mother dragon, who just had one of her eggs containing an unborn child smashed by a reckless passerby. And if she were able, there would definitely be steam blaring out each of her ears and nostrils. *"You WHAT?"*

"What?"

"Are you— Amy, ARE YOU INSANE? Are you TRYING TO GET YOURSELF KILLED?"

"Stop shouting. The echoing is more obtuse in here."

"That is the most— I can't BELIEVE you—"

"Alright, already! Sure, now you mention, it could be a bit risky—"

*"A BIT? You're talking of mastering the absence of light! Our aura **is** our light! The only thing you'll master is a cold pulse."*

"I've done it! Apparently. E'oné's gonna help me perfect. She saw it when it happened."

"E'oné... saw... before me?"

"You look like you have an upset stomach."

"Ames, I can't begin to tell you how much fury I currently have at the fact that my best friend has been trying to off herself for MONTHS, and there's a stranger who knows all about it before me."

"Off myself is a bit dramatic..."

"Amyyyy—"

"When you put it like that... well I didn't plan it!" Demora scrubbed her forehead with three fingers, a rough massage up and down. *"I know you're not going to stop. I see that look in your eye. You're too far in, Amy. I'll help you crack your wild theories, but promise me two things."*

"Okay..."

"Promise me you will not, I repeat, will <u>NOT</u> try it again unless I am there with you. As a last resort, I may have to split my aura to save you."

"Like what..." ...I did for Cloudy?

"Yes."

"Okay. What's the other thing?"

"You'll help me track down the Most Wanted?"

"Deal! I've got you."

"Great." She finally settled from her battle stance. Would she have fought me for the promise? *"So what are you thinking?"*

Amy twisted a loc of her hair as she sat in the question. *"If this prison means we're in Graves' mind, that means she has some type of emotional scars we can expose."*

"Interesting... wow! Didn't think ya had it in ya, Ames."

"Please. We're in a prison. The objective is to break out. Escape. What rules would any prisoner given free will abide by?"

<u>*—LATER, Amy writes in the dirt of her cell—*</u>

Ms. JellyRoll.
If her great-granduncle was a Zhigzi that makes her a Zhigzi as well.

Bloody hell, she's royalty.
One step under the Emperor of Asia.

Chapter Thirteen

Level 2: Stuck Between Levels

World *prize for failure delivered right to my doorstep.* Amy walked in her thoughts down a dirt corridor. Stumbled for a second, caught off guard by the crunch in her footsteps on the much dryer earth in this section of the prison. *Wasted time, spent energy, and nowhere closer to my theory or further clues about the Most Wanted.* She sighed at the lines of insects she trailed behind. *But if I* can *access my black light, I might be able to feel the source of this prison's energy. Bypass it. Unseen.*

Amy's peripheral caught the blue shell of a critter moving along the ceiling and wall, back and forth, frantically. "Tracking insects isn't the type of detective work I agreed to. What are you on, little fella?" She moved closer to the insect.

Its blue head buried itself into the wall, though its crater of a shell stopped the rest of its body from entering.

It's a drybeetle. A stuck drybeetle. Amy's thumb and index finger picked it out the hole and placed it up the wall. She scratched her shoulder and felt something hard. Another drybeetle ran circles on her upper arm. She picked it up, bent to a small hole near her feet, and let the critter crawl off her finger and down the hole. *How was Kassandra able to bypass Graves' system during our Soul Game match? Her 'realm within the Spirit World'. That can't be a coincidence.* Amy wiped the dirt on the ground with a finger and inspected it. *This prison isn't real. Graves has us in some part of the Aura Realm. That's how Kass was able to infiltrate. Makes perfect sense.*

Upon standing, a puzzling sight across the narrow hall caught her attention.

Crudely carved into the dirt wall: MOST WANTED WAS HERE

Amy's left hand on the wall held her up. She chuckled with a tightened jaw. *What's the likelihood? Either Graves is fucking with me or—* "OWah!"

Her left hand grew hot but wouldn't budge from off the wall. As she kept trying to yank it away, a shimmer of light from a nearby crevice hit the side of Amy's face. She turned her head—

An avalanche of crusted and hardened dirt poured out the wall some feet ahead of her. Among the wreckage, a figure covered in spiky stars rose from within the shadows, its arms extending and its fingers clawing at the air. It released huffs of furious exhaustion, the air thick with more dust every second.

Amy's left hand braced the wall, her right aimed at the silhouette moving towards her.

"Number 7?" Dusting herself free of the overwhelming dirt that mucked up her designer jacket, E'oné stepped fully into the harsh lighting.

Amy leaned back against the wall, her nerves falling back into place. "Thank Callisto." *Ugh, why'd I say that?* "Hey E, what the hell happened to you?"

"Just had a wicked challenge. I aced it! Kinda unfair I haven't gotten your name yet." She smiled.

"Oh, yeah? Same. You'll win it in a game soon enough against me, I'm sure." Amy bounced her head back on the crumbling earth. "With my luck."

"Yours didn't go well then, huh?"

"It went—" Amy's mind goes to her challenge 30 minutes prior...

•

.

.

.

{

Amy stood in a vanilla bean bubble of a vast room ten times her size.

A circular off-pink material protruded from the far wall. Its bulbous, multi-ring face swelled and withdrew as though breathing. Numbers 1 - 20 in purple lights dressed its outer ring, all in scrambled order. The inner rings of the *dartboard?* had missing segments leading to blackness.

At the opposite end of the room behind her, four monstrous titanium walls met in the middle.

"Welcome to Pull Your Weight!" Hooooooo-wepaaaaaaaa!

Echos of the weightless, charismatic voice bounced off the plush walls, leaving indents that corrected themselves shortly after.

Who the hell—?

Directly above her head, a red guitar lay sucked into the ceiling's memory foam.

Is that a Fender Strat?

The Fender Stratocaster trembled in its spot— **HA HA HA HA HA HA Haarrrrr HAAAAAaaa!**

Amy's feet left the floor— "What sorcery is this?"

She floated up to the middle of the spherical room, in line with the bullseye ahead and the middle of the now-turning titanium walls behind. *Is that a fan?!*

The wind of the titanium cycle threatened Amy's already unbalanced form in midair— the bottom of her shift flapped away from her torso.

The titanium fan— a soft blur—

Opposite forces. Amy steadied mid-air— her vision blurred at the dizzying sight of the floor *way* down below. *They have to meet somewhere in the middle. Causing stability. Structure.*

BLASTOFF!

"**WAA**AAaaaaaaaaaaaaaaaaaaaaaaaaaa!" She fought the violent force, but before she could twist in time, she found herself propelled through a space near the bullseye.

Start again!

"What?!" Amy clenched her fists and stiffened in the air.

Her body dragged inch by inch towards the dartboard again.

She's quite the fighter! But will she make it again?

Her body shook with the unrelenting gust behind her.

Her body torpedoed through the plush material of the dartboard, tossed end over end to the other side, stopping herself in the middle of the room again.

Another dartboard across the way.

20! There's a start! 281 to go!

Amy's right hand seared. "Ah, fuck!" Her body shot towards the board. "Oh, no! Can't— control—" Her body spun and crashed through another soft spot on the board.

Triple! 51 points shaved off! 230 left!

Amy forced herself to a stop again but she couldn't hold it and her body flew back first— through the board—

15! 215 left!

—and barreled through the next—

OH NO! She hits a missing segment! Plus 40, 245 to go!

"No." Amy's arms and legs shook under the pressure as she manuevered her body to face the oncoming board.

A missing segment awaited her.

Dodged it space and fumbled through the cotton candy mesh.

Triple 18! Quite the recovery at 227!

Her body spiraled towards the next board, stuck in its vortex of flailing limbs—

Oooof! Right through a miss!

Through another space—.

Back to 301!

Amy's hands, white hot, her aura glowing off the edges— Her body's momentum twirled to a stall, still inching forward under the tremendous winds— kicked her feet before her, holding them up as she fought the air's pressure.

Dead ahead, a vacancy on the board—

Amy kicked her feet to the side— side slammed into another fluffy segment.

Triple 20!

She stretched her legs behind her and glued her arms to her sides.

A faint white glow embraced her entire body.

She ducked into another soft segment.

19!

Amy rocked her speeding torso from side to side, teasing her direction—

Gravity can bend light— Her whipping locs stood on end.

But my inner light can defy gravity with a little— push!

Her chest swelled as her body's faint glow grew brighter.

She SPED UP— anchored her body left and right, then through the board—

Bullseye!

— and again— gaining speed through a loop of marshmallow dartboards—

A miss!

—and in her frustration, she toppled her into another—

Back to the root! 301!

Fuck! Focus, aura! Amy's body froze but staggered against the fan's force.

Her efforts only slowed her momentum. *Focus!*

Stop yelling!

"Aura! Shit—" Amy flew through the board.

Uh-Oh! Plus 40!

Amy's body seizured against the cold, invasive winds.

Came to almost a full stop— right in front of a gap on the board.

Her resistance is inspiring! But will it last?

I can do it! She fell backwards into the board.

Triple 17!

"Empty your mind." The words she read in her last piece of literature raced from ear to ear.

Amy edged closer towards a gap.

Be formless. She breathed in deep.

Shapeless. Her white aura sparked around her with jagged edges.

Like water. Eyes closed, she spun her body *and let it go.*

Kicked her feet, propelling her body through the softness of a segment neighboring the gap she grazed.

15!

Amy shot through a gap.

Uh-Oh!

"Come on!" Within the overwhelming glow of her aura, she zipped away.

Triple 18!

Double 17!

127 left!

She flew effortlessly through another segment.

Bullseye!

Double 16!

5!

Her body's flight fought wicked turbulence as it weaved and rode the wind.

5!

I need to crank up the aura.

1!

Soared through a segment—

7! 27 left!

If I blackout... it's over.

14! 13 remain!

Getting tired. Colder... She shook out her fingertips.

Her aura faded from her body's outline, slowing her flight.

The world around her disappeared in blurred blotches.

Oh no! A miss! 27 to go again!

Her consciousness slipped every other second. *Not yet.* Her teeth smashed together and gritted. *Not yet!*

Amy blinked.

Halfway reopened her eyes.

Her aura exploded around her body.

Amy's face— *Giddy from the fever each part of me grew—*

Amy shot to the corner of the dartboard, aiming right for segment 17.

Her eyes rolled back— *My veins are— choking—*

Clutched the migraine that stretched from end to end of her head.

Her perspiration's wetness dried on her with **sizzlesssssssss.**

Could it be? Another miss!
And yet another!
Another!
Another!
Another!
Another!
Another!

}

"Zero gravity? That's pretty stunner."

Amy shrugged at the *guilty sympathy written* on E'oné's face.

"I'm sorry yours didn't turn up how you wanted."

"It's whatever. What was yours?"

"I had the same challenge you helped me with at the start of the games."   "Oh? And you killed it? Sick!"

"Thanks. How's your dark energy experiments going?"

"Not much to tell there. I've thought of this deditrite soil." Amy kicked some dirt up. "The only soil that sparks the growth of false aura particles, right?"   "Something like that."

"This prison's a hot box for aura."

"Why do you call spirit that? '*Aura*?'"

"Just what I was taught."

"You live with your grandmother, right?"

"Yeah."

"Does she know about you you?"

Should I trust her? I've seen what her fears can do to her. I need her help describing my dark energy manipu— hate calling it that. My shadow light. "Yeah. She taught me everything I know about aura."

"And now you're trying to do the impossible. Dark photon manipulation may as well be magic."

Amy cracked a smile. "Maybe. But you saw something. Whatever I did can be replicated, it must be replicable."

"Have you—" E'oné's thinking face wears no costume.

Yes? YES? Come on, I gave a little something. Say it.

"Have you tried... Hm." The girl fussed with her braids as she pondered. "Do you know how they rewrap a weathered mummy?"

"Of course not."

They shared a short burst of laughter.

"I didn't know either until recently," E'oné' said. "New linen is never used by the Necrotide. A mummy's spirit is bonded with their wrap, even past death. So they believe in utilizing the wisdom that comes from the wraps of perished mummies. To share in and carry on the legacies. They use the old school method of spirit splicing similar to twisting dreadlocks."

"If you're suggesting I aura splice, I tried once and ended up with burnt fingertips I couldn't use for weeks. I had to stay home from school that week."

"Your method of reversing your spirit's light is costly. Absence of light is a scary thought. It's the most unbalanced thing I'd never ever want to face let alone induce. If I were you, instead of trying to change something, I would focus on creating a link. Aura is creation, after all."

"A link?"

"It's like the soil here. It creates its own resource to help with growth. What if you did the same?"

Creates its own resource. But with what? My shadow is only affected by its light source. What if I can create new particles? Dark photons are naturally released from my aura but I can't interact with them. But if I can use my aura to draw out the dark photons and then combine them with the surrounding gravitons. There's—

"I can tell you have a lot on your mind," E'oné said. "I'm going to go get some sleep."

"Right. I'll see you later."

E'oné walked in the opposite direction. "Keep me posted on your progress!"

"Will do!" Amy rubbed her chin. *During the dart game, I had to counter the anti-gravity using my aura. If I can create new particles parented from dark photons and gravitons, I could create a physical means of using dark energy. Black light. Or shadow light. I can decide on a name later.* Amy paced up and down the corridor. *It's almost like how a curse's aura is tinted black, but it's really the former color of the creator before their death. It would be like having a personal set of ziccolights— invisible ones— sourced from my aura.* She frowned, coming to a stop at the end of the hall. *Demo's right, though. It's dangerous. It's semi-splitting my energy. We saw what a full split does to a girl.*

—Amy curls her right hand into a fist—

Smoke rises from a growing deep scar, blackening on the back of her right hand—

—Amy sits in an aura ball of her natural orange-—

—the orange drains from the ball—

—the ball, now transparent white—

I lost my aura's original color and former power, splitting it to contain Cloudy's curse. Fracturing the energy I have left into particles doesn't sound so appetizing anymore. Still. Black light may be the answer to bypassing whatever's feeding the prison. How do I get it to function? Why'd it work with E'oné? What was I feeling at the time?

<u>*—Amy's hands push against E'oné's aura prison—*</u>

<u>*—the burning sensation of her esophagus—*</u>

<u>*—Amy's foot shakes off the hot stabbing—*</u>

And then I blinked. She paused, her eyes shyly turning to the wall beside her. *The force within these walls is just as good as E'oné's aura prison. And Graves couldn't possibly have a defense against shadow light.*

She placed her hands on the wall. Pressed into it with *most* of her might. The dirt imprinted with the force of each finger. *Come on, aura, wake up!* Every line in her head creased with her efforts. A small ember flared in her gut, a fleeting sensation that stuck around.

Her standstill with the wall went on for ten minutes of pure focus.

She slammed her hands into the wall. "Fuck!" Rested her forehead on it.

<u>*—A light blue aura rose from far away—*</u>

<u>*—Jonathan's blue aura form scowled at her—*</u>

<u>*—AM I DEAD?*</u> — The echos of her worry haunted her.

— <u>*"Only if you want to be."*</u> —

Amy remembered the nagging shivers from his arrival.

— <u>*"Cloudy had proof to his message."*</u> —

— <u>*"Cloudy had proof to his message."*</u> —

— <u>*"Cloudy had proof to his message."*</u> —

So much anger. Pain. Amy faced the nearest wall, the distaste from her memories wearing her face. *I carry it all the time.* She placed her left hand on the crumbling dirt wall. Stared at her quivering right hand and its gnarly disfigurement. The Scar *watched me.* She most hated how the Scar made her feel. *How it felt.* It felt *pleasure.* The kind of pleasure gotten from relieving one's ear hole of its contents. And The Scar writhed in ecstasy at this moment.

She placed her right hand on the wall.

Veins pulsed out of her temples, moving as though moving

chunky milk through a hose.

Small cracks in her vision *dared* her to blink.

Feel. Empty your mind. Be formless. Like water.

Amy took a breath so deep it scared off the scattering drybeetles nearby.

She exhaled her newfound calm.

Her body shook as its temperature escalated.

Immense pressure forced its way out from behind her eyes.

Her lips dried and quivered from her fever.

The ends of her locs stood at attention.

As she began to close her eyes, the last thing she saw was her aura's white outline flickering around her hands, creating deeper and wider indents in the wall.

The pit of her stomach dropped far beyond its limits, as though her very body was collapsing into the ground.

A circle of typhooning whiteness, both known and unknown to her, lowered her into its depths.

Life & Death

Her intention of connecting with the dirt walls of the prison created this pocket of excitement in her personal bubble that she— *looking back*— had felt when she touched E'oné's aura prison trying to help her *way back on Level 1. That seemed so far away now.* Like the Necrotide, who read the wraps of perished mummies, Amy knew she must similarly read the wall and uncover what secrets the deditrite dirty hide. The waves of energy emanating from the prison walls made her feel *as though I'm wading through a pool on the first Summer day. But—* as she swam through the warmth, she couldn't shake the feeling that something watched her from the bottom of the "pool". And it grew impatient with her. A sauna of desperation wet the air. *I swear the wall knows. It's anticipating my next move. Or is Graves preparing to shut me out from my experiment?*

The world around her drew further away, but she remained on task, hands glued to the simmering wall.

Please work for me, aura. Her abs clenched as she felt for her *stomach's reply.*

Seconds passed before a pit of fire grew within her belly.

It knew it was wanted. Needed. It's you and I, aura. Her heart sent her stomach's reply down her legs into her toes. Her *boneless* arms fell to her sides.

I fell into a dream.

.

.

.

.

.

She plunged in slow motion into a space of milky white. Her pea sized figure, a dot, within the never-ending drop.

Amy's entire body greyed, last the irises, but her pupils faded to white. She knew— *I was dead. No, please.* Her voice echoed her surrounding area, but her mouth never moved. *What is happening?* Her body was frozen in freefall. Only her eyes bounced around in their sockets, taking in the absent world she was in that seemed to go on forever.

Several whispers broke the absolute silence, steadily cranking up to conversational levels.

"The Earth is a living being on its own. You think it's happy with what we've done to it in all these centuries?"

Is someone there? The whites of Amy's pupils moved independently from her irises, catching glimpses of unremarkable faces zooming by as she fell past small scenes of action. Fervid, broken straight lines formed featureless and undefined figures of humans and other beings. Each scene moved at its own pace with pieces of dialogue filling the space with echoes of information.

"We can connect to our collective consciousness. Mediums tap into this by seeing the past and predicting our possible futures based on our free will."

"Memento mori."

"Callisto believed that we are better than we allow ourselves to be."

"Don't fight with peasants when you can smother the royal table."

"Tao tried to teach us, but we wouldn't listen."

The voices diminished as though falling themselves further away from Amy.

Amy's body arched backwards with a snap, ribs straining to

break away from their host. Amy's chest thrust in hyperventilation, each of her ragged breaths making her sternum jut out sharper. Her spine groaned under the tension, vertebrae begging itself not to splinter like wood under the threat. Each limb hung limp, and her fingers twitched in spasms of agony.

A symphony of screams, laughter, argument and crying disturbed the space, causing a warping ring in Amy's ears. Drops of blood fell from them soon after.

Her white pupils enlarged. Black cracks tore in from around their circumference and stopped in the middle, forming inner circles. Raw searing light erupted from them, shooting beams like self-extending magical power poles that blended comfortably with the white zone.

Shadows danced in her eyes' projection. The shadows became concrete, living silhouettes showing features such as hair, torsos, hands, and legs but their heads had no eyes, only noses and mouths.

The silhouette creatures spread from one another across the open space. Scenes made from the same fuzzy shadow material built around the creatures. The squiggling shadows break apart and come together, changing scenes just right. Not too fast or slow, but with enough time to paint clear pictures. Short films suffocated the space.

Like pixie dust, scenes popped into Amy's peripheral.

"It is but a simple price to pay."

[A figure runs into a playground and hops onto the seesaw with another friend. Laughing with the others in the park. Not a care in the World as they all play in the most purest, beautiful harmony. A taller figure slinks in. But vanishes. Along with all of the other figures, flushed away like that dust. All but one. Still on the seesaw, jumping and falling with his own weight. Six small coffins appear. They clockwise circle the lone figure as he continues seesawing along through life.]

[A figure with wavy hair smiles as they leave a house. They

wear a frown returning home, with a figure twice their size placing a hand on their shoulder. Both figures go down into a cellar. The bigger figure smiles as they lean into the smaller as the scene breaks apart. In bed, the big figure sleeps next to its partner and two smaller figures in their own little beds. The wavy-haired figure stands in the kitchen, speaking to their house's Creaevix system. Then the figure leaves the house, no smile or frown worn. Only that narrow in-between remained. The house went up in flames behind them. The wavy hair figure's expression remains— handcuffed through their trial— sitting in their cell— and finally performing manual labor in an overcrowded pit with other tiny figures.]

[A figure shakes their head in protest. A larger ADULT figure in their stupid dress looms over them. Slaps them, sending the smaller figure to the floor. The smaller figure is tied up with bands going over their mouth, wrapping down to the tip of their feet. Encased and squirming. With the older figure smiling over their body. The struggling figure fractures like broken bone and reforms into dozens of teeny gift boxes. Adult figure walks with a cart into a pit, dress flowing behind, and delivers the gift boxes from the cart to a community of bony shadow figures. The community eats the contents of the gift boxes while the deliverer dances, earsplitting **CHA-CHINGS!** exploding over her head.]

The film reel of moving pictures rotated nonstop around her eyes while filling her head with voices in different languages. The worst part: every emotion, strike, thought, and feeling burned through Amy's core, ripping open her veins as compensation for their collected pain.

Amy's mouth remained gaped in a silent scream. The desperation to escape *this hell* softened her eyes. Tears wanted to fall, *but that was impossible here.* All that was left *was to feel.*

HERE'S THE GRIEF YOU NEVER <u>CARE</u> <u>ENOUGH</u> TO SHOW!

Doppelgangers of Amy cried in sobbing puddles, filling the spaces between the backdrop of indie movies of pain.

"Desolation. I reside inside a farce. These shallow forms of comfort and stability consume me."

"Your mother didn't want you. She'd rather die."

The images and Amy's zoomed around her vision faster than she could keep up with. All fuzzed into squiggly lines that shook the way seizures ingested with rabies would.

Amy's eyes rolled back, pulsing out of her sockets. Every pore she had pushed through agonizing labor, expelling something from deep within her, giving birth to something foreign that *I knew belonged to me.*

Chapter Fourteen

Level 2: Common Ground

"**M**ummy, *I'm hot.*" The murmurs came at the stroke of midnight—*3:27 a.m., to be exact. But wait, how could that be?* She tossed with unopened eyes in her half-slumber, cursed to ride between points in time. Torn apart by versions of herself never in agreement—yet her skin prickled with the chill of that evening...

Tormented by the scum of the past.

Cloudy?

He's one; there are many.

Every night in bed, my last breath teases my conclusion. It's closer now.

Choking breaths caught a lick of air in skipping seconds while her ash-kissed eyelids fluttered.

Closer. Thoughts strangle both existences for different reasons.

"Mummy, I'm hot!"

Somehow, She knew what *searing flesh smelled like. How it tasted.*

"MUMMY, I'M HOT!"

"3:27 a.m., the child died." Reddened eyes shot open. Amy jolted up, her fingers tracing her lips and *the statement I just made.*

Death of children haunting my nightmares. Spit and clawed the walls inside her mouth. *What was that?* She wiped her clammy brow, whipped her head too fast for her migraine, massaged the throbbing on her left temple, and shielded her eyes from the heat of the light. *It felt... so real.* She stared at her clawed right hand. *Imagining **a pulpy throat** nestled inside.* Shook the thought from her head.

Around her cell, multitudes of transparent bubbles made from light floated in tight rows. Some floated off on rogue paths; most took up much of the airspace above her head.

"Smaller next time, got it. Might've been the longest I've slept before the nightmares crept in." She counted each bubble and pondered the math. Her eyes widened. "Only four hours passed?" Sighed with a shrug. "Solid sleep on a bad day." Spaced out at the world outside her bars.

All night, up and down corridors. Amy opened her cell and walked down the deserted floor. *That's the last time I stay up late searching for clues in this mausoleum of misery. Didn't find a thing. Useless. Nothing along these stupid cracks.* She broke into a jog, her eyes peeping into each passing cell. "Where the hell is everyone?"

Unable to find a soul for ten minutes, She blew her tired locs out of her face.

And found it. Camouflaged against the wall, a ladder led to heights unknown, too bright above to see where it led.

Another puzzle. She wiped her baggy eyes. *Starving.* Climbed the ladder.

Halfway up, voices echoed from above.

Her head popped into an empty corridor half the width of the level below.

The voices faded in and out as she explored the new hall of boring dirt walls. A few strides later, the volume of the idle chatter lowered, gone within the minute.

"Weird." She turned around and walked in the opposite direction.

The voices came back into earshot. Grew louder. She passed the hole in the ground she came in from and went on for a few more steps until stopping as the voices lowered once again.

She turned around and went the other way. The voices grew.

Then lowered.

Shan fucking hiska. After minutes of altering her direction back and forth, she settled on a spot where the voices echoed their strongest. Her face scrunched up as she stepped closer to the wall before her. Surprised by its warmth, she tapped it and pushed with both hands.

Melted. She became one with the wall as her body mushed through dirt and rock. *Got to be fucking—*

She stepped out onto the beige vinyl flooring of the other side, stumbling into a common room that misrepresented the rest of the prison's aesthetic. The room had four sky-blue walls, one with a faux window painted on the upper half. Quotes and other positive affirmations littered the floors and walls. A quarter of the space was rows of shelves stacked with books, tomes, ancient board games, *Lazer-Fish,* and an Animalia Gems virtual console with two flatscreens from an era unknown to her. In the back middle of the room, three tables overflowed with sugary delicacies, plump fruits, and the greenest veggies.

On the wall to Amy's left, a message in dark ink: 'Mankind does not know how to create without chaos. Don't be chaos.' "What's with all the self-help rubbish?"

"We had a team-building exercise!" Vedessia said, beaming over a teeny book that fit right into her palms. "Ooop—" The arm of the Gyaad girl dragged her into a row.

"Cool." Amy cruised through the room of students immersed in their worlds at various tables. *So studious, this bunch. That's what a good night's rest can do for you.* She stopped at Demora's table. "Hey, what's going on?"

"Hey, sleepyhead." Demora flashed her a smile and then reset her eyes on the chess game she was deep into against Mr. SmartyPants. "How're you feeling? You were basically dead!"

I broke her promise. I can't tell her what I did. Nor what I saw. All those... horror flicks, playing at the same time. Sitting through various films at different showtimes. Everywhere at once. I'll never go back. Nightmares hide in the light. "I feel dead." Amy's chortle into snorting snapped some heads in her direction. The anxiety of social gatherings fathered her next words. "Glad to see some rest has got us all in chill spirits. Look at you all glow. Wow. Your skins are immaculate!"

"<u>Chill</u>?" Mr. SmartyPants moved his last rook. "No wonder you're trailing."

She ignored the odd stares and questioning look of Demora. "Higher than you."

"Check again." He turned to Demora. "And a check for you, too."

Demora studied the chessboard. "Wait a minute."

"What?" Amy frowned.

Across the room, a whiteboard hung on the pastel walls with a leaderboard full of flower art. Scribbled in marker *with ranks still dripping dirt*:

Amy's hand found her hip. "How'd you all gain extra points?"

"We rose when the challenge called," Mr. SmartyPants said. "Checkmate."

"Are you fucking joking?" Demora pushed herself away from the chessboard. "Impossible. You always win."

"Luck, I guess."

"Spare your rubbish for lesser souls."

"How did everyone except me get points?" Amy pointed at the board. "Demo, what the hell?"

One point deducted from Number 7.

"Whole town knows her name by now!" Amy shouted to the ceiling. Closed her eyes *in embarrassment. I'm an idiot.*

Demora stared at the table in front of her. Tight smile. Shook her head.

"Sorry." Amy reached for her but let her hands fall to her sides. "What's going on?"

Demora massaged her forehead. "You slept through a secret prize round." Her eyes stood on the chessboard in front of her. "It was an ass of a challenge that honestly needed the team effort. From <u>each of us</u>. We all got points in the end." She shrugged. "Well…"

"Everyone except me. Great." *I don't care.*

Demora stopped her chin rub and stood to face Amy. "I tried to wake you, but you wouldn't stir. You were knocked! What am I supposed to do?"

"And everyone else went about their business, huh? Some team effort."

"I tried to wake you, too." Vedessia's voice came from behind a book twice her head size at another table. "At your cell, I tried so hard… I ended up bursting your bubbles. I'm so sorry." Her doe eyes dipped behind her literature.

Amy rolled her shoulders. Her fingers' mindless drum across

her thigh was the only source of sound in the room besides flipping pages.

"Manage your rest next time, girl," E'oné said from another table. "We could have used your help back there. That challenge required information from all of us. Can you take your temper elsewhere? Some of us are trying to study." She turned her back to continue her private conversation with her brother.

The Gyaad girl glared at Amy. Opened her mouth. **"Screeeeeeeeeeeee."** Went back to scribbling in a notebook *using her finger?*

Amy opened her mouth. *Maybe not the best time.* Her open mouth turned to Demora.

"Sorry," her *best friend* mouthed. "I—"

Amy dropped her soldiers with a sigh. Marched towards the restroom door. *Here I was, trying to crack the puzzle that would free us all. They're more worried about their points and their games. What. Ever.*

She entered and stopped in front of the wide mirror over the sinks. Sighed into her reflection. "I guess it's you and me out here, old girl."

Her reflection stared back at her.

It smirked.

Steam caked across the entire glass in no time. A single stroke etched into it as Amy pulled back. Stroke by stroke, letters formed: **ARROGANCE**

Demora rushed in beside her. "Listen, I'm sorry..." She stifled a laugh. "Spiegel van gebreken. Mirror of Flaws. Tells you your current... never mind, I saved you breakfast."

Amy's eyes rolled off the mirror and fell over the plate handed to her. It was filled to the brim with an assortment of treats under a steamy glass covering.

"Another prize round bonus. A nice little banquet from an apparently World-renowned chef. Never heard of the bloke, but the dishes are banger. I tried to get back down to you, but the entrance to that floor was already gone. I <u>really</u> tried to wake you..."

"I'm— I—" Amy shook her head. "I paced these halls for <u>hours</u> looking for clues in the dark."

"Maybe that's the point." Demora shrugged. "Just need to play the games. That's the key."

"Then, what, boom? Here's your reward. Now you can leave?"

"She said we could leave at any time. Do you want to leave now?"

"It's not—" Amy eyed the ceiling. "It's what she's <u>doing</u>. How she's doing it." *I know that look, Demo. Don't give me your pity, woman.*

Demora placed a hand on her. "We're here, you and me. Don't forget we're in this together. I'm beginning to understand the team element to Graves' madness now. The others... they truly felt let down today. You're incredible, and I know you have the greatest intentions." She danced her head from side to side, *eyes picking words out of thin air.*

"But?" Amy crossed her arms, her tray of food balanced in one hand.

"You gotta wake up." She held onto Amy's shoulders. "We're not the only ones having trouble sleeping at night here. We can't lose ourselves entirely in this complex."

"Only a little?"

"I want to see both of us come out on top. Last thing you need is the other prisoners riling up against you." Demo winked. "Cuz then I have to smash some heads." Smiled.

Amy fell against the sink, eyes back on the ceiling. She brought them down to meet Demora's. Pushed air out of her pursed lips. "I hear you." She closed her eyes and unfolded her arms. "I hear you. I feel..."

"Feeling's mutual. No sleep for The Unity, huh?"

Amy smiled. "None whatsoever."

"Now eat up. Hm? The next high-stakes game starts in fifteen."

"What?"

Amy scoffed down the last of her cherry scone alone at a

table in the Common Room. Went for another blueberry.

A raccooroach puffed on top of it.

"Shit!" Amy dropped the plate, shattering glass across the floor.

No insects in sight. *Mind playing tricks again.*

The other students watched her with puzzled expressions.

"Sorry." She joined the others in a semi-circle around the glowing leaderboard.

Current Rankings & Points + (Points not added)

1 = 12 (?/15)

2 = 15

3 = 9

4 = 8

5 = 7

6 = 13

7 = 4

8 = 7 (?/15)

9 = 2

10 = 2

Amy shook her head at the message on the wall beside her:

Life's better when you're always live!

"Like that?" Jamari lowered his blockbuster shades a bit to peep at her. "That one was me. A-haa!"

Amy's nose flared up on one side.

Good day, students. Welcome to Level 2 of this Prison Games event. Your next high-stakes challenge will be a modified version of an ever-popular game. Today, you'll be playing Kombat Kabaddi.

"Score! I love Kabaddi!" Vedessia jumped up, fist-punching the air. Froze when she landed. "Combat?"

We'll have four teams for this challenge. Three teams will have three members, while the fourth team only has one student.

"Major ass, mate," Jamari said.

"Where's the advantage in that?" Mr. Stoicism said.

The top five on the leaderboard are team captains, who will take turns selecting a new member to join their team. Previous allegiances will be defaulted if unselected. Number 1, please specify who you would like to join your team.

Demora stepped away from the crowd and peered at the aged ceiling fan. "I choose to work alone."

Really? Not even going to look at me?

Very well. Team A will consist solely of Number 1.

"Are you sure about that?" Amy asked.

"Focus on getting through the rounds, and I'll see you in the finals, right?" Demora winked at her.

"Yeah. See you." Amy's peripheral found Vedessia. *Was that a growl?*

Number 2, please make your selection.

Vedessia locked eyes with Amy. "Um... I choose..." Silent

stare between the two.

What's with her? Pick me already if—

Across from her, the Gyaad stared with folded arms and a tapping foot.

"I choose Number 3," Vedessia said, *keeping her eyesight far from my side of the room.*

Done. Number 3, please make your selection. Note that this will be your team's final selection.

The Gyaad tapped her chin. Opened her mouth.

"Please!" Mr. Stoicism dropped on his knees to her side. "Please, please, I play LuxBall! My stats are stellar! Don't leave me, partner. I promise I'll do better!" He grabbed her hands. "I know I wasn't the best before, but I'll listen. I didn't mean for us to lose. I'll be a better partner, so <u>please</u> give me one more shot! Please! We can do this!"

The Gyaad girl rolled her eyes and opened her mouth. **"Ahhhhhhaaahh ahhhhwwwwwwwwnnn nnnaaaaaannnnnnnn."**

Team B is formed. Number 4, please make your selection.

Kassandra sat at a desk, spinning her token. "Can we drop a member? My last partner was annoying."

Amy's mouth dropped on *the rude little twat.*

No.

Kassandra's eyes searched the room. "Anyone want to trade partners?"

Wow.

No trades allowed.

"Sigh, fine. Dread's everlasting. Number 6."

Very good. Number 5, please make your selection.

Ms. JellyRoll studied the remaining eligibles: Amy, Jamari, and Mr. SmartyPants.

Please get me out of here. Need a new start...

Her eyes stayed with Amy for a while until she turned to Jamari. "I choose number 10." She looked back at Amy. "No offense to anyone. I had to make the best calculation."

And I'm stuck with the Lockheart Girls reboot...

Number 8 will be auto-sent to complete Team D. That settles every team. Team A - Number 1. Team B - Numbers 2, 3, and 9. Team C - Numbers 4, 7, and 6. Team D - Numbers 5, 10, and 8

Amy caught the eyes of her teammates— *both their faces absolutely thrilled to have me on their team.*

Teams, you'll face three rotating opponents today. Your paths to victory will depend on your ability to score as a team. You'll also be given secret grades on identifying your opponent, maintaining strict awareness of your surroundings, and relying on your teammates to help you get the job done. Individual points scored will affect your unique rankings and may affect you in future games. You'll have fifteen seconds to score. You'll be alerted when you have five seconds to reset your position before your opponent takes their turn.

"Still confident, Number 1?" E'oné smirked at Demora. "That'll be wiped out soon."

Amy and Demora grilled her.

Your opponents will rotate every minute, bringing a

new quarter, with a ten-second cool down between opponents. Take this time to revise your strategy, as special rules will be enforced during gameplay. After the fourth quarter, all points earned will be calculated.

"Fast-paced." Mr. Stoicism smiled from ear to ear. He nudged the Gyaad girl. "Right up my alley."

She held her head, and her mouth opened a tiny bit. **"Ooosssssssiiii."**

The more team points earned, the higher the team's rank. The top-ranked team receives five points each, second place receives three, and third place gets one point each. The lowest-ranked team loses one point each. The team with the lowest points will be sent to their prison cells for four hours. The student with the lowest overall grade will also be sent to their cell and will lose two additional points.

"How do we know who's graded the worst?" Ms. JellyRoll asked.

Identify your marks. Maintain awareness. Help your team succeed.

"That's no answer." Amy crossed her arms, glaring at the ceiling.

"It's a must-win," Jamari said.

Students, please spread out and stand with your teammates.

Jamari pulled down his blockbuster shades, eyes on Amy, then Demora. "Good luck."

Demora crept up to Amy's ear. "Be careful. You're close in score. He's trying to expand the gap."

"Heard you."

Kassandra, unmoved from her spot at the back of the room, nodded as E'oné joined her side. She glared at Amy.

Amy sighed and made her way over to them.

Good luck, students.

What do I remember about Kabaddi?

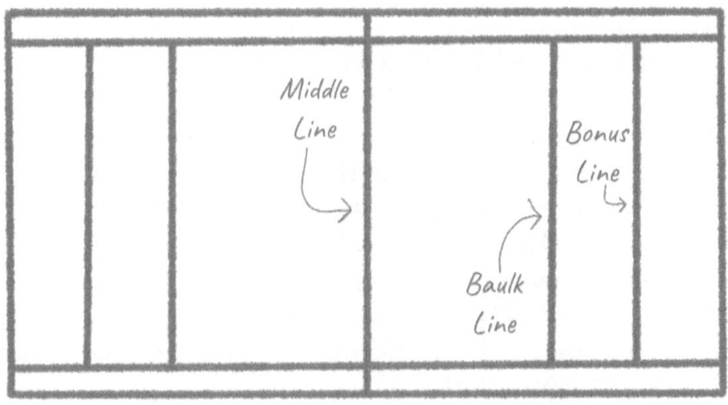

A blur of red light scorched the room.

Amy unshielded her eyes. Scoped the bland room of grey, she now stood in. Ahead, two perpendicular titanium walls almost as high as the ceiling met in the middle.

Those walls look like the giant fan from the other night.

"What now?" Kassandra grumbled at her side.

Amy and her teammates stood on a manicured lawn rivaling the beauty of the open sea.

"This blue grass..." E'oné, on her knees, rubbed her hands over the small blades and took whiffs. "Repressories. They're sharp but don't break the skin. When the blades get through the flesh, it disrupts your occipital lobes." She stood. "Instead of showing you what's true to your vision, you only see what you want to see."

"We'll stay sharper, won't we?" Kassandra glared into Amy.

"Always." Amy's eyes rolled off of her.

"Come on, girls, let's keep it together." E'oné stood between them. "We all want the same thing, right? Avoid those prison cells. Get more points. Escape the prison."

Amy and Kassandra nodded.

"Good." E'oné smiled with her clenched fist up. "Let's get it, Team C."

Kassandra folded her arms. "It's got."

Ooooooh...

WURRRRRRRRRRRRRRRRRRRRRV

Team C turned around to face—Demora.

Number 1 smiled with open arms at her fellow students. "The fact that it's going to take three of you to outdo me says everything it has to already." Demo beckoned them forth.

E'oné stepped in front of the team. "She's mine."

"No problem with me." Kassandra threw a look.

Amy caught it. Her focus shifted from her to E'oné, then landed on Demora, who still smiled, though now with closed eyes. *This'll get ugly—quick.*

"Please!" Demora fanned herself. "You girls would need another half of Amy to match me."

Come again?

One point deducted from Number 1.

Demora chuckled. "And it still wouldn't matter."

"You ain't about business," E'oné said. "You're so blind off your own shit that you can't see when it's about to hit you."

"Don't let her rile you." Kassandra held her back with one arm. "Remember to win."

"Right."

"Listen to Mommy," Demora said in a mocking American accent.

"Hey, sleepyhead." Kassandra nodded to Amy. "You take

middle since you know her best."

"Fine." Amy stomped over to the center position within her team's portion of the field. Her teammates took positions on either side behind her, inches from behind the baulk line.

Please be reminded that two points of contact are needed for a point to count. Outs also give the defending team points. The game will commence at the bell. Chosen at random, the first side's field to glow starts the match.

Underneath Demora, her half of the field glowed a luminous ocean blue.

Team A is on offense.

DING DING DING!

Chapter Fifteen

Level 2: Demo vs. Amy & Everyone There

Demora hopped forward and charged right for Amy.

Oh shit. Amy sped to meet her. *Let's check that speed of yours.* A fingertip's reach away from her friend's shoulder—*Wha*—

She found herself face-first in the cool-to-the-touch grass. *What just happened?*

"Come on, 7." Demora gazed down at her. "You know you're supposed to check your blind spot." Her laughter continued as she ran down the field.

"My blind spot?"

Demora avoided E'oné's tackle in a blur, and *just* missed Kassandra's closing grasp.

Amy shuttered at the sight. "Huh? Fuck." *How is she so fast?*

Demora skipped behind Team C's baulk line and bonus line. Sped back.

Amy bounced on her feet from side to side, anticipating every move. *Bit chilly in here.*

Demora's brows angled into menace, but her smile grew wide.

"Touch her!"

"Touch her!"

"What? I'm ready-ing!" Amy launched at her fast-approaching best friend.

"Not yet, you aren't," Demora said as she faded into Amy's hands.

Two hands tapped Amy's back.

Amy turned around—in time to see Demora cross her base, waving.

DING

Two points for Team A.

"C'mon girl!" E'oné approached with Kassandra sulking behind her.

Amy picked herself off the ground. "I-I don't know what happened."

"She glided right past you." Kassandra rolled her eyes. "How'd you miss her?"

"Wait." Amy stared into space. *—Demo prances up to Amy with a curtsy, followed by a hand reaching the sky as she twirls into her best friend's open arms— "Not yet, you aren't." —Winks as her body vanishes—* "An afterimage." *How did she conjure up the energy to do that? Only a skilled auraist could pull that off without using their aura's full power. Another confirmation we're in some realm within—*

Kassandra's **scoff** broke her daydream.

E'oné threw up a hand. "Please, her sorry excuse for an afterimage was barely pure. Such an amateur move. Ugh." She walked to left field.

Five seconds to start. Team C on offense.

"Zip to us." Kassandra took the center and pointed Amy off. "I'll watch here. You manage the left. Think you got <u>that</u>?"

"Yeah, on it." Amy moved with sluggish feet. "She won't try that twice."

"She did it to you <u>twice</u>." Kassandra pulled her eyes forward, laying into Demora. "Not with me. Our turn to score."

DING

Kassandra charged forward.

Demora strolled forward.

Amy ran up, matching pace with E'oné. She stopped and stooped to a tackle position at the center line. She paced side to side, hands up to guard.

"Gather that nerve, 7!" Demora's ballerina feet shuffled and ran— *at an even more incredible speed!*

Kassandra met Demo with a kick that the blond girl dodged and rolled under. The blond blur dashed to the right, speeding up, eyes locked on Amy.

Amy hunkered down, arms almost on her thighs.

Blinked.

DING

Illegal shove. Extra time allowed for a reset. Keep it clean, Number 7. Team A has two points.

Amy sat up on her ass, rubbing her back, the other hand supporting her up. *Of all times...*

E'oné and Kassandra groaned at her side, also on their asses.

"Thanks, 7!" E'oné said. "Why'd you do that?"

"Push into me again," Kassandra said, face sending daggers.

Amy just stared at them. "What?"

"7!" Outside field lines, Demora dusted herself off. Her fiery eyes dug into Amy. "Watch those hands, friend, or I may not play so nice anymore." A smirk grew. "Fiesty, though." She strolled to her zone.

"What?" Amy threw her hand up. *What happened?*

"Hello?!" E'oné shouted to Amy. "She's only scored on you!"

"We just started!" Amy stared around for help. "We got time!"

Five seconds to start. Team A on offense.

Kassandra stood with her arms crossed, center field, not even looking back at her team. "Let's reset. Switch it up. And keep it <u>clean</u>."

E'oné nodded and pointed Amy over to her side, as they traded places.

Shove? How did she get so fucking fast? Shove? This feels impossible. Fucking amnesia episodes. Ok, breathe, Devine. Lemme stop her <u>once</u>.

Can you?

Who—

DING

"Well, well, well." Demora skipped towards them, moving from left to right, eyes tracking each of her opponents, ending on Amy. "She's starting to come around. Still..."

Amy hopped to her left, digging her feet into the soft grass. *Wait, the grass. Shows me what I want to see. I tried to sense her aura, but I blinked out. Why now? What if I—*

Demora pushed an arm into Amy's chest, smiling as she swung the other hand at Amy's shocked face.

Kassandra grabbed Demora's hand before it clobbered Amy. "Will you focus?!" She roared at Amy.

Demora spun out of her grasp—and got pushed feet away by E'oné.

DING

One point for Team C. Score is 2-1, advantage Team A.

"Sorry girl." E'oné shrugged. "You made nice bait though."

"Happy to be of assistance." Amy stuck her hands in her pockets.

Demora chuckled as she returned to her side. "This won't go on for longer."

Five seconds to start. Team C on offense.

"It won't." Amy readied her fists.

DING DING

Quarter 1 is over.

WURRRRRRRRRRRRRRRRRRRV The titanium walls rotated, taking Demora with it.

"Demo!" Amy launched forward.

One point deducted from Number 7.

"She's bloody fine!" Kassandra's yelled from behind.

Amy groaned into the ceiling. *That's that— Dammit, Graves. She got that one.*

"Wait! 4, hold on—" E'oné's voice pleaded.

Amy turned right into Kassandra's face of murderous intent.

"You always get shaken on the first stir!" Kassandra poked a finger in her chest. "Get over your friend and worry about your own progress!" She threw her arms to the heavens. "The extremes of humanity bore me! Getting sick of this fucking prison..." She stormed off.

*— **You seem to upset most you encounter.**' —*

Amy shrunk and moved away from the others.

The titanium walls ceased their rotation with no new opponent in sight.

E'oné frowned. "That's odd."

"Stay sharp." Kassandra backed towards her teammates.

Their side of the field glowed.

Once again, Team C is on offense.

DING

The three young women rushed forward, bouncing on light feet with eyes darting around.

"Oh!" E'oné went down, head first into the thickening white mist building over the field.

Amy backed up and bumped into Kassandra.

Kassandra's head circled around them. "Stay back to back."

Amy's back met hers. "What type of mist is this? Did something—"

"It grabbed her."

"It?"

The walls of heavy mist enclosed them, leaving nothing else visible.

"That metallic smell…" Amy's eyes went wide. "Vampire."

Kassandra sniffed the air. "Scent is stronger this way." She beckoned in one direction. They ran towards it, arms cutting the air ahead of them as their eyes searched for their opponent. "Can't be Vamp. They can't mist indoors."

"The Counts can." Amy spotted a glint. "Dash over to right field!"

Kassandra cut over, keeping pace with Amy as they booked it for the titanium wall. Only a fraction of the yellow baulk line for Team A was visible.

"Hover the line." The hairs of Amy's skin rose as she studied every inch of her surroundings. "It's a newly crowned Count. There are leaks in the mist. It's also probably too thick for proper hearing. The mist is heaviest over the baulk." Her eyes narrowed. "He's there."

"Go high, I go low." Kassandra wiped a bead of sweat. "Not much time left."

A patch of grass pushed up against an unknown force *as though stepped on.*

"There." Amy sprinted—

"Stay, girl"

—jumped— *Girl?* into a stretching high-kick— *Got you, you bas—*

Kassandra spun her backhand fist down low— but got yanked into the thick.

Amy's high kick connected to meat. She stretched down to

grab onto a sleek maroon pant leg hidden in the mist.

The figure's gloved hands—*beautiful ring*—grabbed Amy's leg.

His thighs squeezed Kassandra's arm.

DING

Three points to the Visitor for Team A. Score is 5-1. Advantage to the Visitor.

"What?" E'oné reemerged from the clearing mist. "Their points all add up?"

"We need to score again, pronto!" Kassandra took the middle and bent at the knees, stalking her opponent's field. "What else do you know about Counts, 7?"

Good question.

Five seconds to start. Team A on offense.

"They take batform in an instant, so prep for that if you're about to grab." *I think?*

"Got it. 6, shift closer to 7. Both of you, line up with me!"

DING

The mist grew instantaneously, as thick as when it left.

"Right side." Amy's eyes locked on a patch of blue grass disappearing. "There!"

Kassandra dodged a gloved hand.

The hand withdrew into the *green?* mist.

"It's changing." E'oné gasped—dodged a blur above her head.

"Why the color change?" Kassandra asked.

"I'm tryna think." Amy nodded to her teammates. "Back to back."

Team C backed into each other, their backs in a triangle. Several patches of the brilliant blue grass around them depressed at an increasing rate, eaten by the mist right after.

"So fast," E'oné said, her mad eyes darting from side to side.

"Watch it!" Amy pushed E'oné to the ground and held her breath as her chest pushed inwards, avoiding the gloved hand's swipe. Stuck out her foot and reached into the mist.

"Unhand me!" The Count's gruff voice yelled, the last of his syllables trailing.

DING

One point for Team C. Score is 5-2; advantage to the Visitor.

The mist cleared at once. The Count, in full view. His gaunt face wore the utmost displeasure of a disproving professor. His arms crossed, with his beady black eyes fixed on his downed opponent.

Amy dusted herself off as she rose to meet his glare.

The Count strode off to his zone.

"What happened?" E'oné wobbled with a shaky head.

"Cyclone mist," Amy said. "Another few seconds, you would have hurled your glorious banquet from earlier."

Five seconds to start. Team C on offense.

"It's a shame." The vampire shook his head. He dusted off his immaculate maroon suit and raised a stern finger. "Only one out of nine can recognize the exquisitely rare abilities of the most dominant species in existence. It's imperative you students catch up on your studies regarding my race's superiority."

"Rude." E'oné's hand brushed him off.

"Vamps are drama faucets." Kassandra bore a hole in the man. "They run on bullshit."

"Deadliest when they're underestimated," Amy said. "And cornered."

DING

"Have you had enough of the mist games, vamp?" Kassandra said.

"That's Count, to you." He disappeared into his gathering white mist.

"There he goes." E'oné backed into Team C's triangle defense.

"Here, dear." The Count's hand fell onto her shoulder. His other appeared from the mist landing on her opposite one. "Terrible."

E'oné's body faded from his grasp. "Think again."

The other girls faded right after her.

"Who wears a ring over their glove?" Amy's leg KICKED his chest and disappeared into the mist before he could grab it.

"A prick," Kassandra's voice echoed.

The Count retreated into his mist before her tackle reached him.

His gloved hands reappeared, and one of them pushed Kassandra into the mist while the other missed as he dodged out of E'oné's closing grasp.

Amy dashed past her. Her eyes followed ruffles in the grass. *Can't run from me, Count. It's not perfect vision but it'll do.* She stopped. Searched her surroundings.

"Where'd they go?" E'oné's voice called out.

Another patch ruffled.

There. Amy dashed over. Swung her arm— caught by The Count stepping out of the mist— she dodged his other arm.

CRACK SNAP POW CLAP WHAP WHAP WHAP SLAP HUUOSH!

The mist separated.

Amy and the Count— their limbs bashed blow for blow, crafting sounds of thunderous determination.

He's no active spar with his ol' rope-a-dope patterns. She threw lightning strikes at his head. *C'mon!* Dipped down and spun into a leg sweep.

The Count's *scrawny* legs jumped over, his beady eyes tracking her every move. "You're good." He chuckled. "It's not your fault I'm superior." ***In every way.***

Maybe, maybe not. But— Amy smiled. "I don't need to beat

you in a fistfight."

The Count frowned. "Hmm?"

E'oné appeared behind him.

Amy's knee met his gut. Placed two hands on him. Ran off.

Kassandra appeared beside him, stepping onto his retreating foot.

E'oné grabbed his other leg.

The Count spun on his heel.

The three crashed to the floor.

Amy passed the baulk line.

DING

One point for Team C. Score is 5-3.

The Count disappeared into his darker green mist. "You have yet to witness true power..."

DING DING

Quarter 2 is over.

The titanium walls spun out of sorts once again.

Amy huddled up with her teammates. "Wonder who's next?"

"Let's stay on their necks," Kassandra said, waving the green air around her.

How is she not friends with Demo? Amy scratched her head. Scratched again.

"My bad, girls." E'oné clenched her fists. "His speed took me off center."

"Vamps are speed junkies once they know you can't catch up." Amy itched her chest. "Trick is to distract them once they're speed-driven." Scratched her back. "Anyone feeling itchy?" Her eyes went wide. "Oh, no."

"What?" E'oné ITCHED between her braids.

Amy shook her hair out. "His cyclone mist can bring— Cuz

he's—"

"Dammit! He got us!" Kassandra shook out her ruined beehive hairdo, pulling long strands in multiple directions. "Fucking hemosects!"

E'oné shrieked on her knees, hands shaking.

"Fuckin—" Amy stamped her feet, slapped her chest, shimmied her limbs, shook anything She could think of to free herself from the tiny invaders exploring her body.

"So much for bats, 7!" Kassandra threw herself onto the field, her back grinding against the grass. "You got the wrong species of vamp!"

"I noticed!" Amy rolled in the grass.

E'oné followed her lead, caught on invisible fire. "Watch the blades!"

"It's only micro tears." Amy slapped her thighs, then both sides of her face. Stared between two fingers. "Think I'm bleeding."

"Only— ugh!" E'oné tore her yellow jacket off. "Hallucinations— bugs— prison games—" She slapped her jacket on the ground over and over. "I can't see them cuz of— this fucking grass! **URGH!**"

— "Repressories— you only see what you want to see." —

"Shit!" Amy threw her sneakers. "I wanna see these fucking— *Language*— adorable little crits!"

The titanium walls ceased again.

Middle line is eliminated. Players may travel sides at will.

Kassandra's eyes found their next opponent first. "What the hell is that?"

"What?" Amy followed her gaze. Jerked back. "Oh."

The field underneath Team A grew bright.

"I hate this prison!" E'oné shook her body out. "Ugh, I'm so done with this." Moved between them, still dusting off. "Who's..." She looked up. Her eyes bulged. "No... anything but...

not that."

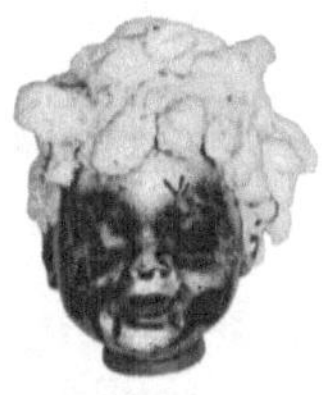

Chapter Sixteen

Level 2: Our Nightmare Fuel

With blackened bone-like fins concealing its head, the creature's baby blue eye darted between its three adversaries. The rest of its body squirmed until it became rigid. A peat-colored fluid with strands of kelp was draped all over as the stench of death invaded the arena. Its maddened eye rested on Amy.

Team A on offense.

"Let's not be rude." Amy stepped ahead of the team, dropping her forearm from her nose. "Though I'm lost on its origins."

"NO." E'oné jumped back, her face telling the story. "They're extinct. It shouldn't be... can't be real."

"Looks real to me," Kassandra said.

DING

E'oné shifted backwards, never taking the creature out of her sight. "No, no, this is not it!" Eyes closed, her palms squeezed the sides of her head. "No, they're not real." She turned and booked it.

"6, get your shit together!" Kassandra said with a finger

point of aggression.

PatterPatterPatterPatterPatterPatterPatterPatter

"Okay." Gaze fixed on the sluggish beast, Kassandra edged backwards and soon followed E'oné's retreat. "We run for now."

The creature's wet fins slapped against the grass as it **SNARLED** its mouth open, bluish globs of drool dangling. Two sockets poked out its head: the first with a yellowish leaking eye and the other socket, three times smaller, with an ever-oscillating baby blue eye.

The beast gained speed. **PatterPatterPatterPatterPatterPatterPatterPatterPatterP atterPatterPatterPatterPatterPatterPatter.**

Amy paused her retreat mid-field. "Is it smiling?" *Moves quite slow.*

E'oné's body shook with cold weight at the end of Team's C zone. "It's a fucking bonemaiden, fuck me!"

Kassandra reached her. "A what—"

"Bonemaiden?" Amy jumped at the *very* last second. Tickling towards her hovering body, a pair of skeletal arms coated in mossy brown syrup crept inches from her spine.

The bonemaiden's spreading torso winked in intervals at her, revealing a fading white light. Inside, teeth angled in various directions, with smaller, razor-sharp teeth atop them, lined the edges.

"The fuck?" Amy, suspended over the gaping, *grabby* torso.

The creature's face bubbled then melted into itself, a mossy mess dripping from its peephole. Its skeletal arms retracted from her falling body, raised *as though embarrassed,* and slurped back into its torso. The bonemaiden beat the ground towards her teammates.

"The fuck?" Amy flicked her hands to her sides. *Hell, was that?* She dashed after it.

PatterPatterPatterPatterPatterPatterPatterPatterPat terPatterPatterPatterPatterPatterPatterPatter

The bonemaiden's expanding body and fins of fury closed in on the other girls, E'oné's screeching body nearest.

"Shit takes up half the field." Kassandra grabbed E'oné's stiff arm. "We have to make a move now!" She raced away, leaving the shivering girl behind.

PatterPatterPatterPatterPatterPatterPatterPatter

Amy's momentum staggered as she dropped face-first into the ground. "Wha—" On her legs, slimy remnants her opponent left behind crawled up to her knees. She crawled forth on her stomach but ceased with shaking eyes. "Oh, no."

PatterPatterPatterPatterPatterPatterPatterPatter

"Please..." E'oné crouched against the wall. "I can't... I don't want to be ripped—"

Amy freed one of her legs from the goop. Struggled with the other. "C'mon!"

The bonemaiden's arms aimed over her ever-shrinking form.

POP! Kassandra's shoulder tackle dug deep into the creature's half-open torso—the two of them soared through the air—

A slight sparkle grew in Amy's transfixed eyes. *Whoa.*

A glint of purple rage grew in Kassandra's irises, blending with hints of amber.

She's incredible.

—the young woman and beast **SMASHED** into the almost immovable titanium, rotating the wall clockwise by a hair.

Amy dashed over to the crumpled *unmoving* bodies.

Sighed as her teammate unfolded.

"Urgh. Dammit." With her slimy hands, Kassandra pushed herself off the fallen bonemaiden and got up. She scrubbed her closed eyes and opened them again.

Her irises SHINED a MOONLIGHT AMBER YELLOW.

"4..." E'oné's unsteady feet hobbled their way towards her. "Your eyes!"

"Fucking seawater." Kassandra bared her teeth. She shook out her dripping hands.

The unconscious bonemaiden's blue tongue flapped outside its foaming mouth. Its eyes dripped black goo, and its body was spread like a taco.

Kassandra continued to scrub her eyes.

DING

One point for Team C. Score is 5-4, advantage, Team A.

"You all right?" Amy approached her with a cautious hand. "Fine."

Amy nodded. *I won't push it. She hasn't grilled me for once. That quiver in her lips... She looked... scared.*

E'oné's mouth hung open. "Are your eyes..."

"Nothing." Kassandra waved her off, crouched and checked out the downed bonemaiden. "The seawater from this beast burnt my natural color back in. This creature must be from beyond Mar de Realeza."

"Someone let <u>this</u> thing get out?" E'oné's body trembled and stirred away from the knocked creature. "So they're not after all." She gulped. "Did you kill it?"

"Barely tapped it." Kassandra poked at the bonemaiden's mouth. "Bet this guy's prey where he's from. Strange, because that toxin foaming from it is natural to the Port Royal division. She stood. "Since when did they get involved in U.K. biz again?" She twisted to Amy. "Why'd it dodge you?"

"I'd love to know as well." E'oné stepped closer to Amy. "Wasn't so murderous chasing after you."

Damn your glamorous brows. "Maybe I need a shower. How the hell am I supposed to know?" *Seriously, the shower.* "We got like ten seconds. Are we going to do this now?"

"Guess that thing is rounded out." Kassandra moved past them all. "The extra break is nice. Last quarter. We've faced three opponents already, so you know who's coming back." Faced Amy. "Are <u>you</u> ready?"

The team needs me. I need <u>me</u> to step it up. "I'll take center." Amy stepped up to Kassandra. "I got you."

Hands up, Kassandra's half-baked curtsy bowed away. "I got

left. 6, stick hard to 7's right!"

"Copy! We sure that thing's—" E'oné looked back. "Oh."

No bonemaiden in sight.

DING DING

Quarter 3 is over.

The titanium walls spun again.

"4!" Amy bent down and grazed her right hand against the blue grass. "She won't come for me right away. She'll take you head-on."

"How do you know that?"

"I do. Trust me."

"Alright…" Kassandra nodded to E'oné and lowered into a sitting position on the tips of her toes.

Bring your best Demo. She'll push herself to the limit this last round of free sparring she's rewarded with. It's not a game to her. If it's a test she wants…

The walls stopped.

Bonus points can now be scored on either turn.

Demora. The Count. Side by side.

She doesn't think I'm ready. Amy ran both hands through the grass. *Why do I want to see you like this?*

Demora beamed with a permanent grin, hands behind her back, twisting on her forefeet.

I swear bubbles will pop out of her ass soon. Is this *what I see in you?* Amy trained her eyes on her best friend and clenched the grass between both fists. *When this is the truth—* She released the grass, and her vision blurred, then snapped back into focus.

—Demora's smile curls into— Demora's cruel smirk on display. She and her partner stared down their opponents with hungry malice.

Her eyes aren't even on me. At all. Amy's face twitched with narrowed eyes on the *objectives. Game's over. 'Half-Amy'.* **SCOFF**

The field under Team A glowed.

Team A on offense.

Kassandra dashed past Amy. "Two-for-one special. E'oné, stick to the plan!"

"Hm?" Amy turned.

DING

Plan? Oh, SHIT—

With E'oné's forceful push from behind, Amy's feet shredded the grass as they dragged along the surface. *The hell is happening???*

Demora's charge slowed at the sight before she pushed forth to meet Kassandra with a flying elbow.

The Count vanished into a mist of purple, reappeared in front of the skidding Amy, and grabbed her shoulders.

E'oné rolled over onto Amy's back—performed a tucked planche, and dropped her butt into the spine of The Count. Her hands pressed off of him, and she moved past them both.

Amy hit the floor hard—The Count's body fell on her stomach. *Dammit, I'm out.* Threw her hands over her groaning mouth.

E'oné rushed past her.

Amy uncovered her mouth and leaned to the side. *I'm gonna be sick.* She stared at the tiny smashed pieces of bug parts in her palm.

"Enjoy."

I— She scanned for the vampire. *Bloody taunt...*

Across the field, Kassandra and Demora exchanged single blows in a flurry, neither able to land a second hand or foot on the other. As she peeked past Demora, Kassandra's pupils glowed purple in the middle of her yellow eyes. "Great job, 6!"

Streaks of brown light flashed in and out of the air.

Demora's glowing pink eyes checked her rear and returned to meet Kassandra's smirk. Let out **a gasp** and swung around—

E'oné's foot met her spine, and her diamond braids

whipped loose as she grabbed Demo. She dodged to the side to escape the falling blond girl's hands on her sunny jacket. E'oné rushed towards Team C's end of the field.

Kassandra squeezed Demora between her arms, lifted and forced her to eat dirt.

E'oné skipped past the bonus line.

DING

Three points for Team C. Score is 6-5, advantage, Team C.

"Let's get it!" E'oné jumped in place.

"Well done, ladies." Kassandra clapped twice, then crossed her arms.

"What the hell was that?" Amy rushed her.

"Figured they'd send more than one opponent for the last quarter." Kassandra's body remained unturned towards Amy, her eyes forward. "So I worked out something with 6."

"They don't call me Tri-Time Planche Champ for nothing." E'oné massaged her buns back in place. "This prison will ruin me."

You— "Could've told me, <u>team</u>!" Amy glared at them, a hand clutched into her stomach.

"Could I?" Kassandra flipped a thick lock of hair that fell down her forehead again.

Team C on offense. Outs are only in effect if the entire team is outed.

"Are you okay?" E'oné gestured to Amy's bent-over position.

"Peachy. Whatever." *Unbelievable. What does it take to gain some respect around here?*

Five seconds to start.

"Good job on that hint, though, 7," Kassandra said.

Amy rolled her eyes.

"How about a freestyle finish this round, girls?" E'oné asked. "No tricks." She faced Amy and laid a hand on her heart.

"Fine. No more tricks, I get it." Kassandra stalked off into position.

"Fine." *Nooow they wanna be teammates. Please. Spare me the dread of Dalestone.*

DING

Amy shot after Kassandra, who already launched straight ahead. *When did she get so fast?*

Demora stood alone at her team's baulk line, the purple mist surrounding her. Her eyes tracked the field at a hypnotic pace.

Amy caught up behind Kassandra, several feet from Demora.

"Where's your partner?!" Kassandra demanded.

"Tag me." Demora, stone-faced. "Tag me, Owens."

One point deducted from Number 1.

"And I'll still end up on top. Tag me."

Amy hustled to catch up. "4..."

"Stay out of this, 7." Kassandra charged Number 1—dodged Demora's hammer punch—her afterimage took the blow. Kassandra hopped *(afterimage)* out of Demora's vicious missed strikes—belly to air *(afterimage)* —cartwheel on grass *(afterimage)* —backflipped *(afterimage)* —landed on knee *(afterimage)* —and kept moving around Demora, quicker with every second.

E'oné cut through the purple mist. Dodged the random limbs of the vampire that retreated into the clouds before being harmed.

The Count chopped E'oné's neck and lifted her by it. Swung his free hand towards her—

—into Amy's grasp. She threw a knee—The Count avoided—and fell into his clouds. Amy threw frustrated chops, separating the mist. *He's gone. <u>Again</u>.*

E'oné shot past at an incredible speed towards Kassandra and Demora's fight.

Amy scrambled after her—swiped the invading mist growing more dense in her face—and jumped over The Count's tripping leg. She raised her arms like a gavel but lowered them pronto and held her stomach. *Oh no.*

"Silly children," The Count's voice echoed through the mist. "I said <u>maybe</u> three of you could provide somewhat of a match for one of me—"

Amy grabbed his swung fist, inches from her face. "I don't care for odds." She caught his other hand with her left—Maaura style—and spun an elbow into his neck.

His arms bent back, he stumbled and hollered. "Wha—" His feet touched the sky.

Amy wrestled him on the ground. Facing each other, they threw blows.

The Count's fist just missed her head.

Amy's chop just missed his neck. She rolled an elbow—

He dodged. Threw a hammer fist—

Amy flipped—placed a knee in his neck. Grabbed his arm. Dodged the blows he threw with his other one. She clasped a hand over her mouth. *No, please—* She fell over.

The Count squirmed up.

Still holding her mouth, she swept his legs.

"Annoying girl!" He grabbed her hands and threw his head at her.

Amy dodged. Her cheeks swelled up. Her mouth forced itself open— a projectile of vomit splashed his chest. She released one of his arms.

"YOU indi—" He whipped off his cloak and struck it against the ground. He lunged.

"Sorry!" *Welp—* She dodged his tackle—right over left? Or is it the other? —her left arm crossed her right— Maaura Lock snatched his arms and held him. Her legs jumped and hooked around his torso— twisted him to the ground. She looked downfield.

Demora snatched E'oné by the back of her neck— wrapped her feet around Kassandra's neck— grabbed the front of E'oné's neck— and spun them around with her. All three crashed to the ground.

An afterimage disappeared from the bundle of bodies.

DING

Streaks of pink— Demora released a giant breath of air, safe behind her bonus line.

Three points for Team A. Score is 8-6, advantage, Team A. All players must be grounded for points to count. All points, including outs, must be scored by passing the baulk line.

"Playing rugby now." Amy marched back to her teammates, shaking her head loose. "4, we need to linger back this round. It's too close."

"So you care about winning now?"

"What's your problem?" Amy followed Kassandra's lax retreat to midfield. "You've been peeved at me ever since you lost that Soul Game."

Kassandra spun on her. "Maybe I'm sick of playing a handicap match. You can't focus on anything but <u>her</u>."

That's not fair.

Team A on offense.

"You reek." Kassandra moved away.

"Thanks."

"C'mon!" E'oné ran between them. "I can't keep playing referee. This is our last chance! No more baits. No more games."

Amy's foot stomped. "No more intra-team aggression."

"Fine!" Kassandra's index finger stabbed towards the ground. "We end this now!" She moved further away. "So I can get **back** to my cell..."

Five seconds to start.

"I will take Number 1." Amy faced E'oné. "If I don't <u>contain</u>—" rolled her eyes away from the girl's bewildered arms " —her, I'll give you both the extra points I earn from the next Prize Fight."

"Your funeral," Kassandra said on the left. "Better hope you don't earn any cuz I <u>will</u> take them."

"The alleged Great Cloudy Container strikes again." E'oné winked. "Let's see it in action."

Amy faced Team A down the field— locked eyes with Demora.

Demora smiled. Mouthed something as she crouched.

DING

Amy galloped in a blur of white light streaks, pivoting left, right, left—ducked to escape Demora's clutching grasp and turned—Demora already in her face.

Chapter Seventeen

Level 2: Amy v. Demo 2: Is it the SUTBAA?

Amy PUNCHED THROUGH HER—an afterimage that Amy wasted no time running past.

E'oné scrapped with Demora near the middle line.

"I've had enough of these games." Demora caught and bent E'oné's arm behind her back, locked it in place with a chicken wing maneuver, and patted her on the back as she tripped her— The Count's arms enclosed E'oné and brought her under his mist.

Demora scurried—into Amy's punch—her face thrown backwards, shook it off—blocked a follow-up blow and came back at her with a lightning-fast hammer arm.

The best friends' hands locked up in the middle, pushing against each other's resistance.

"Think you can ground me, Ames," Demora whispered in her ear. "Or do I have to get you angry first?"

"You're not getting that bonus line," Amy said. "All I need to do is stop you."

"All I need is within. With the occasional assist." Demora ducked.

Behind them, The Count's arms floated back into his mist— Kassandra's body launched into Amy—Demora shoved their momentum to the ground and dashed.

Amy executed a kip-up—landed on her palm and knee and dashed after the blond streak. *Not yet, you don't.*

Inches from the baulk, Demora winked over her shoulder but frowned—

Amy yoked Demora back by the collar at the tip of the baulk line—Kassandra put another hand on the struggling-to-move-ahead Demora—

The restrained girl elbowed Kassandra away and snatched Amy by the arm. "Trying to stop me? Well, I'll never let you cross that line either."

"You don't have a choice!" Amy ducked her a wild swing.

THWOCK Punch connected to punch. **SWAAAAP** Elbow clashed with elbow. **WHOOPT** Shin hit shin. **WHAAM!** Forehead smashed into forehead.

"Ow!" Amy held her clammy head, then stomach. *Not again.*

"Fuck!" Demora shook out her leg and head. "Geez." Wide eyes at Amy's hand over her mouth. "Don't you—"

Amy winked and uncovered her mouth. She wore a smirk.

Kassandra picked Demora up from behind—and dove—with Amy's help, they pinned *Number 1* to the ground. "GO!" Kassandra's half-growl shook Amy's core.

Amy blazed past Team A's baulk line, then spun and bolted in the opposite direction.

E'oné held her own against the Count in the middle. "Go!" She ate a punch as Amy passed by, but her full-body snare held onto the vamp's legs, bringing them both to the ground.

The purple clouds grew to the ceiling, mist eating the entire arena.

Amy sucked her teeth. "aaaaaaaaaAH!" Her arm cut through the mist, clearing part of it. *He was a martial artist.* "Aiyah!" *Philosopher.* "Hyah!" *Scientist of the human form. 'Expressing yourself goes beyond the inner. Outward expression is the natural result of the work done.'* "eeeeeeeeAAAAH!" Arms swiped the air with increased speed and momentum. "Eeee-yah!!" More clouds cleared ahead, pushed back by her efforts. Mist crowded her peripherals, but she rushed forth, her blur of limbs and hair becoming white streaks in the wind—Feet from her team's base—

The Count lifted her by the neck.

"Get… off!" She struggled against his firm hold.

"Enough!" He grabbed her swinging arm.

E'oné slid under them and hugged his waist. "Also split champ—" She split her legs between his and twirled herself, sending his legs in opposite directions.

"Awwwck!" The vamp held his pelvis, eyes wide and mouth agape.

"—five years and counting!" E'oné wrapped herself around his stomach.

Amy freed from his grasp, pushed him back with two hands, and spin-kicked his chest away. Sped off towards her team's zone.

Yanked back by Demora.

Amy swung her elbow—into a Demo's block—slapped it out her way—they exchanged pounding blows.

Kassandra jumped in with a fist, but *Number 1* dodged.

Demora knocked Amy back— "One sec—" and dodged another fist. "Number 4 wants to be a big girl." Fingers curled in, she sent two quick spikes under Kassandra's arm and hit three more jabs up and down her latissimus dorsi before smiling and spinning away—into her best friend's face.

Amy locked Demo's arms in Maaura stance and HEADBUTTED her—lifted her best friend in a wrestling gut wrench, spun—threw her to the ground and stepped back— PUNTED the side of her torso.

Demora, shoulders rotated on the ground, feet in the air— *a spinaroonie? Where did she learn*— one hand on the grass, *the blond wonder* leapt— KICKED— RIGHT THROUGH AMY'S AFTERIMAGE. "What?" Landed on her feet, eyes searching the field.

Amy smiled back at her from afar, sprinted past Team C's baulk— then bonus line— overran the end line— plunged into a rolling ball and crashed into the wall.

DING DING DING!

Three points for Team C. Score is 9-8. With two seconds left, this match is officially over. Winners, Team C.

Amy sighed on her hands and knees. "Drink the wind, my friend." She laughed.

"Alright!" E'oné ran over and helped Amy up. "Not bad, 7!"

Kassandra reached them and plopped down on the grass. "Not bad girls. Not too bad." Her purple eyes dimmed to their natural yellow as she collapsed on her back. "I'm spent."

The mist dispersed, the last vanishing from midfield; The Count stood in the aftermath. With his trademark scowl on Team C, he gave a curt bow. His purple clouds of deception spread from behind and ate him whole, leaving nothing behind as the mist died out again.

Demora stared down the field at her opponents, hunched over, her hands in her pockets.

She smiled. "I am Demora Corbyn-McDonald."

Roots EXPLODED from the ground underneath her, twisted and squeezed around her legs— YANKED her down into a hole— swallowed her whole before it closed itself.

"Demora!" Amy rushed to the spot that devoured her best friend. "What the hell was that?"

"Still, she screams her name." Kassandra wandered off. "Ding, dong. The witch is gone. Better be lunchtime." She moved towards a revealing light behind the rising south wall.

Amy trudged her way towards the light. *She's impossible.*

E'oné caught up beside her. "I'm sure she's fine. Graves' tricks, remember?"

"You know, you gals didn't have to use me as bait."

"We decided before the match to try it if we felt you couldn't get the job done against your friend. That's our bad."

"Marvelous." Amy shook her head. "Least we won."

"Keeping it real, girl. Don't be so attached. Balance, feel

me?"

Amy blew her dampened hair from her face. "I need a shower."

"Did you check your cell?"

"There's one in there???"

"Uh, yeah, girl."

Amy DROPPED into a never-ending hole. Above her, the ground resealed itself, removing the last bit of light and E'oné's screaming voice.

.

.

.

.

Amy's eyes opened. "What the hell?" Her backhand caressed her forehead, first from the sweat, second from the obnoxious light that blinded her. She found her stomach—*fucking vamp bugs*—*language*—its presence finding her feet, enabling her to shift her weight off the bed. Held her head tight between both hands. *My fucking head.* "Not this again…"

"You've already slept for three hours more than you're given." Aura Amy leaned against the cell bars, peeved face on her host.

"Wait, why? How? Not now." Her head fell back into her hands.

"All I know is you were sent to your cell for the four-hour sentence."

"But we won!" Amy's hands glided along the dirt walls, her eyes intense.

"Did we? The numbers are not always worthy of your input." Aura Amy's scolding face loomed over her. *"How's that head of ours so clogged up?"*

"Is there a shower in here?"

Aura Amy rolled her eyes and pointed to the adjacent wall. *"Move further left. More. More. More. Okay, why'd you go that far? Come back a little. Little more. More. There. Push."*

Amy moved back as part of the wall slid open to the side.

The sparkling stainless glass shower, sink, and toilet gleamed inside the bathroom with silver walls and tiles. "Incredible." She faced her aura. "You get snarkier every time we meet. What happened after our match?"

"Ol' girl Graves has got me running around doing yada yada, and I'm not supposed to be here past your sentence." She tossed a weary hand at Amy. "But I couldn't watch you do this to us again, my oblivious HOST."

Amy inspected the shower. "What's wrong, coach?"

"Why are we here?"

"SO glad I don't have to truck my way up a floor anymore for the loo." Pants half down, Amy sat on the spotless toilet. "Better education, I guess."

"Let's pretend that's true for a second. Why do you keep allowing her to get in our way?"

The host shrugged. "Gonna have to be more specific than—"

"Exactly! Why go through all these strenuous tasks without giving our full potential? Got me clockin' overtime here! You roamed these halls for hours the other night, yet you still missed the key!"

"Stop yelling!" Amy flushed with one hand, used the other's finger to dig her *punctured* eardrum out, got off the loo and pulled her pants up. Washed her hands for— *24, 25, 26, 27 seconds. Yeah, I've got a problem.* "How are you even functioning?" She exited the bathroom. Lifted her aura's shirt, but her hand got smacked away. "Why do you always wear our favorite shirt?" Her finger outlined the words on the shirt: FUCKERY. "That's what this prison is. You know anything about it? What's Graves hiding in here?"

"You're not even hiding it anymore! Your incessant need to uncover anyone else's truth—"

"I take it you know—"

"You're crazy! You are crazy! Can't even hide your—"

"I take it you know nothing about— One sec." Amy chugged a glass of water.

Aura Amy's face of disbelief and rage watched her host take a big gulp.

Amy placed the glass on her lumpy dirt chair."—human relationships."

Jaw clenched, temples lit white, arms and hands clawed, Aura Amy crept to her. *"You can't even hide your incessant need to uncover anyone's truth in spite of honing your own."* Aura Amy stomped. *"She isn't you! It's not only her, though. It's her. And her. And him. And they. It's EVERYONE else!"* She orchestrated her arms in grabby motion in random directions. *"We SHARE a conscience! Your thoughts are like goobling babies infected by rambunctious loathing!"*

"I was not a goobler. Take it back. I know why you said that."

"Then know this! You may be my host, but that does not mean you control me."

Amy collapsed on the bed. *They never understand.*

"I heard that, you drama show!" Aura Amy held her forehead and took a deep breath. *"Okay. Think back to the other night. Roaming the halls. Scratching your tits."*

"Yeah, yeah, lemme think." Amy scratched her head. Then, her undertit. *Hate thinking this hard...*

"I know!"

"Will you—" Amy shooed the *fly* away. Her eyes widened. "Wait..."

"Yes?" Aura Amy leaned forward, tapping her knees together.

<u>*—Amy stalks the hall—a step and sneeze—these walls, a tease—*</u>

"That rhymed." Amy sat up on the bed, blank eyes on the wall.

"Focus!" Aura Amy threw her hands up. *"Ridiculous, like I'm your mother..."*

"Our. Rest her soul."

<u>*—Amy stalks the hall—sits on her butt against the wall—*</u>

Will you cut that out?

Get out, I'm trying to remember! Then there was the "family photo room" I found.

—Amy scrolls through slabs of pics of spurts with flowing red skirts and lots of spurts getting birthed from the earth—

Yeees...

Shh!

—I sniff and sniff—only the smell of my drawl and—oop, what's that?

"Where I sneezed..." Amy's finger tapped the side of her temple. "I saw it. I think."

"Yes, yes?"

"I kept running into one hall in particular. Sneezed in that same spot thrice."

"Yes?" Aura Amy leaned like a hungry canine. *"Soooo...?"*

—Amy leans on the dirt wall—sucks her teeth—a critter creeps on her shoulder—she picks it off and puts it down into the hole her body stood over—leans back up—

With her frowning crown and empty head down—

Shhh!

I thought we were rhyming? Pooper.

—took the chuckle of the message left by a poor clown—

—MOST WANTED WAS HERE—

—Very funny, Graves. So SCARY—Amy spots a long crack in the wall— a glint inside of it—

"The glint in the wall!" Amy yanked her hair. "I can't believe I missed that. Idiot!"

"Hey." Aura Amy placed a gentle hand on her shoulder. *"We're all idiots until we grow."*

"The insects I saw the other day all traveling in a row." Amy's back hit the wall. "Must lead to a secret room." Slid down on her ass. "I am unagreeable. Even with myself." *Me? SUTBAA?*

Check the source.

"Hush, aura."

"That wasn't me! And there are about one hundred cases of SUTBAA worldwide right now. You should get that checked out, for OUR sake."

Amy sighed. "I will." She grabbed her migraine. "So caught

in my ass that I'm blind to my blunders yet so caught in the asses of others I lose the plot."

"That's what I've been telling you." The aura form's hands went up in the air.

"E'oné said something that stuck. Balance. How about we try it?"

Aura Amy smiled. *"That's more like it."* Her face turned serious again.

Amy wore the same face. "Question is, what will <u>I</u> do?"

Aura Amy swung the cell bars open. *"Let's find out."*

"Shower first."

Chapter Eighteen

Level 2: Enemies Everywhere in the Non-Existent Prison

Mumbling to herself, Amy slipped closer to the noise coming from the Common Room. *Couldn't find that hall again. These rooms must be shifting. Oop—His voice is annoyingly louder than usual today.*

"Now, why would I devolve myself to an algorithm?"

"You love riddles." *The usually well-reserved* Ms. JellyRoll faced down Mr. SmartyPants, eyes narrowed and a shaky fist at her side. "I didn't agree to win like this."

"You agreed to win just the same, no? Never thought you were one to give in when the heat was on."

"And I never thought someone would be foolish enough to try and conquer a Dragon or Phoenix, let alone both. Man proves us wrong every day." She marched away *still with graceful strides taken towards* the exit. She took Amy in. "Watch yourself." Exited.

"Sure," Amy said, watching Ms. JellyRoll disappear into the darkness behind her.

Mr. SmartyPants' eyes stayed on Amy before losing himself behind a book at his table of solitude.

Kid can't keep a friend, huh?

"You think the others got lost after their cell sentences?" E'oné asked her brother.

"Or they're held hostage by something other than the prison..." Jamari's *obnoxious shades* followed Amy's path down the middle of the room.

"Sleeping beauty has no worries," Mr. Stoicism said, eyes on the table he sat at with the siblings.

Amy stopped. Looked him up and down. "Excuse me?"

"We were the weakest team," he went on. "I was released after four hours, but my team hasn't returned." He spun in his seat to face her. "You go through the floor and end up sleeping peacefully in your cell. That's rather interesting, isn't it?"

"Yeah—no. You just said I was in my cell. What are you implying?" She pointed at E'oné. "You were there when it happened."

"Wasn't there after." E'oné leaned back in her chair, resting her jacket's hood over her head.

"You're looking well rested, spring chicken." Jamari jumped to his feet and circled Amy. "What's your incarceration deal? I want in."

"Lay off!" Amy found herself in the middle of them all. "Can't you all see what's happening?" "Graves is sending us mad!"

"You've been mad." Jamari wagged his finger and banged it into his palm like a gavel. "You're the only one not complaining about cell time. We've been rollin' with Graves. Now you come tryna throw Prof under the bus, Newcomer?" His finger judged her, top, down, left, and right. "Trapped with your aura, not a scratch." His finger shot at his E'oné. "My sis is as callus as sharkfin, as vain as the diamond-shelled krhyzos in Maasai Mara—"

"What?" E'oné's head shook in confusion.

"That's facts, sis, but I meant well by it." His eyes refocused on Amy while still pointing at his sister. "And even she couldn't sleep right after her cell time."

"You were sent to your cell, too? Why? We won."

E'oné sighed. "Do you know what happened to the others, 7?"

"I don't."

"Numbers 2 and 3 have been away far past four hours. Lucky her, though!" Jamari wagged a finger at Amy, clasped his palms together, and rested his cheek against his prayer hands. "Sleeping in her cell; a baby on mother's milk. And her rallymate, best chum, girl of the hour! She's been dogging us from the jump! Was sent to her cell, too, yet came back without a care in the World. Whistled off on her own tune once again." He slid in front of Amy. "I sense a conspiracy. You're not even one bit rattled!"

"My aura's been haunting me long before I met you, so she and I are just having cups of tea at this point."

"She?!" Jamari's arms attempted to rally the room's support. "This mad bat gave her <u>aura</u>— that word, **blech!**" He quivered, his blockbuster shades almost falling off his nose. "She gave her spirit a persona! Proof's in Callisto's seed!"

"Ugh." Amy rolled her eyes *away from the child* and searched the others' faces. "Where did Number 1 go?"

Silence.

In her world, in one corner of the room, Kassandra's feet stretched on top of her table. She enjoyed a glassed bubbly beverage.

"Anyone?" Amy asked in her nonchalant former teammate's direction.

Mr. Stoicism's callous face remained as he got up and sunk onto a couch leaning against the wall on the far side of the room. Closed his eyes.

Amy's eyes narrowed on him. *Pompous shit.*

Jamari, hands behind his head, *too royal for this room,* bounced in and then out of his seat. He flipped his token as he strolled his way between some bookshelves.

Amy's eyes examined the room. Her insides boiled. "Where is she?" A bit of blood drew from her pam as her nails dug in.

"Look," E'oné said, "Little Miss Universe couldn't bear to hear from us commoners anymore, so she wandered off. <u>Like</u> my brother said."

Amy's fists relaxed. *Didn't we have a moment? Least that's what it felt like. I shouldn't...* "You know what, 6? I'd like to see how you'd fare if some bloody monsters kidnapped you and were still at large." Amy pulled herself away from their society of great expectations. "I'd like to see <u>any</u> of you survive what she did." Her eyes caught one of the positive affirma—*fuckalls*—on the wall above the exit. *'Your aura will never outgrow its age without alignment of One'*—oh, please! She trailed out into the exit's shadows.

She roamed through the darkness. *Why bother attempting to live under their rule? Won't keep me in a box. Although I may feel cornered, my internal shouldn't be. I need to recall the time. Now I'm lost in this maze of—Why can't I recall the fucking time?*

Amy stopped in the middle of absolute darkness and gazed above. She screamed.

"Uck—" Held her throat and buckled over. Sighed. Threw her head back with closed eyes. *FUCK! AHHHHHHHHHHHHHHHHHHHHHH FUCKING SHITFACE DREAD OF— AHHHHHHHHHHHHHHHHHHHHHHHHHHHHHHHHH*

Looked over her hands. "How can our physical bodies exist in the Aura Realm?"

Maybe we aren't. .... *What's a bird without its voice?* ...... *YOU NEVER <u>CARE</u> E<u>NOUGH</u>*.........*connect to our* *collective consciousness*......... *CHA-CHING!* ......Desolation. .... *You said you'd be there* .... *Tao tried to teach us*...... *CHA-CHING!* .... *believe that Cloudy had proof to his message* ....*The Earth is a living being* ......*we wouldn't listen*............... *smother the royal table*...........

CHA-CHING!... ......Your mother didn't want you ....
Memento mori......She'd rather die.........a simple price to
pay......She'd rather die............... you've got breath............ for now
....

"SHUT UP!" The final syllable of Amy's demand cut through the bleak void. Ripples of her cry washed over the blanket of darkness, bending it in jagged, rhythmic waves, folding and unfolding like an accordion. The sea of black that was the ground rose in crests and sank in troughs, as the atmosphere around her stretched and contracted.

Amy squeezed her throat. Let go of a strained cough and endured with a glare, licking her lips to stop specks of blood from escaping her mouth. Her protest, stronger than the razor-sharp slashes in her burning throat.

The darkness broke form and convulsed into a tide. The obsidian ocean splashed before her, a nose tip away, then converged and menstruated over her entire form. Amy's body sunk in a twirling water dance, falling to the end of the sea's belly. The silent stillness dug at her insides, *eating* like the bonesaw teeth of the Screwworm Tickbeetles. It reformed into the licks of raccooroaches skittering across and around her entire flesh.

Amy opened her eyes. Finding herself— *ARE YOU BLOODY FUCKING KIDDING ME?!* Her eyes said what her mouth wouldn't. "Unbelievable." She stood up and her depraved eyebrows roasted the orange veil separating her from the *faux* darkness of this Prison Games challenge— *in this FALSE "prison" in its silly little portion of the Aura Realm!* "Let's get it to it, yeah?"

She stood in the middle of an orange aurabox twice her size, that had a <u>cloudy</u> mist shrouding its exterior. "I should have left this place when I had a chance." She beckoned the glimpses of darkness she caught within her shrouded visual to *come at me! Let's rumble. Who's the monstrous threat stalking me inside my prison?* She thought of the undead. Her grandmother passing away. Or Demora's. Or the small lives whose cost to live is far too much. *They're just bloody fucking children. Come off, man!* She thought of everything wicked hidden in the shadows before and still in her future, *if not short.* She thought of death's embrace; that cool hand that runs your body cold, leaving your mind last to feel your aura siphoned from your being. *At least that's how Gma once described it. But how would she know?*

Amy thought of Cloudy.

—Cloudy's silver face slashes across like paint—his chittering, itching laughter breaking the realm of her mind— tiny silver thumbs, grouped by the dozen crawling down her skin in centipede fashion—

For all She thought... nothing came at all.

It took her *three minutes exactly* to realize she was already losing the battle with her number one opponent. Amy watched the vague shadows of herself in the sliced patches across the reflective— *but not as refined as E'oné's*— self-made prison.

She considered her options.

"I don't have the magic key to myself just yet! I haven't— haven't got it figured." Her eyes got lost in the cotton shrouds revolving around her. "If I forfeit and leave the prison now, that's a bit of ego I must swallow." Her nostrils flushed out her frustration. "Fine. I—"

The *unthinkable* clicked.

Swallow. Swallow light. Shadow. She *couldn't help* but grin. *Sometimes your shadow must suffocate the light. Can only be harnessed by sacrificing my consciousness. All chips on the table then.* "Fuck it. Alright Aura, let's supercharge us up and take a nap." She sighed. "Just don't kill us."

Her knees bent, her stance crooked, *visually, but firm. Spoke to her heart first. Translate to the belly. Let the warmth spread throughout. Past is no more. Future unset. It's here, it's now.*

The ache started in her fingertips, gathering white specks of her inner power dancing around them. *—Amy charges into Demora during Kombat Kabaddi—* She breathed the tasteless air in deeply and allowed her chest to fall in relaxation. *—Amy tumbles through a cotton mesh in the anti-gravity room—* A soft, white glow faded into existence around her body. *—The arms of Eaglot's Nest snatch purple auracards falling from Amy's hand—* Amy clenched her fists. *—Amy slammed her scarred right hand against E'oné's auraprison—* Her eyes closed as the heat inside of her reached a boiling point. *—Cloudy's everlasting smile fills the frame—an orange glow grows from within its hollow eyes—*

Amy blinked. Still conscious, she opened her eyes. "Come off it. Don't tell me <u>now</u> it won't wor—"

She blinked.

Chapter Nineteen

Level 2: Understanding

Amy woke up shivering, *the icy grip of an invisible giant* on her chest spreading across all her limbs. She sat up in the lonely darkness. *Did it work?* Her expression hardened. Graves. *Forcing me to bring up all this trauma over and over. Trapping me in a prison inside a prison. I don't know what your endgame is, but I'll find out, Professor.* She hunched over, *oblivious to time or whereabouts,* and traced a finger on her knees. Echoing footsteps behind her didn't disturb her peace.

The steps grew louder. Closer.

I could turn around. Or let whatever it is eat me. It's my prison, anyway.

A shimmering blanket of white light stopped beside her, blue feet sticking out underneath. The Gyaad girl bent down, watching Amy's undeterred face stare ahead. She opened her mouth. "**NiiiiiiiiiiiiiiiiiiiingooooooooAAAAAA.**"

Amy covered her ear and scooted away. "Wha—3? You're alright! What happened in your cell?"

Number 3 grabbed her arm and pointed behind them. She reached into the nothingness.

Amy watched the girl mime her surroundings. "I don't—"

Number 3 GRABBED onto the darkness. She pulled it back,

yanked and ripped an uneven square portion of it down like paper, revealing the blinding white light underneath.

"This place gets bonkier every turn." Amy leaned towards the exposed patch of light.

Using the shadows like chalk, the Number 3 drew black characters into the white light.

I HEARD YOUR SCREAMS FROM MY CELL THEY HELPED ME FIND MY WAY OUT HELPED ME FIND A WAY TO ACCEPT MY LESSON I CHOSE TO REMAIN

"Huh? You wanted to stay in your cell?"

Number 3 nodded. She wiped the shadowy words away. Drew more of them.

YOU HAVE AMAZING VOCAL STRENGTH! CAN I TEACH YOU HOW TO UNDERSTAND MY LANGUAGE ¿

Amy smiled. "I'd love to."

3 jumped for joy. She ran back to Amy's side, plopped down to a crossed-legged position in front of her, and beckoned Amy to join her.

After what felt like hours, Amy's face scrunched up. "Hold on…" She stared at the musical notes written into several ripped-out portions of white light around them. "So that's how the word aura would sound. And this over here means spirit."

Number 3 nodded enthusiastically.

"Training my ears is another thing. Another mission for the road." Amy stroked her chin. "But what you've shown me today proves we're in the aura realm." She smiled at 3.

3 grinned with a shrug.

Amy stood up and circled the spot. "You are a genius, 3. Now, we have to find the path to an exit." She froze. "The Most Wanted. What if they're the key to escape?"

3 beamed and shrugged.

"I'd have to find that hall from the other night again. You said you mapped out some stuff in here. Can you help me find a specific hall I'm seeking?"

3 shrugged but nodded with excitement.

Students, please return to the Common Room. Your next Prize Fight will begin shortly.

"Oh, bollocks. How about it, 3? Let's say we'll exchange any useful information we gather from here on out, yeah?"

3 jumped to her feet with her fists raised high. Opened her mouth. "Thank—**AAAH**—brilliant—**skreeeeee**—my ally, you are—**FERAAAAAAAAAAAAAAA—**"

"I'm getting better." Amy recoiled in slight agony. "Yup, still not there yet, but we're a work in progress." She searched the darkness. "How do we get out of here?"

3 linked arms with Amy and waved her along. Opened her mouth.

"Oh! You're a cheeky blinder! What's your name, by the way? I'm Amy."

"**Aaaameeeee HEYYIIWS SSSSSSSSOooooo oooooooooooooo RAEWwwwwwKKKK!**"

Amy sighed. "We'll get there." She followed *her new friend's* fervent lead.

Greek elites would be proud of this lavish display of sports architecture. How is Graves doing all of this without diminishing her aura reserves? What day is it?

The ten students of Graves stood in a lineup, facing a seating area of Panathenaic grandeur. Sandwiched between Number 3 and Demora, Amy wrinkled her nose, taken aback by the heavy air amongst the group. *Who isn't beefing at this point? What's that smell?* All eyes kept straight except for her, Demora, and the Gyaad.

Demora's face scrutinized Number 3's enthusiastic wave at her and Amy.

High up in the audience stands, three figures sat a few seats apart, peering down at the students.

Welcome, students, to your Prize Fight. You'll engage in a game of Triple Threat Red Rover.

Vedessia gasped. "I suck at this."

Kassandra eyeballed the curly-haired girl's foot, which was stepping on hers. "Please, tell us more. We're dying to care."

"Sorry."

The Gyaad grilled Kassandra.

Jamari scoffed at them all.

The ground broke apart under the students, becoming a platform as it lifted them.

For this challenge, you'll have a bit more of your spirit available to you. Fifty percent, to be exact.

"Score," Jamari said. "Now we're talking."

The platform rose higher before it bent into a boomerang shape.

Balance is everything. However, the strength of your team crafts the result.

The platform stopped, still beneath the eyes of the small audience in the stands.

The judges you see before you will each command a team. These leaders will vote on who moves next for their faction during gameplay. Your leaders for tonight: Count Maclyvtch, Professor of Anthrobotany and Anthropology Sciences.

One of the audience members rose. A spotlight shined on *his ever-lovely disposition, silently chastising them: The Count.* Nose upturned, he gave a curt bow, then sat down.

Mr. Steedleshrien, Professor of Environmental Safety.

The Dashing Man— *my wrestling opponent on Level 1!* —got to his feet and waved. "You're all so wonderful! Watching your lot has been a thrill. Bravo, students!"

"Sit down, Steedleshrien." Count Maclyvtch, chin on his palm, groaned.

And last but well admired, leader Nu'rik'rumboo, our specialist from Port Royal.

PatterPatterPatterPatterPatterPatterPatterPatterPatterPatter The bonemaiden slapped its fins against the seat in front of it.

"Ugh." E'oné groaned with shaky brows. "Why is it back?"

"Show some respect." Demora rolled her eyes.

"Teach me if you dare."

"Oh, I've been doing that. But I see you're still in need of discipline."

"I'll show you discipline—"

Time to decide the teams. Team A and B will comprise four players, while Team C will only have two.

"How is that any fair?" Mr. Stoicism *moaned.*

Mr. SmartyPants shook his head. "Are you always this obtuse or simply a man-child for life?"

Your objective is simple: Don't allow your opponents to break your barrier, or you'll defect to their team. The length of this game depends on your efficiency.

Players who break through a team can steal one player from the broken links of that team. You join that team if you cannot break through an opponent's line. Teams A and B leaders can send their players through the other two team lines to try and steal a player from each. Or they can choose to go through only one team for their turn. Team C will be in the middle, and their Leader has three options. They can send their chosen player through one team's line and, if successful, send that player to attack the other team's line. Or Leader C may have that player tag out to a new teammate, who can then make a run for the other side's team. Leader C's final option is to make their chosen player run through one team for their turn.

"Team C has a strenuous battle ahead of them," Ms. JellyRoll said. "May prove effective if run with precision and acute strategy."

Return to your position if you're successful and done with your team's turn. Once one of the teams is out of players, elimination will be in effect for all players who fail to cross their opponent's barrier.

"Gotta be joking, mate."

"Hope I'm not too <u>vain</u> for your team, bro. Ugh."

"aaaaahheeEEeeeeaaaaAaa!"

"Let's keep civil, friends!"

"Hope you all end up in the right alliance."

"Super."

"This is exhausting."

"The first few rounds make or break it!"

Amy grilled the ceiling. "Childish games."

One more note. You'll be competing for a prize pool of 50 points.

"Stellar."

"Who's hungry?"

"I hope we all play well!"

"Splendid!" Mr. Stoicism's eyes brightened like a child on Yuletide. "My comeback begins now."

Winners left standing will also be given a reward that is worth several lifetimes. Additionally, survivors who win at a player deficit will receive five extra points each.

"Let's get it!" Jamari and E'oné said. She turned away. He cracked his knuckles, unstirred by her stamping foot.

Leaders already have their voting order. Team C, please make your selection.

Pa-Pat-Pat-Pat-Pat The excited Nu'rik'rumboo's skeletal arms escaped its chest, wiggling forward.

Team C has selected Number 1. Number 1, please make your way to the red box on midfield.

Demora walked out of line and along the raised platform. She stopped on top of a red rectangle at the midpoint between both ends of the platform.

Team A, make your selection.

Count Maclyvtch rose to his feet, flipping his cape off his shoulder. "Number 4."

Team A has chosen 4. Number 4, head for the green box on your left.

Kassandra eyed the Count, holding eye contact as she walked. Stopped on the green rectangle.

Team B, make your selection.

Mr. Steedleshrien leapt up, clapping. "I choose Number 2! Such a bright girl."

Team B has chosen Number 2 for the last of the first picks. Head for the blue box on your far right.

"Great!" Vedessia skipped her way down the field. She passed an eye-rolling Demora and bounced her way to a blue rectangle at the end of the platform.

Team C, your final selection, please.

Pa-Pa-Pa-Pa-Pa

Team C has chosen Number 5.

"That's odds for you. No time for sour." Ms. JellyRoll floated by a snickering Mr. SmartyPants. She stood by Demora.

"That's a solid team," E'oné said. "You ready to conquer, brother?"

"Ain't nothing," Jamari answered. "We've survived 125th and Lex. We can survive anything."

Team A, your second pick awaits.

"I choose Number 7." The Count's eyes stayed locked on.

Amy ignored him, Mr. Stoicism's obnoxious **scoff**, and the **raspberry** from Jamari on the path towards Kassandra.

Team A has chosen Number 7.

Amy stood beside Kassandra, shaking her head at the low growl under her recurring teammate's breath. "Let's try to be civil, <u>please</u>."

"Play to win." Kassandra's eyes zipped onto Amy. "Or stand in my way and see what happens. Your choice."

Sigh. *Here we go...*

Team B, please select.

"Oh, yes!" Mr. Steedleshrien leaned forward. "I choose the ever-lovely Number 3."

The Gyaad girl opened her mouth and went on her way.

"Oh, I concur!" Mr. Steedleshrien died of laughter. "That ancestral spunk!"

Team A, your turn.

"I choose Number 6."

E'oné stopped in front of Jamari. "Good luck, brother." Fist-bumped him, then made her way.

Behind her, Mr. SmartyPants winked at Demora.

Demora's upturned nose left him, and her gaze fell into the pit below the platform.

Amy folded her arms. *What's that one about, Demo?*

Team B, your move.

"I absolutely LOVED your new single! Of course, the ever eminent, The M—"

No names, please, Mr. Steedleshrien.

"Oh right, right, my apologies again." He laughed. "Okay, I choose Number 10! A rank that's a crime to his untapped potential!"

Number 10, the other way, please. Number 10?

Jamari walked over to Team A and stood face-to-face with Amy. "This has been a long time coming for you. This game's my jam. Typically, I keep my hitlist private, but you and your blond friend, The Pink Wonder, are <u>both</u> going down this time around."

"Tell me, Wyst." Amy closed in on his ear. "Are you the Most Wanted?"

He leaned in. "If I were, you'd already be in your cell faster than I can drop an album." Turned to his sister. "Sorry, sis, but I gotta win this one." Jamari shrugged.

Huh? Amy's eyes squinted. *Wait...*

"Hope we end up survivors in the end," he cheesed at E'oné, walking away backwards with open arms. "If not, nothing personal for the loss." He turned around, throwing a cut-throat gesture in the air. "The <u>ship</u> has to go down."

"Ugh." E'oné shook her head, staring at his back. "He's so dramatic."

Spotting E'oné's raised eyebrow at her, Amy closed her hung jaw and threw on a quick smile with flushed cheeks. *I've been here before.* Her eyes wandered over E'oné's sporty yellow jacket. *I've seen this before. Seen them... Partially...*

She smirked. *If I'm right...*

Chapter Nineteen

Chapter Twenty

Level 2: Someone Always Breaks The Rules

Amy stared at the cover bound in aged leather with a shimmering steel framework along the edges. Intricate embossments of several magnificent beasts surrounded the title: *TOME OF ANIMALIA*. "I swear I have no problem sharing it with you." She flipped through its yellow pages. "We can each take a day. I'm just gonna start reading right now!"

"Wow. First time I've seen you starry-eyed about <u>anything</u> since we got here," E'oné said. She moved a dirt jigsaw piece into a slot on the wall. "You can have it."

The piece she placed emitted a warm, yellow glow as it seamlessly fit into the unfinished puzzle. AAAAAaAAAAAAAAAAAaAAAAAAAAAAAaAAAAAAAA AAaAAAAAAAAA

E'oné opened her eyes. "So this section's yellow. Can you mark that down?"

"Yup." Amy squeezed the abdomen of a white, bulbous inkinfela. "This guy's out." She crouched, eyes landing on a few trails of inkinfelas rolling around the ground. Picked one up and squeezed it, squirting pale blue liquid from its tip into the corner of an open page.

The white bug dropped on the page, and its rounded tri-body parts rolled its momentum in a circle.

Amy dipped her pinky into the small puddle the bug created and wrote inside the tome's pages. "I wonder—" She flipped through it. "Yes! The bonemaiden is here." Her head dove deep between the open pages.

"Ugh. Tell me when you know how to ward them off. Your turn."

"Oh, yeah." Amy shook some inkinfelas off a jigsaw piece on the ground, picked it up, and fit it over a slot.

OOOOOOOOOOOaEEEEEEEEEEEEEEEEEAAAA!

Red, green, and purple light flashed upon Amy's shocked, strained face.

Amy held her temple and reopened her eyes. "Oh, no." She stooped and held the tome over the inkinfelas, who changed course and scattered towards her. "Three colors; where are you?" The critters leaned up, their tiny mouths nipping at the pages. "What's your dig with them?"

"All these crits seem to love that tome a little too much for my liking; hence, it's yours."

"No, I meant bonemaidens." Amy helped the insects roll onto the open pages with a smile. "I wasn't aware they existed before that game."

E'oné groaned.

The silence lingered for several jigsaw turns, with only screams from the open white-lit space on the wall to break it.

Sigh. "Everyone loves my brother's story. What they don't know is that my father remarried outside of his lifeform."

Amy shut the tome and gave her undivided attention. "Didn't he settle with a spouse somewhere in the countryside?"

"'Writing letters to his loving son till his dying day before passing from natural causes.' Yeah, it's a cute media story. The hell that went on in that house said otherwise."

Both young women stepped back, the jigsaw completed, and all its pieces illuminated in a dazzling array of colors. The lights dimmed to a picture of a mermaid with a spear aimed towards the sky while she rode a winged tigerfox.

"On to the next," E'oné said.

They moved down the corridor, passing a pair of golden Pegasus statues meeting at the corner.

"Where's your Mum?" Amy asked.

"My mother died when I was eight."

"I'm sorry."

"It happens. I was studying the equilibrium theory of ancient cats while at uni in the States, but everything stopped after her passing. Moved back to London right after. "

"Oh, you're not from here?"

"Born and raised in America with my Mom and a British nanny. I moved back and forth between here and the U.K. to spend time with Jamari. Whenever my brother had to tour, his mom let me crash at hers. We got along well. Still keep in touch."

"Jamari's cool with that?"

"He doesn't care. His beef with his mom is his. I've tried to bring them together over the years. Everyone knows where they stand."

"Yup. I hope they can work it out someday."

"Me too. Once I moved here full-time, I decided to move on from the cat studies. Waxology."

"No way, far out."

"Dad wasn't too fond of the choice. I could never live up to Jamari's glory in his eyes. Even in my life, my brother was the star. I wanted to show Dad I was a master in my own right. Have you ever read that anonymous essay published in *The Yorker* that went viral about the link between the 9 Live Theory and mummification?"

"That was a doozy." *I sound like Jimmy.* "Brilliant analysis."

"Well, meet the author." She pointed at herself.

"No way!"

"Way. You're not the only one with secrets."

"Why anonymous?"

"The only person I needed to know would catch the hint because he knows his daughter." E'oné frowned at her feet as they passed another golden Pegasus. "Except he didn't. It took two months for Father to notice the article. I had to bring it up casually over brunch one day when I was sick of waiting."

"Rough. What he say?"

"No matter. I knew I was onto something once I realized the restorative powers of wax could help prove my theories. And I missed my mother."

What did she do?

"It had already been a week since she passed, so I needed to act fast. Luckily, she was buried in the family plot. So I robbed her corpse and brought it home."

"My grandmother knew a well-versed waxologist who once attempted and failed to do what I think you're about to tell me."

E'oné smiled. "The wax mended her broken body back to form and healed most of the deteriorated tissue. Since we buried her spirit with the body, I placed her soul back in her body by splicing it with pieces of the wax mended with her body. Took forever. It takes some time for the soul to recognize the body as a suitable host. She started regaining her memory around the third week."

Incredible. Aura splicing at her age? Gma would be proud; she does it for breakfast.

"My mom used to read me fairytales from around the world, and we created an exhaustive list of places we would go and the things we'd do." E'oné smiled into space. "Started mapping out trips and setting dates. Then she..." Closed her eyes.

Never knew my mum, I can't imagine..."You brought her back to form. You're a genius."

"Life and death are intertwined in obscurity. Mom learned both sides, and it changed her. It showed a month in. She couldn't understand how to live as part of the undead. She remained dedicated to the life she had before her death. I needed time away from her because I only knew life. That's when I took up planche and threw myself into split competitions."

"Something went wrong."

E'oné nodded. "Father found her one day sneaking into his

bed. His new wife was away visiting family."

"Did he… was he upset with you?"

"The opposite. Probably the proudest he's ever been with me. They continued seeing each other like they never were apart. He'd see my Mom late at night and his wife during the day. Soon, Mom wasn't too keen on sharing anymore. Nights left alone in a shack down by the river ate at her. Especially those nights when he couldn't sneak away to visit her, which became more frequent. She kept obsessing about it for weeks, telling me how much she despised that fraud who took her place. One day, she disappeared. We couldn't find her and assumed she had moved on. I hated it but was grateful she was doing something for herself. And I hated my father's position in all this."

"Horrible position for a daughter to be in."

E'oné shrugged. "I went on with life. Things remained quiet until I arrived home one day alone in the house, which was uncommon since Dad would usually be on the couch or in his studio waiting for my stepmother to come in. What a night that was." She paused, taking in the golden statue to her right. "Haven't we passed these already?"

Amy inspected the Pegasus. Shrugged.

"Ugh, I think we found a loop."

"A what?"

"Some others and I stumbled into these looping corridors now and then." Her eyes checked up and down the hall. "I'm sure there's a door nearby. Check those walls over there."

Amy headed to the section E'oné pointed her to, grazing her hands along the dirt. "So what happened that night? And what's this got to do with bonemaidens?"

"Father came up from the cellar and wanted me to bring him some Daemonorop tarps from the garage."

"Where the hell did he get Daemonorop in London?"

"Stepmom's a botanist, and my father loved entertaining UnderCity crevents with Jamari's money."

"Oh."

"So I did what any good daughter would and brought the

tarps, following him to the basement. Thinking we're going to do some amazing father-daughter project, maybe draining some mummified spurts with the tarps for study. Silly girl's fantasies—"

My nightmare.

"Only to find blood on the stairs going down. And in the cellar—this way."

They turned another corner and found a green Pegasus statue.

"Ah, progress. What happened in the cellar?"

"Two bodies on some more Daemonorop tarps in the middle of the floor. My mother was unconscious. He drugged her. The other body was my stepmother. She had her throat ripped out and part of her lower jaw missing. Both chained to the floor."

"Your Mum... killed her?"

E'oné took a seat on the ground. "And he wanted me to do it again. Bring back the dead. Father wanted his two wives. I wanted to make him happy."

"Unreal. I can't believe he put you through that."

"Took us two hours to find her soul wandering about twenty minutes away."

Amy leaned on the wall across from her. "So you did it again." *A tortured genius.*

"Except I wouldn't have if I'd known she was a descendant of a bonemaiden. When a demi-maiden passes on, they transfigure into a full-on maiden. From that point on, my house was occupied by the four of us. The nightmares are still fresh. Stepmom hated me."

DOMMMmmmmm

Across from them, a part of the wall pushed in.

DOMMMmmmmm

The girls approached the opening as the wall continued pushing into the darkness until eaten by its depths.

"There's our clue." Amy pointed ahead as she dipped first into the uncertain.

DOMMMmmmmm

"Is that obnoxious noise necessary?" E'oné covered her ears, following Amy in.

DOMMMmmmmm

Amy slapped her hands on her ears. "I'm literally going to go deaf in this place."

The pitch dark ate them whole.

Green lights washed over them, followed by white spotlights circling their personal bubbles.

"Excuse me, fellow students. Congratulations to the pair of you! Real champion performance." A square green aura platform descended from above and zoomed over their heads. Mr. SmartyPants sneered down at the two young women from on top of it.

"Thanks?" E'oné said. "How are you accessing spirit?"

"Still haven't figured out some things since our last conversation, E'oné?"

"Hey! You haven't earned my name!"

"Knowledge gained is knowledge earned, Ms. Wyst." The platform zoomed around as he cleaned his decagon eyeglasses with his shirt.

"Wait, is this another challenge?" Amy asked.

"Only if you make it one, 7."

"If it's a fight you want, 8, let's stop talking and make it happen." Amy got her fists at the ready.

E'oné held her back. "Careful, he's with spirit."

"I don't care if he's with aura or the Emperor!"

"You didn't answer, 8! How are you accessing <u>your</u> spirit?"

"I told you all before. Don't you get it?" His platform stopped over their heads as he peered at them through his translucent aura podium. "It's Alien Science. It's inevitable, and I study frequently." He walked down his aura as it created steps to meet his feet. "It's calculated mastery you can't begin to comprehend. Right after the Red Rover match, as you grabbed your <u>prize</u>..." His eyes lingered on Amy. "I trapped you two in my own little loop. Gave you some meaningless tasks."

"You little creep!" E'oné grabbed the platform—only for her hand to phase right through.

The platform and Mr. SmartyPants faded from existence.

He reappeared, sitting behind a green aura table of magnificent length. "Now, let's talk business. 7, you owe me a favor, and I'm cashing in."

"Lemme guess." Amy folded her arms, eyes closed. "You want some points for your trouble? You didn't have to go through these extremes. I'm willing to deal."

"I'm ecstatic to hear it! The deal I want is that tome." He pointed directly at the tome she cradled close to her heart. "I'll hold on to *Tome Of Animalia* and make sure that knowledge goes to great use."

"HA! Absolutely not!" Amy laughed. "You must be clinical if you think I'm giving this to you!"

"Ah." Mr. SmartyPants leaned back as a chair manifested from his aura. "You lack the knowledge needed to make the ideal decision."

"If you say knowledge one more time, I'm gonna puke." E'oné rolled her eyes. "She's not giving up the book, so get over it!"

"Seems you may get your fight, 7. Because this **tome** is worth the effort, isn't it?" Mr. SmartyPants stuck out his chest. "You see, I'm one of the Most Wanted...

"What?" The women shot looks at each other before turning back to him.

"Amy Devine. Nineteen years old, living in her mortician grandmother's home surrounded by the dead. A study of events over her history dictates a fear of the dearly departed that stems from childhood. 'Ames', as only her best friend Demora Corbyn-McDonald calls her, exhibits a quirky knack for getting into trouble, racking up at least 13000 UDs in civil charges over her years. Twelve of those years hitting five strikes out of six on her offenses, with the highest charge being a recent Class C civil with a slight pardon—intriguing. Don't get me started on Demo's record. Did I miss anything?"

Amy's hung jaw quivered, her airborne fists shaking.

"You—Don't call her—How do you—you're whaaat?!"

"One of the Most Wanted. Keep up, dear classmate."

"You're shitting on hallowed grounds, 8!" E'oné stepped back, her fists raised. "We're not—"

"Let's cut this out, hm? I'm not the original MW and could care less for the concept, but I can't let you pass. Not unless you honor your favor and give me the tome. Check your rear."

His aura shot high above and curved around them. Two 20-foot giantesses formed.

"We have little time for this debate. Though I manipulated the professor's light to contact some of my own, her protections are quite substantial, leaving me unable to configure certain aspects. So simple "prison points" wouldn't suffice either way."

Amy clutched *her* tome, *imagining his neck in its place.* "What if we waited you out?"

"I'd still have you trapped." He leaned towards them. "Here's a freebie. As Most Wanted, I'm able to harbor more of my spirit and have a technique Graves allows the MWs. Using your word, 7: the <u>Aura</u> Pinch."

"What?!" Amy's breathless voice caught in her throat. *Bloody, sniving, inconsequential little—*

"The what?"

"A simple pinch to the shoulder. A pinch packed with a considerable amount of <u>aura</u>."

"<u>Aura</u>." Amy mocked his drawl. "You will not get away with this." She squeezed the tome as she fought back the building wetness in her eyes.

She softened at a gentle touch—E'oné's hand on her shoulder.

"Balance. Can't beat him this time. We take our lesson in the loss and recoup." She spat in 8's direction. "I can't believe we're getting punked by. All those hours buried in books—trying to compensate for something, are we? Maybe it's time you grew up and aimed for a maturity level higher than your IQ."

"Lemme give you a free tip, Ms. Wyst." Mr. SmartyPants used his index fingers to perform a short push-up sequence atop his aura table. He backflipped and landed with precision. "True geniuses don't enjoy being referred to as geniuses. It's degrading. Trying to measure my ever-expanding intelligence on a scale."

"I didn't call you a genius!" E'oné stomped towards him, nearly launching out her *cute shoes, forgetting to lose in grace.*

"Spare me the drama." He waved her off. "So tell me, Ms. Devine. Do you have honor? You see, I come from a people who deeply believe in honor. Do you... Amy?"

Amy's blank stare was somewhere between murder, insanity, and sorrow.

"I can't believe this shit," E'oné said. "I'm sorry, girl. It's not the end. I promise."

"Clock's ticking." Mr. SmartyPants tapped his watch. "I unfortunately have to go back down a level." He threw on a faux face of distress. "What if I have to face some hideous beast? You would want to help out your fellow students, no? Oh, how I wish I could let you pass, but I just can't. It's knowledge, after all." He held his hand out. "The tome. I must have it."

I'm going to murder him twenty-seven times inside three hours. Amy held the tome up.

One of the aura giantesses picked it like a cherry with two massive fingers.

"Excellent." Mr. SmartyPants took the tome brought over from his loyal subject. "Would love to stay and entertain more, ladies, but I must take my leave. I've got to spend some more time in this dreadful place, as there's still so much to research."

The darkness behind him spiraled into an opening, revealing the dirt walls outside of it. "Oh, and ladies? Please keep this little "hang time" between us?" He moved to the opening. "Or I'll be forced to send you to your cells for an unspecified amount of time." Threw a careless hand back. "Cheers to your brilliant victory!" He faced them again, raising his *painfully* straight index finger to push his glasses higher on his nose. "My name is Hideko Ang, and I am the number one chess master in five of the seven regions."

Chapter Twenty-One

Level 2: You'll Never Find...

"He's a bastard," E'oné said behind a despondent Amy.

Voices trailed from afar as they walked *through the ever-dreary* corridor. *Fucking sick and tired of these dry walls of earthy mounds suffocating my every turn and triumph.*

"Wonder what's for lunch," E'oné's *uncomfortably nervous eyes on me.*

Amy groaned. *Don't feed my peripherals that pity. Stupid games and stupider rewards.*

Except for the one you lost.

"Shut up."

"<u>Excuse</u> me?" E'oné's neck struck an angle.

"Not you." Amy shook her head. "It's my head. Trying to swallow the pride I have remaining."

"Oookay. I could use a massage."

Amy sulked forward.

"Can I ask? Back at Level 1. Why'd you help me?"

"Cuz you were clearly under mucho distress."

"But you gained nothing from it? Well, besides my name, which I willingly gave."

"Yeah." Amy threw a side glance. "Why do I have to gain

something for me to help another?" She stopped and scanned the melting, muddy landscape ahead. "Fuck's sake, what now? E'oné?"

Surrounded by a liquifying world, Amy stood alone as the scene melted away.

She whipped around, staring at her new location within a room full of memorabilia from ages past. An Olympics poster on the wall stretched from end to end, the words Hosted by the Oktoberfest Capital of the World splattered across the top. She wandered the room full of objects from a time before disco balls, like the ones hanging above her head, became weapons of mass destruction in The First Peculiar War. A pulsating rhythm grew around her, and the floor pounded to life with a cascade of psychedelic light matching the tune's beat fading into play.

"What are you doing here?" Jamari strode over with his puffed-out chest pointed at her.

"Let ya know as soon as I find out. This prison is bonkers."

"Wow." His blockbuster shades searched the floor. "It's like a multi-colored checkerboard!"

"It's a disco room," Amy said, brows furrowed as she searched the air around him for common sense.

"The hell is disco?"   "You're joking."

"Wonder what this challenge is?" He pointed at Amy. "I'm not dancing with you."

Amy rolled her eyes. "I'd be so lucky."

Several squares on the floor split apart. Toddler bots rose from the holes left behind, their boxy chrome bodies changing colors faster than the floor's squares. They shimmied in place, wagging finger guns in the air as they spun at the stretch of the looping beat.

"Hey!" Jamari bopped. "Lil dudes! Go, little robo! Go, little robo!" He followed the movements of his new friends.

Amy just stared at him. "I must be dead in Hell already."

Good day, students. Looks like you've stumbled on a puzzle.
Prep your singing voices!

Amy gulped. Grabbed the swell over her heart as her chest heaved. Her surroundings became pixelated with each passing second. She averted her gaze to a corner of the room.

A red Fender Stratocaster guitar with googly eyes and a crooked smile on its body stared back at her. Its grin curled far too upward. Eerie shadows cast under the eyes.

For this secret prize round, you'll have two seconds to follow along with the cadence of the vocals while keeping your body moving to the beat. Don't stop moving. Unlock pieces to the puzzle using clues your ears give you. Complete all four rounds. Good luck.

"That's it?! Those are all the instructions?"

"What'd you expect?" Amy sighed.

DING

Bow

Bow

BOW

"Dear…" Amy swayed in place with limbs moving like wet noodles.

"C'mon, girl!" *Jamari had a grand time,* shoulders shimmying, knees buckling, then bouncing back to form. "Making our people look bad." He threw up the Black Power salute.

You'll never fiiind… A booming, suave voice echoed.

"You'll never fiiind…" Amy and Jamari sang with voices a touch in harmony.

You'll neveeer fiiind…

"You'll neveeer fiiind…"

"Hey, I know this song!"

WuaAlaWuaAlaWuaAlaWuaAlaWuaAlaW uaAla

Bellowing on and on as the tune scratched and screamed in reverse order.

Silence.

Bow Bow BOW The tune began from scratch.

"Ah, shit." Jamari adjusted his shades. "My bad."

"You don't know about disco floors, but you know this song. So happy for you." Amy crossed her arms. "We're starting over!"

"No shit!"

You'll never fiiind...

"You'll never fiiind..." Amy grilled him.

"You'll never fiiind..." Jamari folded his arms.

You'll neveeer fiiind...

"You'll neveeer fiiind..."

"You'll NEVeer fiind..."

WuaAlaWuaAlaWuaAlaWuaAlaWuaAlaW uaAla

Bellowing on and on as the tune scratched and screamed in reverse order. Silence. **Bow Bow BOW** The tune began from scratch.

"What?" Jamari threw his hands up.

"Keep in cadence! She <u>literally</u> said that."

"Oh yeah."

You'll never fiiind...

"You'll never fiiind..."

"You'll never fiiind..."

You'll neveeer fiiind...

"You'll neveeer fiiind..."

"You'll neveeer fiiind..."

You'll never fiiiiind...

"You'll never fiiiiind..."

"You'll never fiiiiind..."

You'll neveeeeeer fiiiiiind...

"You'll neveeeeeer fiiiiiind..." Amy's hips flicked. She wiped the pool of sweat off her cheeks.

"You'll neveeeeer fiiiiiind…" Jamari shimmied harder, baring teeth at Amy.

The dance mates moved several squares away from one another.

The tune hit its bend.

You'll never fiiind…

"You'll never fiiind…"

"You'll never fiiind…"

You'll neveeer fiiind…

"You'll neveeer fiiind…"

"You'll neveeer fiiind…"

You'll never fiiiiind…

"You'll never fiiiiind…"

"You'll never fiiiiind…"

You'll neveeeeer fiiiiiind…

"You'll neveeeeer fiiiiiind…"

"You'll neveeeeer fiiiiiind…"

The tune hit its bend.

You'll never fiiind…

"You'll never fiiind… wow."

"You'll never fiiind… jokin, man…"

You'll neveeer fiiind…

"You'll neveeer fiiind…"

"You'll neveeer fiiind…"

You'll never fiiiiind…

"You'll never fiiiiind…"

"You'll never fiiiiind…"

You'll neveeeeer fiiiiiind…

"You'll neveeeeer fiiiiiind…"

"You'll neveeeeer fiiiiiind…"

"Can't expect us to go nonstop with this." Amy thrusted her body with impatience.

"…gonna kill me…" Jamari mumbled as he dragged his feet.

The tune hit its bend.

You'll never fiiind...

"You'll never fiiind..."

"You'll never fiiind... Fuck!"

You'll neveeer fiiind...

"Calm down! You'll neveeer fiiind..."

"You'll neveeer fiiind... No."

You'll never fiiiiind...

"You'll never fiiiiind..."

"You'll never fiiiiind..."

You'll neveeeeeer fiiiiiind...

"You'll neveeeeeer fiiiiiind..."

"You'll neveeeeeer fiiiiiind..."

"Wait, the pitch in the OG song... isn't this?" Jamari scratched the sides of his shades.

"Can you even see in those?"

The tune hit its bend.

You'll never fiiind...

"You'll never fiiind..."

"You'll never fiiind... Aye!"

You'll neveeer fiiind...

"You'll neveeer fiiind... What?"

"You'll neveeer fiiind... It's in A key!"

Amy shrugged and mouthed, "Okay?"

You'll never fiiiiind...

Putapoo-tsssssssp! Putapoo-tsssssssp! Putapoo-tsssssssp! Putapoo-tsssssssp!

Amy's eyes lit up. "You'll never fiiiiind... nice!"

"You'll never fiiiiind... new part!"

Putapoo-tsssssssp! Putapoo-tsssssssp! Putapoo-tsssssssp! Putapoo-tsssssssp!

You'll neveeeeeer fiiiiiind...

Putapoo-tsssssssp! Putapoo-tsssssssp! Putapoo-tsssssssp! Putapoo-tsssssssp!

"You'll neveeeeeer fiiiiiind..."

"You'll neveeeeer fiiiiiind…"

"Stellar! Whooa." Under Jamari, the word AGE blinked in and out of existence within the squares his feet danced on.

"Age?" Amy's eyes rolled up. "19?" Squares under her blinked with ??? as she moved. The music grew louder, the tune hitting its bend.

You'll never fiiind…
Putapoo-tsssssssssp! Putapoo-tsssssssssp!
Putapoo-tsssssssssp! Putapoo-tsssssssssp!

Maybe? "You'll never fiiind… Song age?"

"You'll never fiiind…" He shrugged.

Putapoo-tsssssssssp! Putapoo-tsssssssssp!
Putapoo-tsssssssssp! Putapoo-tsssssssssp!
You'll neveeer fiiind…
Putapoo-tsssssssssp! Putapoo-tsssssssssp!
Putapoo-tsssssssssp! Putapoo-tsssssssssp!

"You'll neveeer fiiind…"

"You'll neveeer fiiind… 78?"

Putapoo-tsssssssssp! Putapoo-tsssssssssp!
Putapoo-tsssssssssp! Putapoo-tsssssssssp!
You'll never fiiiiind…
Putapoo-tsssssssssp! Putapoo-tsssssssssp!
Putapoo-tsssssssssp! Putapoo-tsssssssssp!

"You'll never fiiiiind…"

"You'll never fiiiiind…"

Putapoo-tsssssssssp! Putapoo-tsssssssssp!
Putapoo-tsssssssssp! Putapoo-tsssssssssp!
You'll neveeeeer fiiiiiind…
Putapoo-tsssssssssp! Putapoo-tsssssssssp!
Putapoo-tsssssssssp! Putapoo-tsssssssssp!

"You'll neveeeeer fiiiiiind…"

"You'll neveeeeer fiiiiiind…"

This is insane. "Wait, age, year, 19… 1970?"

"No…" Jamari lit up. "I know—1976!"

The music's increased volume prompted both students to

slam their hands over their ears.

The tune hit its bend.

You'll never fiiind... Putapoo-tssssssssp! Putapoo-tssssssssp! Putapoo-tssssssssp!

HAAAAAAAAAAAAAAAAAAAAAAAAAAAAAAAAAAAAa aaaaaaaaaaaaaaaaaaaaaaaaaaaaaaaaaaaaaaaa h

"You'll never fiiind... fuck?"

"You'll never fiiind... blasting me, mate!"

Putapoo-tssssssssp! Putapoo-tssssssssp! Putapoo-tssssssssp! Putapoo-tssssssssp!

HAAAAAAAAAAAAAAAAAAAAAAAAAAAAAAAAAAAAa aaaaaaaaaaaaaaaaaaaaaaaaaaaaaaaaaaaaaaaa h

You'll neveeer fiiind... Putapoo-tssssssssp! Putapoo-tssssssssp! Putapoo-tssssssssp!

HAAAAAAAAAAAAAAAAAAAAAAAAAAAAAAAAAAAAa aaaaaaaaaaaaaaaaaaaaaaaaaaaaaaaaaaaaaaaa h

"You'll neveeer fiiind..."

"You'll neveeer fiiind..."

Putapoo-tssssssssp! Putapoo-tssssssssp! Putapoo-tssssssssp! Putapoo-tssssssssp!

HAAAAAAAAAAAAAAAAAAAAAAAAAAAAAAAAAAAAa aaaaaaaaaaaaaaaaaaaaaaaaaaaaaaaaaaaaaaaa h

You'll never fiiiiind... Putapoo-tssssssssp! Putapoo-tssssssssp! Putapoo-tssssssssp!

HAAAAAAAAAAAAAAAAAAAAAAAAAAAAAAAAAAAAa aaaaaaaaaaaaaaaaaaaaaaaaaaaaaaaaaaaaaaaa h

"You'll never fiiiiind..."

"You'll never fiiiiind..."

Putapoo-tssssssssp! Putapoo-tssssssssp! Putapoo-tssssssssp! Putapoo-tssssssssp!

HAAAAAAAAAAAAAAAAAAAAAAAAAAAAAAAAa aaaaaaaaaaaaaaaaaaaaaaaaaaaaaaaaaaaaa h

You'll neveeeeer fiiiiind... Putapoo- tsssssssssp! Putapoo-tsssssssssp! Putapoo- tsssssssssp!

HAAAAAAAAAAAAAAAAAAAAAAAAAAAAAAAAa aaaaaaaaaaaaaaaaaaaaaaaaaaaaaaaaaaaa h

"You'll neveeeeer fiiiiind..."

"You'll neveeeeer fiiiiind..."

Amy blew hot air. "What a trip—"

"Yo." A sweat-covered Jamari collapsed to one knee.

"Are you alright?! We gotta keep—"

The tune hit its bend.

"Yeah, yeah."

WuaAlaWuaAlaWuaAlaWuaAlaWuaAlaW uaAla

Amy closed her eyes, fingers to forehead rubbing with vigor. Bellowing on and on as the tune scratched and screamed in reverse order.

"Fuck!" Jamari punched the dance floor.

"It's alright—*it's not*—we know where we're at. Let's just get back into it."

Bow Bow BOW

Their bodies swayed back into the groove.

You'll never fiiind...

"You'll never fiiind..."

"You'll never fiiind... A key!" Jamari waved a weak hand to "go on."

You'll neveeer fiiind...

Putapoo-tsssssssssp! Putapoo-tsssssssssp! Putapoo-tsssssssssp! Putapoo-tsssssssssp!

"You'll neveeer fiiind... 1976!"

"You'll neveeer fiiind…"

Putapoo-tsssssssssp! Putapoo-tsssssssssp! Putapoo-tsssssssssp! Putapoo-tsssssssssp!

HAAAAAAAAAAAAAAAAAAAAAAAAAAAAAAAAAAAAAAa aaaaaaaaaaaaaaaaaaaaaaaaaaaaaaaaaaaaaaaaaaa h

You'll never fiiiiind… Putapoo-tsssssssssp! Putapoo-tsssssssssp! Putapoo-tsssssssssp!

HAAAAAAAAAAAAAAAAAAAAAAAAAAAAAAAAAAAAAa aaaaaaaaaaaaaaaaaaaaaaaaaaaaaaaaaaaaaaaaaaa h

"You'll never fiiiiind…"

"You'll never fiiiiind…"

Putapoo-tsssssssssp! Putapoo-tsssssssssp! Putapoo-tsssssssssp! Putapoo-tsssssssssp!

HAAAAAAAAAAAAAAAAAAAAAAAAAAAAAAAAAAAAAa aaaaaaaaaaaaaaaaaaaaaaaaaaaaaaaaaaaaaaaaaaa h

You'll neveeeeeer fiiiiiind… Putapoo-tsssssssssp! Putapoo-tsssssssssp! Putapoo-tsssssssssp!

HAAAAAAAAAAAAAAAAAAAAAAAAAAAAAAAAAAAAAa aaaaaaaaaaaaaaaaaaaaaaaaaaaaaaaaaaaaaaaaaaa h

"You'll neveeeeeer fiiiiiind…"

"You'll neveeeeeer fiiiiiind…"

"Alright, that's three parts, right?" Jamari asked, out of breath, with slow to gyrate hips.

Amy swayed, side to side, shaking off the sweat beads. "Two more to unlock."

"Fuck…" Jamari's hunched shoulders and shuffling feet *did their best*. "I'm useless in everything…"

Amy threw her arms. "Bit late to lose your confidence, superstar!"

The tune hit its bend.

You'll never fiiind… Putapoo-tsssssssssp!

Putapoo-tsssssssssp! Putapoo-tsssssssssp!

**HAAAAAAAAAAAAAAAAAAAAAAAAAAAAAAAAAAAAAAAa
aaaaaaaaaaaaaaaaaaaaaaaaaaaaaaaaaaaaaaa
h**

"You'll never fiiind..."

Jamari rubbed his chin. "You'll never fiiind... two! No, three—"

**Putapoo-tsssssssssp! Putapoo-tsssssssssp!
Putapoo-tsssssssssp! Putapoo-tsssssssssp!**

**HAAAAAAAAAAAAAAAAAAAAAAAAAAAAAAAAAAAAAa
aaaaaaaaaaaaaaaaaaaaaaaaaaaaaaaaaaaaaaa
h**

**You'll neveeer fiiind... Putapoo-tsssssssssp!
Putapoo-tsssssssssp! Putapoo-tsssssssssp!**

**HAAAAAAAAAAAAAAAAAAAAAAAAAAAAAAAAAAAAAa
aaaaaaaaaaaaaaaaaaaaaaaaaaaaaaaaaaaaaaa
h**

"You'll neveeer fiiind... What?!"

"You'll neveeer fiiind... Three keys!"

**Putapoo-tsssssssssp! Putapoo-tsssssssssp!
Putapoo-tsssssssssp! Putapoo-tsssssssssp!**

**HAAAAAAAAAAAAAAAAAAAAAAAAAAAAAAAAAAAAAa
aaaaaaaaaaaaaaaaaaaaaaaaaaaaaaaaaaaaaaa
h**

**You'll never fiiiiind... Putapoo-tsssssssssp!
Putapoo-tsssssssssp! Putapoo-tsssssssssp!**

**HAAAAAAAAAAAAAAAAAAAAAAAAAAAAAAAAAAAAAa
aaaaaaaaaaaaaaaaaaaaaaaaaaaaaaaaaaaaaaa
h**

"You'll never fiiiiind... Three what?!"

"You'll never fiiiiind... A, something—E..."

**Putapoo-tsssssssssp! Putapoo-tsssssssssp!
Putapoo-tsssssssssp! Putapoo-tsssssssssp!**

**HAAAAAAAAAAAAAAAAAAAAAAAAAAAAAAAAAAAAAa
aaaaaaaaaaaaaaaaaaaaaaaaaaaaaaaaaaaaaaa
h**

You'll neveeeeer fiiiiiind... Putapoo-tssssssssp! Putapoo-tssssssssp! Putapoo-tssssssssp!

HAAAAAAAAAAAAAAAAAAAAAAAAAAAAAAAAAAAAAaaaaaaaaaaaaaaaaaaaaaaaaaaaaaaaaaaaaaaaaaaah

"You'll neveeeeer fiiiiiind... C?"

"You'll neveeeeer fiiiiiind... Three keys!"

Their deadweight dancing grew heavier with every forced step.

Jamari swallowed air, his head to the ceiling. "Three keys! A! C! E! That's it!"

"Please work..." Amy cleared her dry throat.

The music grew louder.

"FUUUCK—"

"FUCK, mate—"

You'll never fiiind... Putapoo-tssssssssp! Putapoo-tssssssssp! Putapoo-tssssssssp!

HAAAAAAAAAAAAAAAAAAAAAAAAAAAAAAAAAAAAAaaaaaaaaaaaaaaaaaaaaaaaaaaaaaaaaaaaaaaaaaah

Burm burm-nim! Burm, burm-nim! Burm burm-nim! Burm, burm-nim!

"You'll never fiiind... Nice work!"

"You'll never fiiind... thank Callisto..."

Putapoo-tssssssssp! Putapoo-tssssssssp! Putapoo-tssssssssp! Putapoo-tssssssssp!

HAAAAAAAAAAAAAAAAAAAAAAAAAAAAAAAAAAAAAaaaaaaaaaaaaaaaaaaaaaaaaaaaaaaaaaaaaaaaaaah

Burm burm-nim! Burm, burm-nim! Burm burm-nim! Burm, burm-nim!

You'll neveeer fiiind... Putapoo-tssssssssp! Putapoo-tssssssssp! Putapoo-tssssssssp!

HAAAAAAAAAAAAAAAAAAAAAAAAAAAAAAAAAAAAAa

aaaaaaaaaaaaaaaaaaaaaaaaaaaaaaaaaaaaaaaa
h
Burm burm-nim! Burm, burm-nim!
Burm burm-nim! Burm, burm-nim!
"You'll neveeer fiiind…"

"You'll neveeer fiiind… wish she told me that…" He kicked his sneakers off.

"What?" Amy mouthed.
Putapoo-tsssssssssp! Putapoo-tsssssssssp!
Putapoo-tsssssssssp! Putapoo-tsssssssssp!
HAAAAAAAAAAAAAAAAAAAAAAAAAAAAAAAAAAAAa
aaaaaaaaaaaaaaaaaaaaaaaaaaaaaaaaaaaaaaaa
h
Burm burm-nim! Burm, burm-nim!
Burm burm-nim! Burm, burm-nim!
You'll never fiiiiind… Putapoo-tsssssssssp!
Putapoo-tsssssssssp! Putapoo-tsssssssssp!
HAAAAAAAAAAAAAAAAAAAAAAAAAAAAAAAAAAAAa
aaaaaaaaaaaaaaaaaaaaaaaaaaaaaaaaaaaaaaaa
h
"You'll never fiiiiind… Four keys?"

"You'll never fiiiiind… betrayed the fam…" Pulled a sock off.
Putapoo-tsssssssssp! Putapoo-tsssssssssp!
Putapoo-tsssssssssp! Putapoo-tsssssssssp!
HAAAAAAAAAAAAAAAAAAAAAAAAAAAAAAAAAAAAa
aaaaaaaaaaaaaaaaaaaaaaaaaaaaaaaaaaaaaaaa
h
Burm burm-nim! Burm, burm-nim!
Burm burm-nim! Burm, burm-nim!
You'll neveeeeeer fiiiiiind… Putapoo-
tsssssssssp! Putapoo-tsssssssssp! Putapoo-
tsssssssssp!
HAAAAAAAAAAAAAAAAAAAAAAAAAAAAAAAAAAAAa
aaaaaaaaaaaaaaaaaaaaaaaaaaaaaaaaaaaaaaaa
h
Burm burm-nim! Burm, burm-nim!

Burm burm-nim! Burm, burm-nim!

Amy's eyebrow raised at his bare foot. "You'll neveeeeer fiiiiiind…"

"You'll neveeeeer fiiiiiind… maybe if I…" Jamari shook his head. "I didn't mean to—"

The tune hit its bend.

"Fuck it all up." And took off his other sock.

WuaAlaWuaAlaWuaAlaWuaAlaWuaAlaW uaAla

Bellowing on and on as the tune scratched and screamed in reverse order.

"Jamari, you can't stop dancing!"

"Easy for you to say." He sat on his butt. "Just cuz you earned my name last game don't mean shit, New Girl." His arms hugged his knees. "People have been trying to take away my voice my whole life, man…"

"What are you talking about?" Amy's eyes searched the ceiling. "Come on, we're one piece away!" *There's no time for this!*

Bow Bow BOW

Amy moved to the jam. Still sitting, Jamari shuffled his feet on the floor, rotating like a Clenzbot 9K.

You'll never fiiind…

"You'll never fiiind…"

"I will never find my peace…"

WuaAlaWuaAlaWuaAlaWuaAlaWuaAlaW uaAla

Bellowing on and on as the tune scratched and screamed in reverse order.

"Fuck!" Amy slapped her forehead.

"I ain't mean it all." Jamari's head hung between his legs. "My mum married one of them. Divorced. Always does whatever she wants, fuck the consequences."

"What are you talking about?"

The music grew louder.

Jamari continued to mumble to himself.

"This is the perfect time for a mental breakdown," Amy half-whispered. *Shan hiska.* "Ok. Jamari? Listen to me. Your mother isn't here. If she were, maybe she'd let us out the back door—"

Bow Bow BOW
You'll never fiiind...

"You'll never fiiind..."

Jamari twiddled his thumbs.

WuaAlaWuaAlaWuaAlaWuaAlaWuaAlaW
uaAla

Bellowing on and on as the tune scratched and screamed in reverse order.

"FUCK!" Amy pounded her knees and massaged her throat.

"Look at me now, father!" He flung his shades across the floor and raised one hand to the heavens while the other rubbed the ever-oscillating tiles.

Bow Bow BOW
You'll never fiiind...

"You'll never fiiind..." Amy stared in horror as—

Jamari performed a snow angel on top of the dance titles.

WuaAlaWuaAlaWuaAlaWuaAlaWuaAlaW
uaAla

Bellowing on and on as the tune scratched and screamed in reverse order.

Amy's palm slapped her forehead several times. Closed her eyes and took a *very* deep breath. "Do what you want, Jamari. She isn't you. You can't control your Mum, but you can control yourself. Make yourself happy."

Tears welled in his eye sockets, pooling, not wanting to fall. "Everyone already knows everything there is to know about me." He turned to her with begging arms. "What left do I have to offer?"

"I can't do this." Amy searched for help. "There's gotta be an answer." *Think, Ames. What would Gma do? What would Demo do? Stupid ass room—*

The Fender Strat's eyebrows angled on her with its mouth

wide open.

She scanned away and everywhere else as the track continued, Bow Bow BOW *repeating its obnoxious restart sequence* between Jamari's blubbering sobs, *one loop after the fucking next.* Bow Bow BOW

Amy closed her eyes, mind raging at every non-solution thought filling it.

Slit his throat, end his misery.

She gasped at the voice, and the breath She *thought* brushed her ear.

**Bow Bow BOW
You'll never fiiind...
WuaAlaWuaAlaWuaAlaWuaAlaWuaAlaW
uaAla**

"Come on." Her begging eyes lay on her **USELESS** partner.

Bow Bow BOW

—*"She isn't you"*—

Amy's right hand massaged her temple. She turned over the hand to view the scar She won at last year's dance with Cloudy, still fresh despite its age. *Truth in spite of honing your own. What would I do?*

Die, die, die.

Embrace.

Amy nodded. *We embrace. Thank you, Aura.*

Poor Jamari wrapped himself in a ball on his side, retelling a story only he could hear in its full context. He swam in place, hands rubbing the floor provocatively.

What is he doing?

I do not care to find out.

Bow Bow BOW

"Jamari, what are you doing? "Stop— Wait, the floor. Ever since he touched it, he's been whacked out. Come off the floor! Jamari, stop rubbing the floor! It's making you like—this!"

WuaAlaWuaAlaWuaAlaWuaAlaWuaAlaW uaAla

"It was only one movie!" Jamari bawled. "Ma-maybe it was the time I-I-I—But... Did that <u>really</u> make her screw around on Pop?" His blank eyes found Amy's. "Did I make her? Is this on me?"

Amy sighed. *I can't believe I'm gonna do this...*

Bow Bow BOW

"Hey there, baby boy..." Amy leaned down to him and placed a gentle hand on his back. "It's okay. Mum's here for you. Always. You're a star, you know that?" *Fuck you, Professor. Making me—* Her eyes grilled the ceiling before returning to Jamari. "You're my shining little eminent star, you know that."

His eyes lit up. "I am, Mama?" He frowned. "But you said I burned out all the stars with my impoverished antics."

Ouch. The hell did she do to you?

WuaAlaWuaAlaWuaAlaWuaAlaWuaAlaW uaAla

"There's never been a brighter star than you. I'm so proud of you, my love."

"Mama—" Jamari jumped into Amy's unprepared arms. She cuddled him to a more appropriate stance, though he was still on his knees.

Yup, this is my new nightmare. Gma would never. I can never tell anybody about what I'm about to do, not even Demo. "That's right, my love. Now come. Let's get up."

His hand rubbed the tiles.

"No, no. Noooo. We rise to the challenge every time, yeah?" Amy helped him to his feet.

"Yeah..." His boyish smile grew as his eyes adored her presence.

"Let's catch the next loop. Move those hips."

He did.

"There we go. *Kill me.* The start is coming up—"

Bow Bow BOW

You'll never fiiind...

"You'll never fiiind..."

"Do we have to do it again, Mummy? My feet hurt."

**WuaAlaWuaAlaWuaAlaWuaAlaWuaAlaW
uaAla**

Amy's eyes shut—*with patience. Steady. Patience.* "Ok, my boy." Amy dusted off his shoulders and held him by the arms, eyes locked into his. "Before this music leads Mummy to mayhem, can you think of anything in this room that might help solve this riddle?"

He took it all in. Shook his head.

"That's okay. It's oookay. Now, let's move to the beat and keep moving. Don't stop." She forced a tight smile. "Okay?"

Jamari cheesed and nodded. "Let's end this, Mum. Together." He rocked his body into motion, getting in tune with the beat. Danced faster.

Amy nodded. Moved her body with bare minimum effort.

**Bow Bow BOW
You'll never fiiind...**

"You'll never fiiind... A key!"

"You'll never fiiind... A key!"

You'll neveeer fiiind...

**Putapoo-tsssssssp! Putapoo-tsssssssp!
Putapoo-tsssssssp! Putapoo-tsssssssp!**

"You'll neveeer fiiind... 1976!"

"You'll neveeer fiiind... 1976!"

**You'll never fiiiind... Putapoo-tsssssssp!
Putapoo-tsssssssp! Putapoo-tsssssssp!**

**HAAAAAAAAAAAAAAAAAAAAAAAAAAAAAAAa
aaaaaaaaaaaaaaaaaaaaaaaaaaaaaaaaaaaaaaa
h**

"You'll never fiiiind... A, C, E!"

"You'll never fiiiind... A, C, E!"

**Putapoo-tsssssssp! Putapoo-tsssssssp!
Putapoo-tsssssssp! Putapoo-tsssssssp!**

HAAAAAAAAAAAAAAAAAAAAAAAAAAAAAAAa aaaaaaaaaaaaaaaaaaaaaaaaaaaaaaaaaaaaa h

You'll neveeeeer fiiiiind... Putapoo-tssssssssp! Putapoo-tssssssssp! Putapoo-tssssssssp!

HAAAAAAAAAAAAAAAAAAAAAAAAAAAAAAAa aaaaaaaaaaaaaaaaaaaaaaaaaaaaaaaaaaaaa h

Burm burm-nim! Burm, burm-nim! Burm burm-nim! Burm, burm-nim!

"You'll neveeeeer fiiiiiind…"

"You'll neveeeeer fiiiiiind…"

Jamari's cheesy smile diminished into a frown. He pointed at the square underneath her. "Regret."

Music, flashing lights and echoes ceased to nothing.

BERM-BERM-BERM

Both students raised a brow at the ceiling.

BERM-BERM-BERM

Jamari stared at his discarded footwear.

BERM-BERM-BERM

Amy's eyes widened at the tongue hanging from the guitar's mouth.

Silence.

NOOOOOOOOOOOOOOOOOOOOOOoooooooooo ooooooooooooooooooooooooooooo

The students' hands shot to their ears.

NOOOOOOOOOOOOOOOOOOOOOOoooooooooo ooooooooooooooooooooooooooooo

Amy, on her knees.

NOOOOOOOOOOOOOOOOOOOOOOoooooooooo ooooooooooooooooooooooooooooo

Jamari, on his back.

NOOOOOOOOOOOOOOOOOOOOOOoooooooooooo

ⵔⵔⵔⵔⵔⵔⵔⵔⵔⵔⵔⵔⵔⵔⵔⵔⵔⵔⵔⵔⵔⵔⵔⵔⵔⵔⵔ
Oh.

Congratulations on completing the challenge, Numbers 7 and 10! You have both been awarded five points! See you all soon.

Silence, except catching breaths. Amy and Jamari stared at the ceiling, then at each other.

Jamari faced the ceiling again and closed his eyes. "Bloodclot."

Chapter Twenty-One

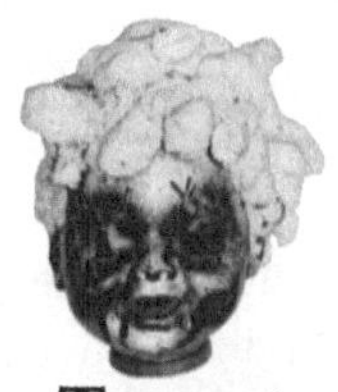

Chapter Twenty-Two

Level 2: Alien Science

"I'm no different from you." Amy picked at her scar. "When you're feeling lost, I think it means you outgrew the person you were. Take it one step at a time."

"Yeah." Jamari put his shades on and flipped his token in the air. "People are still being sent to their cells, regardless of positioning."

"It's Number 8. He's one of the Most Wanted."

"What? How do you know?"

"Unfortunate run-in. He's not the original, though. Wish I was paying more attention to the game. It may very well be the thing holding us all back."

"Find the Most Wanted, huh? And it's <u>definitely</u> not you, right?"

"If I were, I would've already sent you to your cell faster than you could reach the studio." She winked.

He smiled. "Fair play."

They walked into the noisy Common Room. Several faces couldn't hide their surprise at their joint arrival.

"Where were you two?" E'oné ran up to her brother. "Are you alright?"

"Clappers!" Jamari popped his jacket collars. "Nothing stops me. 7 and I just had a challenge to conquer. Ain't that right, 7?"

"I never want to hear that song again." Amy sighed. "Let's see where we're at." She locked eyes with Mr. Stoicism across the room.

He took his eyes away from her and put them on Jamari. "Must you flip that thing so incessantly?"

Jamari nodded to him. "Yo, remember when we first met?"

Mr. Stoicism stared at the token, flipping with disgust. "What about it?"

"We recognized each other. Respected each other's game. You said, 'Great thinkers pace, but I rock back and forth in my seat like a pendulum,' kinda like you did right before a Luxball match. Caught a chuckle out of me cuz you were real for that."

"I didn't say that for your amusement."

"I know. But I related cuz of those late-night studio seshes where I couldn't pull a lyric out my ass. This—" Jamari flipped his token higher, caught it, and repeated. "It helps me cope, mate."

"I apologize if your eminence doesn't gain my sympathy."

"It's what came before, my guy." Jamari grabbed a jelly doughnut from the table full of delicacies. "I ran from home once when my Mum was going buggers. Third time that week. 'Cept this time, I ventured a little far and came round this bridge that crevents liked to frequent." He took bites from his doughnut. "Could've been real dicey for me. I was scared out of my wits." He smiled in his memories. "Luckily, I met some cool COIC kids who hung out underneath the bridge daily. They loved playing this tossing game, trying to see who could create a bigger dent under the bridge's metal frame."

Jamari sat, still flipping his token, half-eaten doughnut in his other hand. "The game also intimidated any weirdos that may try to muck with um. Those kids had power, man. I was gone for weeks, learning so much. They taught me to harness my," he pointed at Amy, "<u>aura</u> into any limb at will. Tossed massive stones so hard I cracked the bridge's foundation. I got invited to join their community but declined." He stopped flipping, finished his snack and leaned forward, rubbing his hands together. "It helps me think, especially when I'm at my lowest. I'm more aligned when I'm... flipping to my own beat. I remember the power I have inside. Sometimes I forget to listen."

Silence.

Me too. "Keep your head up, king." Amy smiled at him.

He smiled back. "We should all be kings and queens of our own." He tipped his shades to her. "Queen. Listen—" Jamari hopped out of his chair and over to Amy. "One more thing..." Pulled her aside, earshots away from the crowd. "What you did back there... I was itching to say, but—thank you. Got us out of a hot spot."

"Don't mention it." Amy closed her eyes, head shaking. "Please. Don't mention it. <u>Ever</u>."

"Right on." Jamari chuckled. "I have to ask..." He leaned in close. "You're a performer, aren't you? Your voice. You're that singer popping through town on her own melody."

Shut your mouth.

"Follow in your precious light and all that lovely jazz. I remember that joint. Performed in the town square, too."

"No idea what that means." Amy's eyes darted around for listening ears. Shared a nervous smile with Demora across the way. *Ok, time to exit.*

"Can't fool a musician's ear," Jamari said. "We don't have to talk about it if you're embarrassed, but I just wanted to let you know I can help you take it to the next step." He leaned in even closer. "I'm a member of The Light. Listen..." In her ear. "Our head, Madame Blé, she's retiring next month."

Amy leaned in. "Oh?"

"She's looking to leave her legacy—" he made two clicks with his mouth, "—cemented. Missing a strong act after ya one and only." He patted his chest. "M.Blé loved the vocals of the mysterious Singer rolling through. She said, her words, 'the deep, expressive, eclectic vibrance of that voice sprouted wings on my back and warmth elsewhere.'" He quivered. "I left the room shortly after, but whatever floats her boat. When you're ready to stop lollygagging with your talent, hit me up. Let's talk."

"Oh, I—" Amy's eyes went mad, searching for an escape. Her

gaze lingered in Demora's direction, but her best friend was engrossed in a conversation with Ms. JellyRoll.

E'oné walked out of the room.

Vedessia's nervous smile and glance left Amy and returned to the Gyaad girl.

Kassandra being Kassandra.

In a corner, Mr. Stoicism pouted, his gaze fixated on the painted faux wall-long window.

Mr. Fucking Shit-Faced SmartyPants, Hideko sat with wandering eyes over a novel in hand and threw a wicked grin at Amy.

"Yeah. Mhm." Amy didn't register the words Jamari said, *more concerned with—my fever—*

She blinked.

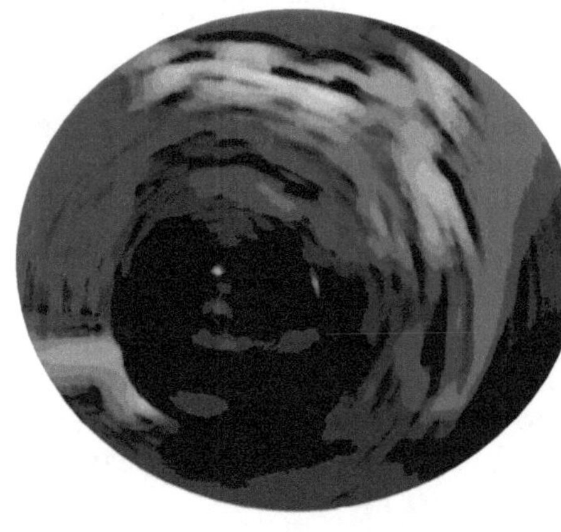

Amy gazed at the stars leaving her vision as Demora and Jamari helped her off the floor.

"You good, mate?"

"Hey, look at me." Demora grabbed Amy's face and maneuvered it side-to-side. "What happened?"

"I'm good." Amy steadied herself. "Got a little lightheaded, that's all."

"Let's get some food in you, yeah?"

"Don't you <u>love</u> to see it?" Mr. Stoicism strolled over, hands in pockets, chest pushed towards the lot. "Everyone's so cozy all of a sudden." He stared at the leaderboard.

CHAPTER TWENTY-TWO

Current Rankings & Points + (Points not added)

1 = 29

2 = 18

3 = 15 (2)

4 = 14 (2)

5 = 17 (1)

6 = 22

7 = 19

8' = 19

9 = 7

10 = 14

"Extra points to top it off as we head into Level 3. I don't know why all these alliances are allowed, anyway." He grilled Amy. "It all surrounds you, doesn't it?"

"Say what you've got to 9, but don't blame me for your poor play."

"You mean the unfair play by others?!"

"I must say I agree." Hideko walked up beside Mr. Stoicism.

"Lay off, 8," Demora *warned* before her stern eyes fell on Mr. Stoicism. "Who plays fair in prison? Perhaps you should spend more time sharpening your skills rather than complain, complain, complain."

His cheeks reddened. "I challenge you!" Mr. Stoicism's chest got *way too close* to Amy's. "I'll take your points and run to the top!"

"Someone's got a fire." Demora yawned. "Finally."

Mr. Stoicism's eyes lowered, but his firm stance returned seconds later. He slammed his fist onto the leaderboard. "Right now!" A red circle of electric-charged light grew underneath his touch.

"Oof! Getting quite noisy in here," Vedessia said, munching away from her chaat dish and sipping from a chalice. "Maybe we enjoy our break, peeps. Lil' rest before the next game?"

Across her table, "**Yes—Ahhhh**," the Gyaad girl nodded, her mouth full of pakoras.

Hideko snickered. "This should be fun. I say alliances be damned." He offers a hand to Mr. Stoicism. "Mind if I join your cause? It'll be worth your while…"

"Done" Number 9 shook his hand.

Jamari stepped forth. "Why don't you—"

Demora's arm held him back. "If you're gonna jump my best friend, I have no choice." She stepped between the warring sides.

"More points, the merrier." Mr. Stoicism nodded, eyes peered through *his crush*.

"On second thought." Hideko backed away. "Maybe we should target this from a diff—"

"Oh, no!" Mr. Stoicism grabbed his hand and slammed it next to his, a red circle illuminating under it as well.

"You bastard, are you insane?!" Hideko tried to yank his hand away unsuccessfully. "You've locked me in!"

"What is this?" Ms. JellyRoll studied the red circles under their hands. "This isn't a part of Graves' prison. Is it 8?" Her cold eyes dug into him.

Hideko smiled while trying to pry his hand off the board.

"Prison Rules!" Mr. Stoicism shouted. "We can settle scores amongst ourselves thanks to 8's ingenuity!"

"Under whose authority?" JellyRoll stalked Hideko's presence. "How could you?"

"Fine." Hideko threw his free hand up in surrender. "Prison Rules are in effect, thanks to me." He shot a look at 9. "And since this fool sealed my fate, I suppose we'll just have to take those points."

"This is wrong." Ms. JellyRoll said. "You do not know what siphoning from Graves' aura will do in the long term. I say we counsel the Professor on how this factors in— **AAAa**hhhhh..." She DROPPED through a hole that rebuilt itself and closed up within seconds of swallowing her.

"What the hell?!" Jamari dashed over, checking the spot. "Where'd she go?!"

"Where's Number 5?" Vedessia bolted towards Hideko, side by side with the Gyaad girl, both glaring at him.

"Challenges can be enacted at will by all prisoners. You're welcome." Hideko took a bow. "You've seen me standing right here. 5's on her own now. This prison's tests never truly cease, yet you all point your fingers at each other, fulfilling your premature adolescent attitudes and behaviors. It's laughable." His grin turned to chuckle and washed over them all. "The absolute test of humanity's nerve in my hands. Sure, I activated Prison Rules, but the code was already there. Activation was crucial in my continuing pursuit of—"

"Alien science, blah, blah, blah!" Amy waved him off. "What's the challenge?"

Hideko waved his hand toward the board. "Place your hand and find out. Ten points wagered each? I'll cover Number 9's missing ones."

"That's criminally more high stakes than we've gotten from the professor," Vedessia said. She raised a finger in the air with a smile. "Maybe we have a conference to settle our—"

"Is there a switch that we can flip off for you?" Demora gave her back to the deflated girl and placed a hand on Amy's shoulder. "I see that look in your eye. Think about it before you—"

"Done." Amy slammed her hand on the board.

A blue circle formed underneath it.

"Right." Demora opened her eyes and sighed. "Alright then." Smacked her hand next to Amy's. "Let's make them regret their decision."

"Since 9 roped me in this." Hideko opened a compartment

on his utility belt and lifted out a shiny tube. "I choose the Spitebug Challenge."

Wrinkles flexed on Amy's forehead. "The what?"

"Known to harvest on the insect Planet Mercury, spitebugs are known to awaken your soul's innermost transgressions, bringing them to light. The first team to react <u>loses</u>. Reactions count when your spirit or <u>aura</u> enters its reactive stage. You'll know when it happens. Ready?"

'*Your auuuuura.*' "Whatever." Amy shot a finger at him. "And I want those points, 8! No games! <u>Honor</u>, <u>remember</u>?"

"I appreciate the confidence," Demora looked between them, "but I don't know about his little alien bugs."

"Too late." Hideko flicked the cap off his tube.

Within seconds, they came. Spitebugs: pink flurries of fuzzy fluff too tiny for the naked eye to see in detail escaped the tube and flooded a quarter of the room in under thirty seconds.

Crazed arms around the room flew through the waves of pink dots. The students' cries of pain filled the air from the nibblings at their flesh.

"Ow! Shit hurts!"

"They're biting!"

"Stop! Little pink bastards!"

Sound left the room. Only visual panic through a pink filter remained.

"The hell?" Demora pressed her nose against a wall of pink. "What did you do, 8?"

"Inside this bubble..." Hideko pointed to the gum texture forming a bubble around him, Mr. Stoicism, Amy, and Demora. "Outside influence doesn't matter. Best to keep the game fair, no?"

Amy yanked her finger back from the sticky bubble. "What is this?"

"Yuck!" Demora pulled the sticky mess off her nose.

"The fluids in the abdominal sacs of my spitebugs craft this bubble. Their <u>secretions</u> create a near-impenetrable texture that doesn't just block sound; it soaks it up, reverberating it back at the hosts. Those little friends of mine are keeping the others occupied so they won't have the chance of attempting to disrupt our game <u>or</u> snitch to Professor Graves."

"She's always watching, you leech," Demora said.

"Everyone's watched someone to get ahead. Call me out, but I deliver the truth, not hiding in the shadows like Graves. I suppose she's watching now, curious about how the students will get through this one. This whole operation is her experiment. Her design. You said it best, 7."

Amy's eyes fell from his pointing finger. *Like she watched Jamari's breakdown last game. And Kassandra's possession... E'oné's trauma...*

"She manipulates us into corners and expects us to find our way out," Hideko said. "Despite the stakes, we're her students, simply here to learn from her. Well, she learns from <u>us</u>, as well, <u>growing</u> her power and evolving herself at <u>our</u> expense. All that power in the knowledge she gains in exchange." He nodded. "It's admirable."

Fucker. "You're a sneeving bastard, <u>Hideko</u>. How are you bypassing her aura?"

"Why thank you, <u>Amy</u>," Hideko responded. "However, that knowledge is for me to retain."

"What?!" Mr. Stoicism faced his partner. "You know each other's names now? This better not be a trick, <u>Hideko</u>, or I will report you to the Professor."

"Relax." Hideko rolled his eyes. "Hey, Number 1, are we still avoiding any challenges with <u>Amy</u>?"

"What?" Amy searched between them. "What's he talking about?"

Demora's face stared straight through Hideko's soul.

"<u>What</u> is he talking about, Demora?" Amy stood straight.

"Ames," Demora said through grit teeth. "No reactions or names, remember?"

Amy scoffed. "Right. Nice try, Hideko. You're not winning that easily!"

"Really?" Hideko checked his watch. "Well, it's like you said,

Number 1. She's only half the woman she needs to be."

"You, <u>WHAT</u>?" Amy spun to her side—

She and Demora DROPPED— through the gaping hole in the ground.

.

.

.

Chapter Twenty-Two

Chapter Twenty-Three

Level 2: TICK TOCK: Undeniable Fear

Amy scurried off the ground, thrashing, and gathered her footing. "I fucking HATE when that happens." Forced her throat to clear.

Demora pointed at her. "Your voice, Ames. Well." She took in the dirt walls and bars of her/*Number 1's* cell. "We'll lose some points, but at least we're away from that narcissistic little—"

Amy **SLAPPED** Demora. *Why did I—* She stared at the stinging palm of her scarred hand.

"Bloody FUCK!" Demora held her cheek. "Dirty cunt, why did you—"

"Bloody BITCH!" Amy shook her head. *What's wrong with me?* "I'm sorry! I didn't—"

"What the HELL was that for?!" Demo pushed her.

Amy's stance hardened. "Half-Amy?! Another half-Amy to match? You said that during the kabaddi game, too, Demora!"

"Well, it's been true, HASN'T it?!" Demora stepped back, rubbing her reddened cheek. "That hurt. What I meant was only you're a match for me—they might as well not be there." Demora gave a tiny shrug. "You just haven't been your true self."

"You're so arrogant! You've been acting in shades, and I've done nothing but defend you!" Amy paced the cell. "Over and over and over and over and over again!"

"I would never spit on your name for anyone! All I said was that you were unfocused!

"**Ugh**, I can't deal." Amy stared at Demora's throne-like chair. "This is all bullshit."

"Amy, that little weasel sent me here because he had to! Even with my points taken, I'm almost eligible for the next level."

"Eligi— Is that all you care about? What do you mean eligible for the next level?"

"Hideko worked out that you move up to Level 3 by accumulating twenty points, even if you haven't finished all Level 2 challenges."

"Of course he did. And you kept that from me, too. Guess I'm too weak for your bother. <u>So</u> happy your alliance thrives ever. Congrats!"

"You're not happy, that's been clear!"

Silence devoured the cell.

Amy chewed on her bottom lip. *How can I be? How can I ever be happy again?*

"I was going to inform you, but you went off accepting challenges without knowing what they are." Demora sighed with deep deliverance. "Look. We're here now. Let's figure this thing out together. I'm sure Graves is still watching. She sent us here together for a reason, no?"

Amy sat against the wall and stared out the cell bars. *Here she goes. Rambling on about Graves like she wasn't her personal lackey way before my knowledge.* **Sigh**. *What am I doing? I'm doing <u>it</u> again. Clocking truth despite honing my own. Doesn't matter what she does, doesn't do, says, etc., etc.*

"I mean, why else would we end up here together?" Demora went on. "It doesn't make any—"

"Because I'm <u>exactly</u> where I've wanted to be this entire time. At your side." Amy sulked into her hands. "The prison sent us here. It's all just '<u>code</u>.'"

"Little MS. Drama Queen..." A voice echoed around

them. Pink lights sprinkled from the walls at all angles and formed a human figure.

Demora, in aura form.

Amy stared between the two. "You too?"

Demora raised an eyebrow at her. "What do you mean 'you too'?

Aura Demora cleared her throat. She studied Amy from head to toe. "There she is. The woman of the hour."

"You stay out of this!" Demora's finger shot at her aura self. "This is <u>not</u> the time!"

Aura Demora strolled around the cell, hands behind her back, taking in the essence of it all with her hungriest eyes for the two best friends. "You prepare. You evolve. Become your best self so you're more than ready when the time comes to take a stand. Question is: which of your auras is the strongest?"

"You're out of your depth, and I've dealt with you enough times today already." Demora pressed her nose to nose. "This is between us. Get. OUT."

"You're right." Aura Demora peeked over her host's shoulders at Amy. "It's between you two. Here's the deal." She pushed past and sat on the throne. "I think everyone's had enough of you two over the years. Bickering, kissing up, bickering, on and over and under with each other. Obsessed." Rolled her eyes. "Ugh. So far beneath me."

"She's a darling," Amy said. "Like her mother."

"One more time." Demora's eyes pierced her translucent fuchsia-pink aura self. "Remove yourself or be removed."

"Say..." Aura Demora jumped up with starving eyes and circled Amy. "Why don't I spar with Ames? That should be quite interesting since I'm the uninhibited version of-" her eyes narrowed on Demora, "you."

"Why am I here?" Amy asked. "This has nothing to do with me. You two clearly have some issues." Her eyes scanned the ceiling. "Can I get out of here now?"

"I second that, Professor Graves!" Demora demanded into the ceiling. She pointed back at her aura. "You listen here. I told you to <u>leave</u>. I will not be made a fool of by my aura or anyone else." She moved closer. "I own you."

"And I told you." Aura Demora circled her before moving to the cell bars and looking out of them. She turned her head, wearing a wicked grin. The outside corridor behind her dimmed to darkness. "It's time for you two to settle this right here and now, or neither of you will leave this prison you've crafted."} She scooped dirt from the ground with a face full of glee that only she understood. "This game has many names. I like to call it the Game Of Undeniable Fear."

More games. Amy's eyes rolled. "What's so undeniable about it?"

"The what? I am not playing games with you, you irritable spirit." Demora spat.

"Geez, can't even talk in turn. Listen. Roll the dice. Withstand your fear." Aura Demora opened a palm. Three dice made from dirt floated from her hand, remnants falling off. "On arrival, your fears will be at their most powerful. Withstand them and keep rolling for the next to appear or yield to your opponent. Either action weakens the fears you placed that round. When you yield, your opponent scores a point. Hold the dice for too long, and you may find it... expensive. At the end of five minutes, whoever has the highest score wins."

"You're mad," Demora said through clenched teeth.

"Why are you delivering the game to us and not Graves?" Amy asked.

"Like I said, it's your prison." Aura Demora laughed.

Beside her, white lights spiraled into a single form: Aura Amy. She crossed her arms, side-eyeing her host.

"You!" Amy's fists clenched.

"Don't blame the Professor for everything," Aura Amy said.

Aura Demora threw her hands up. "The winner gains twelve points while the loser loses six and gets sent back to Level 1. Let's create some space, kiddos."

The aura forms faded from view. The cell darkened.

The space between Amy and Demora expanded, placing them several feet apart.

Aura Demora's laughter echoed around them.

Clocks ticking...

"What the bloody hell? I can't believe this shit." Demora scanned the nothingness. "How do we know when five minutes is up?"

The three dirt dice flew into Amy's hand.

TICK

TOCK

Aura Amy's *TICK TOCK* boomed throughout the space.

TICK

TOCK

TICK

TOCK

Demora massaged the bridge of her nose. "Ugh. Auras."

"Your aura has a brilliant sense of humor," Amy said.

"Seems we have no choice, Ames."

"Or we could just wait out the five minutes."

Aura Demora's voice CACKLED.

Do that; you'll both end up losing twelve points and be sent to Level 1-together.

"You have a lovely child," Amy said. "Rubbish." Demora unfolded her arms. "Let's get on with it, Ames."

"No." Amy folded her arms. "I'm done playing these games."

"Don't be stupid. You heard her. If we don't play, back to Level 1."

"Don't call me stupid. So be it. Maybe we can figure this thing out from the bottom."

TICK

TOCK

"Have you lost your mind? You've been complaining about this prison, yet want to return to the start? You're absolu—"

"—lutely joking, yeah, yeah. Demo, we gain control if we don't play into their game. Think about it. Why send us back to Level 1 unless there's more to uncover?"

"You sound like Mr. Spitebug."

"He may be on to that <u>one</u> thing," Amy said. "There's tons of hidden shit in this place. Look around! This proves we're in the Aura Realm! The levels aren't even levels. It's one plane that we need to navigate—"

"Amy, enough! Roll the dice."

TICK

TOCK

Amy squeezed the dice in her scarred hand.

TICK

TOCK

Demora threw her arms to the sides. "I don't care about all the secrets. It doesn't matter! Advancement is the path I'm on. The objective has always been to escape the prison. Find what you can along the way, but escape the prison as Number 1. Now, roll the dice. I'm not returning to Level 1."

TICK

TOCK

TICK

TOCK

"Roll the dice."

"Nope."

"I think those spitebugs have gotten into your head."

"You can't be this obsessed with winning—"

"**Why not?!**" Demora's voice reverberated throughout *the realm*. "My entire **life!** I've stood on the sidelines in the shadow of something. Someone. Watching my value taken for granted. Our people, auraists everywhere, are being tossed in prison without regard. London, America, Asia— it's everywhere! I win this, I secure favor in the SOGL, and I can help our people overcome the World's prejudice. But more than that, I can prove that I am, without a doubt, worthy. I am— I will be the <u>best</u> of the <u>best</u>."

Amy studied her fiery, *unfamiliar* eyes.

"Besting the handpicked brightest young auraists of the revolution. All the secrets I need lay in victory." Demora pointed a shaky finger. "Now roll the dice!"

TICK
TOCK
TICK
TOCK

Amy juggled the dirt dice in her left hand. Tossed them to her right hand.

Each side of the dice— blank.

"You always talk about what's best," Demora said. "Best for this one, best for that one. What's best for you, Amy?!" She stomped her foot.

Rippling vibrations left it and coursed throughout the dark space.

"Aheeeooooooooooo."

Amy searched the darkness for her. *Number 3?*

"Dammit, Amy, just roll the fucking dice!" Demora squeezed a fist. "We don't have time for this. At least let me go on, and you can stay behind and solve your riddles!"

"Fine." Amy shook her head. "I yield." She tossed the dice Demora's way.

TICK
TOCK

One point to the home team. Zero for Ames.

Aura Demora's laugh flushed the air with winds lifting both opponent's hair.

Demora shook the dice in her hand. "You're impossible." She threw them down.

The dice rolled, spun on their tips once, twice, three times, knocked into one another, and continued rolling. One by one, they each landed on a side.

"**Hark!**" Demora buckled. "Shit." The dice jumped back into her open palm.

"Demo?" Amy stepped forth. "Are you okay?"

Demora trembled as she stared at something above her. She tossed the dice again. "Fuck!" Leapt to one side, avoiding *something?*

"What do you see?"

"Nothing!" Demora raised her hands again, staring all around her. Dropped the dice. "FUCK!" She buckled over.

Amy sped— closed the space between them in seconds and caught Demora right as she fell to her knees. "Demo, let's end this. We don't have to fight—"

Demora shoved her back. "Enough!"

The darkness expanded between them, placing them several feet apart again.

"I did tell 8 to avoid our team going against you!"

TICK

TOCK

Amy's face shifted through phases—worry—rage—pity.

TICK

TOCK

"Because you are nowhere comparable to my strength since you lost your aura's color! You haven't been the same since Cloudy! Before we ever went head-on again, I needed you at your best. Back to form. Otherwise, it wouldn't be a fair fight. Which Amy will I get next?" She threw the dice across the open field.

One point for Number 7! Score tied at one! Two minutes left, girls...

She's right. "How noble." Amy shook the dice, one almost spilling out of her hand. "Feeling sorry for me, huh? No bother. I'll show you and anyone else who thinks I'm <u>weak</u>."   T o s s e d the dice and stood in silence.

Eh-heh. Eh-heh.

CHAPTER TWENTY-THREE

Sobbing from somewhere far but also near came in and out of earshot.

Amy's mouth moved, but no words came out. She held her throat. Her hands shook.

Hogging the dice for too long there, Ames.

The dice hopped back into her hands. She flung them down. They rolled.

UUUUUUUUUUUUUUUUUUUUUUUUUUUUUUUUUU
UUUUUUUUUUUUUUHHH

Dozens of decaying corpses moaned and reached toward her, closing in inches from her.

Amy caught the dice again and rolled.

Her arms stiffened and stuck to her sides. *Shit, I can't move!* Her eyes darted at the corpses closing in. The dice flew into her hand again. *C'mon, roll.* She dropped them.

Her undead tormentors froze in place, their rotting fingers barely grazing her lips, ears, and shoulders, with one of them holding a lock of her hair from behind.

They all flew back. Stopped feet away, stood at attention, eyes locked on Amy.

A rotting, scarred hand similar to hers squeezed her shoulder from behind. Its owner: a drooling corpse without hair or facial skin but with features comparable to Amy's. It smiled. Shoved its broken jaw back into place.

TICK
TOCK

Chapter Twenty-Four

Level 2: Betrayal In The Works

Still a stiff board, Amy's feet pattered in a circle until facing away from her corpse version. Dropped the dice again.

Another Amy smiled at her. "Peeling back the flesh will give you nightmares." A coin-sized piece of her cheek peeled off with a sizzling tear. The doppelganger's flesh continued peeling in searing bits.

Dice in her hand, Amy closed her eyes. Dropped the dice.

One of the dice rolled an X.

SWOOOH! A spinning metal plate SLICED through the doppelganger's neck.

The laughing head nicked Amy's thigh before rolling away into the darkness.

Another Amy DROPPED in front of her, a noose strangling her as she reached for Amy.

Another double walked up beside Amy and bowed. CRACKED its neck at an unforgiving angle before collapsing.

More Amys flooded the scene, demonstrating flashes of death predicaments: An Amy sunk into the floor, gargling and blowing bubbles of blood; engulfed in flames, an Amy fell to her knees; a katana pierced an Amy through her heart.

Stop, just make it stop... Don't think. Feel. Don't think. Feel. Her right hand jerked away from her body. Her knee buckled. *FEEL!*

Bodies collapsed around her, littering the area with corpses piling on top one another.

Amy's hands squeezed the sides of her head. *I can move again.* Closed her eyes. *Don't think, don't think, don't think.* Opened her eyes. *Feel.*

Something tugged against her weight. Held her back. "What—"

Several white strands of light wrapped around her waist, shoulders, and legs, pulling on her from behind.

Demora struggled against her own set of white light strands, panting but with a smile on her face. "There she is! Fight um off, Ames!"

"What—is—happening—argh!" Amy fought and pulled against her captivity.

"Keep— fighting!" Demora's teeth smashed together, pulling herself forward. "Don't let the fears win. We're better than they'll ever be!"

The two best friends fought against their restraints, sweat pooling down their faces and drenching their shirts. They took labored steps towards each other.

Their eyes never left one another.

Amy bared her teeth—*The Unity.*

Demora nodded—***The Unity.***

Inches apart, their fingers reached for each other.

The Unity!

The Unity!

TICK

TOCK

TICK

TOCK

Amy glanced at her scarred right hand clutching the dice. *If I yield now, she'll win. She should.*

A tune **WHISTLED** in the distance.

"What is that?" Demora paused her struggle with searching eyes. "Where have I heard that tune before?"

TIME!

Blinding light swallowed the pitch black as everything spun out of focus.

Amy and Demora struggled to stay on their feet as time and space bent around them.

Their bodies fell— and kept falling, stretching into the void beneath them—

I'm so proud of you two.

Congrats, my muses. Even score. As always. As forever.

Back in Cell 1 on their hands and knees, Amy and Demora stared into space, catching their breaths. They collapsed on their butts. Their eyes met.

Shallow breaths escaped Amy's mouth. *I've never seen her that scared before. Her fears... What did she see?*

"Mental," a breathless Demora said. "Are you good?"

Amy shook her head. "Peachy. How about you?"

"We're still here." She smirked.

"Yes, we are." Amy smiled wide.

They erupted into laughter. Got to their feet and examined their bodies.

All back in one piece. Felt like I was getting stretched apart.

Demora **SLAPPED** Amy off balance.

Amy shook her cobwebs loose. "**Ow**—Bloody fuck!"

"Earned it. We're even now."

Amy rubbed her flushed cheek. Nodded. "Fine. Fair."

"Amy, I'm sorry. I've been a pain in the ass over the past year, for sure. We've been doing this for too long to not get on each other's nerves now and then." She held Amy's hands in her own. "You're my muse. My greatest ally. My perfect rival. My best friend." Demora stared at her feet. "If you're not at your best, who can I trust to push me to the edge? I get worried about you." Her eyes trailed Amy's scarred right hand. "This world's a danger to our kind, and if we're not excelling, leveling up daily, we'll be eaten alive. I know I can count on you at the end of it all." Her eyes found Amy's again. "I believe in you, Amy. Always and forever."

"I love you." Amy raised the back of her scarred right hand. "It's all been a circle. I've felt so alone ever since..." She gave a small smile. "But you're always there, even when you're not. Believing in me more than I believe in myself. Thank you."

"I love you."

The two best friends hugged. Tight. *Forever.*

WHISTLING

Demora's smile curled the opposite way. Her eyebrows furrowed. "That annoying whistle..."

It echoed through the halls outside the cell.

"Way to ruin the moment." Amy punched her arm. "For some tune."

"I've heard it before... but where?"

"Well, if it was top ten on the Stroker Hits List, I'm sure I've heard it too." Amy shook her head. "No, but—"

Jumping bits of dirt on the wall pulled back as a hole expanded violently.

Above the large hole, words formed:

Beside the hole:

Amy folded her arms. "So much for twenty points to move forward."

"Hideko, that little conniving bloodant. Serves him right, losing points. Looks like we each got six points for this little nightmare fuel adventure." Demora winked at her. "Never count

LEVEL 3

Must have twenty-five points to enter.

out a Devine. You'll be there in no time, I know it. Gonna <u>catch</u>

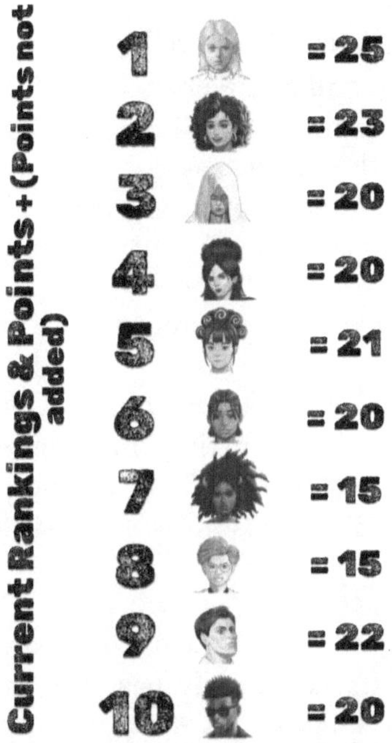

<u>up</u> with your Egyptian honey on the third level?"

"How do <u>you</u> know she's Egyptian?"

"Have you heard her accent? It's like breathless ponies in heat dominating the sad lot of us wet for them."

"You're disgusting." Amy suppressed a smile.

"You like it."

"Tell me what I like."

"I did."

"Fuck off." Amy pushed past her. Peeked through the cell bars. "Your master alliance with SmartyPants still in effect?"

"Please, he'd be so lucky." Demora hugged her from behind. "For real. No more alliances? Keep everything out in the open? You and me?"

Amy embraced the arms wrapped around her. "You and me. Think that's best."

"Off I go then." Demora started towards the gaping hole in the wall.

Whistling from outside the cell grew louder.

Demora stopped and looked back. "Wait, where… where?"

The whistling stopped. The source whistled another tune. "You'll never find…" the voice sang.

Amy sighed and shook her head. "Jamari." She pressed her face against the warm cell bars. "Surprised he's singing that one. Nevermind, I said I wouldn't talk about—"

"Shh, sh sh sh." Demora's scrunched face watched the floor. Scratched her chin.

"Don't shush me." Amy slapped her arm away.

"Wait." Demora backed further into her cell. Her hung jaw swayed, her teeth gnawing together. She pointed a trembling finger past Amy. "That whistling. It tortured me for nights on end."

"Was he that bad?"

The lighting in the cell crackled. Dimmed.

Demora's eyes stared blankly past the bars, her face half covered in shadows. "I heard that whistling outside the chamber my captors kept me in. Jamari… That first tune he whistled… I remember it now. "Callisto's Harmony" The unofficial anthem for The Light." She grabbed her chest and buckled. "Jamari."

Oh. "Hey." Amy reached out to her. *Oh, no.* "Be here with me."

Demora gripped Amy's arms for support. "<u>THEY</u> did it." She nodded, looking through Amy's chest. Her stance hardened. "That gas filled my nostrils over and over until I wanted to spill my guts." She held Amy's face in her hands. "I can't leave yet. We can't. I need your help."

Ok. OK. "I got you, anything you need. Always." *That's right, Demo, stay with me.* She held Demora against her tight. "I've got you." *This is going better than expected. A year ago, she would've had her hands around his throat already.*

"I will <u>kill</u> him. <u>I will kill all members of the Light.</u>" Demora pushed past Amy. "Bloody bastards, COME ON!" She pushed the cell bars.

NOPE! Amy grabbed her arms and pulled her deeper into the cell. Shut the bars again. "Demo, I'm with you. Let's think this through. Jamari is a nitwit—*sorry, J*—but even he wouldn't whistle that tune knowing that you're in here IF he knew anything about your captivity." She *tried to* lead her best friend to sit on her *throne* chair. "<u>We</u> will get them. Let's be smart about it. We'll dig up some dirt—"

"**Yoc!**" Demora threw her hands up, left her seat and paced. "I see you're back to detecting." She closed her eyes and took a deep breath. Reopened them, gazing into Amy's. "Ames, I stood by you when you took on that smartypants asshole's challenge that got us here. <u>Please</u>. Stand by me now!"

"Okay." Amy nodded. "Okay, let's do what we have to." Raised a finger. "<u>Smart</u>. We do it smart."

"Smart, it is." Demora smiled and hugged her. "There's my girl."

Amy winced at the fingers being clawed into her back. *Fuck. Fuck me.*

"Alright, come on." Demora led them towards the bars. "Let's corner the bastard and—"

Amy, arms locked in MAAURA STYLE, grabbed Demora's arms from behind.

"Hey! That's tight—What are you—"

Amy spun towards the hole in the wall— PUSHED Demora through it.

The hole compressed as bits of dirt zipped closed up around the opening.

Demora's hand shot out of the hole, dirt closing around— then OVER it— dirt encrusted her arms in seconds.

The wall retracted her dirt-coated arm until it flattened to normal.

Amy's backed away from the wall. Staring at it. *What now?* Her arms trembled towards the cell doors. Swung them open. *There was murder in her eyes. I had to... Right?*

Amy dashed out, eyes searching up and down the empty

corridor. *Where's his cell?* She charged down one end. *C'mon.*

Zipped past her cell— doubled back, head cocked to one side, peering in—

A book. On her bed.

She zipped inside and snatched it up. *Hallow's Journey. Awesome.* "I don't have time for this." She side-eyed the ceiling. "Had enough of these games," she mumbled. With the book clutched to her chest, she ran out of her cell.

This prison's the worst.

She glanced at the book in her arms. *Could be a solid clue.* Quickened her pace. *Or another deceitful test.*

She hit the brakes, stumbled, and crashed into his open cell.

Inside, Jamari, head-bobbing, with wooden, square blocks connected by an arch shape over his ears, faced her. "Ay—" Nodded and waved her over.

Amy stepped in, jaw dropped at the pastel influence around the spot. *Beautiful posters*— in the center of each, prominent artists of their time and before. "So glad I caught you." *Before she did.*

He pulled his blocks off his ears. "Just got back from my interview. Had yours yet?"

"What? What interview?"

"With Graves, mate. She's doing a roundabout, like on our first night." He scrunched his face up. "Was that yesterday? This is the third day, right? Huh."

Second—no—maybe? "No idea." *Interview? Great. About time I had words with*— "I was wondering… I wanted to ask you more about The Light."

Jamari bolted up, shut his cell bars, and plopped back down on his uneven mound for a seat. "What's up with it?" His hand offered Amy a place across from him.

"Why the nerve?" Amy sat on the bed's edge, her book still clutched to her chest. *If you did play a hand in her bout, I'll—*

"Oh, I keep a low profile on my affiliations. Too many sponsors and too many headaches about this, that, and the other. You won't have to worry about that either. Got chu."

CHAPTER TWENTY-FOUR

"Still think I'm The Singer?"

He smiled and tossed his shades on the bed. "I know it, mate."

Amy sighed. "I've been lost." She glanced at her scarred right hand. *For Demora.* "I've fought my demons, so I know what it's like to feel yourself on wit's end. But for my Gma, my best friend... I find strength."

Jamari nodded. "The Light felt like a second home after mine was destroyed."

"It's still not always easy. Needing guidance... You know, like, like an—"

"Alright, stop. Cut the shit, mate."

Amy closed her mouth. *Oh no.* She squeezed her book tighter. *Get ready—*

Jamari jumped to his feet, eyes peering out of his cell bars. Popped back into his seat and leaned in close to her. "They took me in without judgement, mate. There's no judgement in The Light. None. And trust me," he chuckled, "I spit at the judges." He frowned. "I've been judge-y, too. I've reflected." He leaned back. "So, cut the noise, real talk. The Singer in town with the "Follow In Your Light" joint, all that jazz. That you?"

Amy's nostrils sucked air that her mouth released in a puff. She nodded. "Yes."

"Knew it!" Jamari jumped and pumped his fist. "Damn, I'm good!" He relaxed in his seat. "So are you. Sorry. Getting my head under swell is a work of art I'm still unraveling."

"You got me." She wore a tight smile.

"It's cool! I'll keep it chill." He leaned into her again. "And last year. All those kids. All that media. It's true? Has the <u>real</u> truth been hidden?" Leaned closer. "Are <u>you</u> <u>really</u> the one who gave it to that Cloudy curse?"

Amy scratched at the scar on the back of her right hand. *For Demo.* Stared him dead in the eyes. "Yes, me again."

His palms **SMACKED** together. "Far. Out." He slow-clapped. Head jerked to peer out his cell again. "That's stellar. Sick, sick."

Whatever you say. "You think The Light can help me?" *Sick to my stomach—*

"Stick with me, I got you. Trust. If you want to lend a voice to The Light, I'll help you. I'll be there every step of the way, fam. One— <u>auraist</u>, you say? To another."

Students, be advised that one of you has advanced to the third level.

"Aw, what?! No way, c'mon."
Amy squirmed in her seat. *Demo, if you're waiting for him...*
We can't stop her, dear host. You know she's—
I just need a little more time to figure this whole thing out.

On Level 3, your first challenge will be the Prize Fight. It'll be unlike previous challenges, so I suggest you rack up points before you enter. Make sure you brush up on your Skully skills.

"SKULLY!" Jamari sprung out of his seat.

Number 7, please make your way to your cell.

Fuck. Stay put, Demo, please. "Guess it's my turn."
"Good luck, fam. And remember. You've got a friend in Jamari Wyst. Trade digits later."
"Digits?"
"Call IDs. GCID caller IDs." He picked up his wooden block device.
"Digits. I like that."
"I dig aura."
Amy lingered by the bars, fingers tapping her thighs. "What are those?" She nodded to the blocks. *Stop stalling, Devine.*
"Headphones. For music listening."
"Headphones? How'd you get those in here?" *Clocks ticking.*
"Oh, I got a guy on the outside. Slipped them through

commissary."

"There's a commissary?!"

Jamari put on his blockbuster shades. "You haven't explored the prison much, have you?"

"Interesting. We'll tackle that another time. Thanks, J." Amy zipped out of his cell.

Chapter Twenty-Five

The Interview: Cell 7

Graves: [Eyes warm, searching.] What takeaways have you gained from your prison experience so far?

[The student. The teacher. Sit within arm's length of each other within the tight cell.]

Amy: [Eyes straight, poker.] It became more alarming along the way… given how authentic the experience became.

Graves: Was it what you were expecting?

Amy: I'm not sure anyone expects much from prison.

Graves: So you're disappointed?

Amy: In Me. But I'm glad we finally have this time to converse.

weR-Kaaaaaaaaaaaaaaaaaaaaaaaaaaaaaaaw

Graves: Sorry about that. Maintenance.

Amy: [Runs her hands along her thighs. Scratches.] *TICK TOCK TICK TOCK TICK TOCK TICK TOCK* I spent the better half of the past year searching for what's next. I'll admit I tried to ignore the World, convinced of its loss.

Graves: Where do you think it's led you?

Amy: Nowhere.

Graves: So you think your progress went nowhere?

Amy: That doesn't make any sense. It can't be progress if it— **[Head cocks.]** Why do you always do that? **[Hands scatter through the air, twisting knobs, flipping switches...]** You twist and turn every little thing around with all your puzzles and your lectures. *It's like I'm not even allowed to be human.* I don't know, Professor Graves, I don't know what I'm doing most of the time, and then I-I thought I could at least solve the riddle of your little aura realm, and you turn the entire cast against me. **[Sits back in chair, folds arms.]**

[Graves laughs.]

[Amy's tongue presses the insides of her cheeks.]

Graves: You've spent so much time trying to find my secrets. Running from what you know and what you were told from the very beginning. All you had to do to escape the prison is ask. There's no secret here about what I'm doing. I've kept it straight with you since the beginning. Strengthen your spirit. Overcome your self-prophesied limitations and play through the games, leaving the prison with something you, and only you, can define.

Amy: [Leans forward.] I watched Kassandra play one of your <u>friendly</u> games and get possessed. What happened?

Graves: I genuinely do not know. She's stable. It is possible that what has been going around town may have afflicted her.

Amy: [Shakes head.] I understand I chose to be here. My body shit in and shit out through dirt and junk more times than I'd like to recount. In and out of cells. I chose to be here. **[points at Graves]** You're an educator. Why are you trying to recruit late stage teens, or at least one of us, into some shadow organization? Us yolks in here losing our minds to receive acknowledgement from the unheard of Society Of Great London?

Graves: I'll admit, I had reservations about introducing your lot to the Prison Games. Spirit wielders, or Auraists, as you'd say, have always navigated a thin line between insanity and reality. The World has shown you what it can do to you. The Society, that shadow organization was built from nothing to create something. A safer World requires a better heart. Your soul— your aura, is your true heart. The less connected you are with your aura, the more vulnerable you will be.

Amy: [Covers her scar.] I just— over the past year I'd constantly questioned every single decision I made in that hole at the bottom of our old school, knowing... **[Averts eye contact with Graves. Closes and reopens eyes with a sturdy gaze into the Professor.]** Knowing that no matter what path I took... **[On Amy's thigh, her clenched fist tightens. Bloodlets drop on her dark denims. She maneuvers her fist over the discolored spot.]** it would be the wrong one

Graves: [Lowers somber eyes.] No, I don't.

Amy: It's not just about me. Demora was <u>kidnapped</u>. Do you think the best course of action after that was to bring her into some prison for games?

Graves: She wanted this, Ms. Devine. You and I both know that.

Amy: What about what's best? I watched E'oné almost get choked out by her own aura. Then you trap me in a box too. Jamari's in a box with his own mother. Sorry, J. What's the endgame for you, Professor? What do you get out of this?

Graves: [After several moments of contemplative silence] The things I've seen. The love I lost. I've learned one thing through it all. You're only as destructive as your mentality. Indeed, I introduced the Prison Games to you, but I have not been its true master. I have heard snippets of conversations but provided no outside interference. I mostly answered replies about the games. Your spirits reported back anything they found worthy of my ears. They never betrayed you, and they did it all free of will. **[Rises.]**

[Amy, frozen. Leans back in her chair.]

Graves: I value the protection of innocents. Give your spirits more credit where it's due. They are your essence, after all. Nothing you all have been through was anything your spirits thought you couldn't handle. **[Paces the cell.]** We can often endure more than what we allow ourselves. Each student is at the heart of this prison's design. Your minds make the matter.

Like I said before, you are the crafters of your prison. I am simply a programmer, moving things according to your unique blueprint. Your auras made everything here possible. They would have never let anything happen to you as they are tied to everything you are. Protection was the number one priority above all else. Protection is why you all are here.

Amy: [Indexes scratch her thighs.]

TICK TOCK TIC—

Amy: Felt like you were playing with our lives. Using our minds as weapons against ourselves.

Graves: The games, the lifeforms involved, each puzzle, books, and secrets that you find are all parts of our hidden world that many great spirit-wielders have encountered in the past. Some of the most challenging spectacles were crafted by what your spirits knew you all needed to go through to strengthen your weaknesses. To overcome your fears. Every fear you have and every obsession... Your spirits— You— are the strings here. I'm the puppet. **[Smiles.]** Gratefully, I get to watch your souls shine in brilliant light.

Amy: [Eyes search hers.] Why'd you leave me this? **[Lifts her *Hallow's Journey* book off the bed and faces the cover to the Professor.]**

Graves: I didn't leave that for you, but I'm sure you'll enjoy it.

Amy: [Places the book back down.] Do you know who left it?

Graves: [Shakes her head.] I wasn't always watching. I caught tidbits here and there to check-in. Made sure things were progressing safely. You'd be surprised how well some of your spirits can mimic my voice. **[Smiles—*proud mother.*]** Charming bunch, your auras. The point of all this is what you make of it. Your lot entered these doors with your demons and then asked who was responsible for blocking your light.

Amy: Demons blocking the internal. External forces further shedding light.

Graves: It's never that simple. I believe you have discovered that the light can sometimes hold you back more than darkness.

Amy: [**Her eyebrows raise.**] *Did she see my shadow work?* Did you see… did you see when I…

Graves: Your students are a clever lot, much more than I can even comprehend at times. What you uncovered here is yours and yours alone.

Amy: Right, but can you describe what you saw me do in my challenge right before Red Rover? The box of aura.

Graves: [**Nods.**] Respectfully, Ms. Devine, sometimes we can't see because we're looking in the wrong direction.

Amy: Another puzzle, prof? *Of course, she's gonna do this to me.*

Graves: [**Brows furrowed.**] You wouldn't know who got past my security measures, would you? The prison's gained some blind spots due to ingenuity. I'm sure you've heard the blaring. [**Points to the ceiling.**]

DOMMMmmmmm

Amy: Oh, that noise. *Hideko. He's mine.* I don't have a clue. I guess I wasn't ready for prison life. Or I came here for all the wrong reasons.

Graves: Now that is quite the takeaway. Where does it lead you?

Amy: [**Shakes head.**] You're only as destructive as your mentality. [**Sighs.**] *I don't have time to play games. I'll train my aura later. Demo's obsessed with her truth, and it'll destroy her unless I get out of here. Find them first. Unless she's… No. Maybe.* [**Nods.**] Feeling like I've been here before. I want out of the prison.

Graves: [**Closes her eyes and nods.**] Only a few on this Earth possess inknowledge. Your dreams can sometimes reflect possibilities you haven't yet known. Visions come to you of the future. Whether they're valid or not, they always feel genuine to you. [**Cocks her head with raised brows.**] Mostly fractured bits of those. It's a concept formally referred to as Déjà vu by our ancestors.

[**Graves runs her hands along the walls. The red of her aura lights the crevices between the dirt.**]

Graves: It's your spirit's calculations, the ripples from experiences. Naturally connected to the Earth, your spirit feels the ripples of others and creates connections between the two—potential paths. For example, I always planned to introduce your lot to the Prison Games. Based on moments of yours I did catch, it seems you realized some things you could never explain. Your spirit may know more than you can wonder.

Amy: [Patient eyes traced her teacher.] That I found out.

Graves: [Rises.] I admire the concept. One bright star of our society once said, 'It's like mathematics and science forming a love child that becomes the biology of your intuition & perceptions.' [Wandering eyes on the ceiling.] When you have a deep understanding of who you are, you'll see a clearer reflection of yourself in others. Their actions, emotions, thoughts, feelings, and more—all seen from a higher level. You can almost move through them. As them. Inknowledge.

[Picks Amy's book off the bed and caresses the front cover.]

Graves: I suspect you possess this inknowledge on a grander scale than I've ever seen. [Eyes on Amy.] You're an accomplished— what word did you use to describe us spirit-wielders?

Amy: Auraists?

Graves: [Nods.] You're an accomplished auraist. Don't let the World destroy what's brewing inside you. Cultivate it. See what happens. [Returns the book to Amy's hands and moves towards the cell bars.] Your exit has been granted. Pass these bars, and you'll return to the real World. And just so we're clear, you've been there all along. This is no spirit realm.

[The cell doors swing open.]

Graves: Farewell, Songbird.

Amy: Songbird?

Graves: Why yes. That's what I called your lovely character parading through town.

[Amy's jaw hangs— frowns— slight smirk— lips tight together— head shakes.]

Amy: [Scoffs and rises.] No light show today?

Graves: [Smiles, shrugs.] Your experience has taught me a lot. I think I'll take the more scenic route. [**Whistles**—*a familiar tune*—**Strolls out of the cell and out of sight.**]

[**Her whistle of** *Follow In Your Light* **echoes throughout the corridor.**]

Amy: *A tune I crafted on a whim as I paraded through towns. I can't figure you, Graves.*

DOMMMmmmmmmmmmmmmmmmmmmmmmmmmmmmmmmmmmm

[**Amy flinches.**]

DOMMMmmmmmmmmmmmmmmmmmmmmmmmmmmmmmmmmmmmm

Amy: What the hell now?

DOMMMmmmmmmmmmmmmmmmmmmmmmmmmmmmmmmmmmmm

DOMMMmmmmmmmmmmmmmmmmmmmmmmmmmmmmmmmmmmm

DOMMMmmmmmmmmmmmmmmmmmmmmmmmmmmmmmmmmmmm

Graves ran back in front of Cell 7. "Quickly gather your things, Ms. Devine, and follow me."

DOMMMmmmmmmmmmmmmmmmmmmmmmmmmmmmmmmmmmmm

Amy clutched her book to her chest as she raced to keep up with Graves down the corridor.

Lights faded in sections behind them.

"What's going on, Professor?"

"I don't know."

DOMMMmmmmmmmmmmmmmmmmmmmmmmmmmmmmmmmmmmm

"Have you seen Demora?"

Graves eyed her for a second but looked forward.

The wall ahead of them split open, revealing the night outside.

Freedom.

Seven of the students waited outside the structure with Count Maclyvtch.

"What's going on?" Graves approached the Count.

He groaned. Peered around at the others. "They're too young."

"Speak, Maclyvtch."

"That's <u>Count</u> Maclyvtch."

"Count Maclyvtch, speak. Please." Graves shared his eye contact without a stir. "They've earned it."

Off his ever-longing sigh, "Half of New Enfield has been blown to bits."

The Gyaad girl fell to her knees, mouth agape, with tears streaming down her face. Ms. JellyRoll and Vedessia stooped to either side to console her.

"Count. Maclyvtch." Graves' icy stare shot right through the Count's forehead.

Easy, Professor. "What happened?" Amy asked.

Count Maclyvtch tightened his folded arms. "An explosion of sorts. I heard whispers it could have been a bomb."

"What?!"

"Seriously?"

"Several uncompliant pipelines were involved. There were some casualties."

"That's awful."

"No…"

"Duat claims again," Vedessia said. "Let us pray for them."

"Who bombed what?" Jamari asked.

The Count shook his head. "That's all the info I have."

Amy found her limbs again, shook off the dizziness from what she had just heard, and turned to the sobbing Gyaad girl still being consoled. "Is she okay? Did she have someone—"

"She's been crying like this since last night," Vedessia answered.

"She said she had a bad omen," Ms. JellyRoll said. She tore off the bottom half of her *already tattered* dress. *What happened there?* Used the cloth to wipe the Gyaad's face. "It's okay. Everything will be alright. No harm will come to you." Faced the others. "She sees herself dying, often."

Same.

"Oh shit!" Jamari's eyes were glued to a device in his hand. "Shit's real, man! Mad buildings lost in the blaze. Shit."

Students gathered around him, eyes on his device's screen. Jamari flipped it open, doubling the screen size.

"A GCID-og? How'd you get that old relic in here?" Mr. Stoicism asked.

"Commissary," Jamari answered, nose still in his device.

Mr. Stoicism looked at Graves. "There's a commissary???"

"They said a Gyaad's in the hospital. Critical condition." Jamari's shades peeled up and looked over at the sobbing Gyaad girl and her comfort circle. "Oh..."

"What?" Vedessia asked.

Ms. JellyRoll's shaking head moved from Jamari to Vedessia. It tipped to the Gyaad.

Count Maclyvtch whispered in Graves' ear.

Jamari flipped his GCID-og shut. "Not my place to say."

"Oh!" Mr. Stoicism's face *found an epiphany we all figured sooner.* "Her sister's in the hospital!" He *stupidly* gestured at the Gyaad girl.

Jamari pushed his arm down. "My guy." He threw hopeless hands up.

"What? It's all over the news!" Mr. Stoicism said.

"Mr. Pudersmitt, please." Graves shook her head. "Of course it is." She reached down to the sobbing Gyaad girl. "Come with me, Vyaila." Beckoned Ms. JellyRoll to follow. "You too, Ms. Ling."

They helped *Vyaila* to her wobbly feet.

Graves faced *Ms. Ling* and Count Maclyvtch. "Take Vyaila to The Center. I'll meet you there later." She turned to the others. "As for the rest of you, please return to your homes. You'll hear from me soon."

"Where's Demora?" Amy's eyes narrowed on the professor.

Graves studied Amy with *painful* eyes. "She left the structure after her last challenge." Graves looked over at something behind them.

Amy followed Graves' eyes; her attention brought to a spot near the bushes.

Hideko trembled in the fetal position on his butt, staring at the prison structure with slow, controlled pants.

A rumble rolled under them all, waking them. Breaths cut in throats all around, the students bracing themselves *for something worse. Is it another bomb?*

The force grew louder behind them—

The Prison Games structure burrowed into the ground.

"Count, please take Mr. Ang, as well." Graves' eyes wandered over them all. "Students, consider Level 3 of the Prison Games paused for the time being."

The Prison Games

Will Return

in

BOOK 3

ABOUT THE AUTHOR

Hailing from the depths of NYC, W.K. Phoenix has lived a life full of intrigue. The horrific and supernatural have always fallen onto his radar, leading him to record these instances of inspiration. Although ignoring the writing craft for some time, inevitably, the stories and characters that roamed in his mind would spill out into reality. Now the Phoenix universe is here to stay...

Please take the time to leave a review after reading!
Thank you!

You can connect with me on:

https://linktr.ee/Wkphoenix
https://twitter.com/wkPhoenixLegacy
https://www.facebook.com/wkPhoenixLegacy
https://www.instagram.com/wkphoenix
https://www.amazon.com/author/wkphoenix
https://www.goodreads.com/author/show/21979218.W_K_
Phoenix

Subscribe to my newsletter:
https://wkphoenix.wixsite.com/waynebaptistejr/contact

COMING

Peculiar Cases Of Something Devine:

Gravity Of Devotion

(Book 2, Part 2)

"If you're reading this... it was nice knowing you." - Amy

Amy Devine should be dead. Stripped of her aura's essence, she's left vulnerable to the threats *I know are coming.* Her life spirals further into chaos after a terrible accident, mysterious disappearances, and a beloved and powerful cult with terrible power gets locked into a bitter feud with her grandmother. As strangers flood her town, Amy can't escape the consequences of The Prison Games—the twisted trials that left her scarred. Murders and disappearances are piling up again, and the fractures between her and those she loves are deepening.

Time is running out. To save her allies and herself, Amy's key to survival is clear: *I must reclaim the core of my aura* and confront the growing darkness within her—*or embrace it entirely.*

iii

COMING ALSO

Peculiar Cases Of Something Devine:

****

(Book 3)

?

Follow for updates and more...

www.ingramcontent.com/pod-product-compliance
Lightning Source LLC
Chambersburg PA
CBHW030758210726
48290CB00002B/327